THE LAST TRANSACTION
SCOP

BARRY N. MALZBERG

Stark House Press • Eureka California

THE LAST TRANSACTION / SCOP

Published by Stark House Press
1315 H Street
Eureka, CA 95501, USA
griffinskye3@sbcglobal.net
www.starkhousepress.com

ISBN: 979-8-88601-132-6

Cover & text design by Mark Shepard, shepgraphics.com

First Stark House Press Edition: March 2025

THE LAST TRANSACTION

Ex-president William (Wild Bill) Springer is dictating his memoirs. Now 80 years old, he lives in medical seclusion, tended by his two devoted, phlegmatic keepers, and growing more senile by the day. He had been a powerful U.S. Senator, a majority leader, then fell into the role of president when no one else wanted to tackle the 20-year-curse. But that was years ago. Now, having outlived his son and both his wives, having outlived his own history even, Springer is tended by Dr. Goodenough as he spools out his life on a tape recorder. It is his final compulsion, his setting the record straight….his last transaction.

SCOP

Scop thinks he can change history. He is living in 2040, a brutal time. If only he can keep Kennedy from being assassinated in 1963, Scop figures he can transmute his present. So Scop keeps going back in time, trying one plan after another—and failing with predictable consistency. The more often he returns to the Grassy Knoll, the more he seems to reinforce the events he is trying to change. He tries to talk Zapruder out of taking his pictures. He even kidnaps a tourist and returns her to his present. But just as nothing that Scop does makes any difference, so too, nothing in this situation is exactly as it seems.

The Last Transaction
Back Story

By Barry N. Malzberg

Somehow Roger Elwood persuaded Chilton Press (publishers of *Dune*) to take on a science fiction line of which this would be the initial volume. A senile, fading USA President (defeated for a second term) is drafting his memoirs; he is half crazed, overwhelmed by regret and a sense of betrayal and purporting to make this memoir his definitive statement. The novel, framed as a diary of self-justification, wanders through his shattered life, two marriages, repudiation for re-election as a result of his manhandling of a student uprising which ended with troops and bombs used on the rebellion. Students die, the nation trembles and the President is repudiated by the next election.

It is a brutal novel which obviously anticipates the kind of disastrous social and political convulsions to follow. Chilton paid the second part of the advance and put it into production at which point, unanticipatedly, Chilton's publisher got hold of the galleys.

Said publisher was enraged by what he took to be shenanigans designed to embarrass him. He told his editor-in-chief "Get rid of this. Presidents don't talk or write this way. [There are rambling, unhinged descriptions of sexual intimacy which I would hardly deem "erotic" and reviewers agreed.] Let him keep the advance and dump this."

Chilton dumped it. And the next week the (expletives deleted) Presidential transcripts were released.

Through what might have been blind luck (or editorial courage) Elwood was somehow able to talk it into Pinnacle Books whose very new editor-in-chief was an old college classmate, Stanley Corwin. (Syracuse 1960.) The novel was published. I received another advance. Maybe Corwin too had second thoughts but the novel emerged. You can find reviews online.

The novel was never published again after the Pinnacle edition.

In retrospect *The Last Transaction* looks madly predictive. I won't go beyond that.

—Teaneck, New Jersey

THE LAST TRANSACTION

BARRY N. MALZBERG

Dedication
For Nathaniel Wisch, M.D.
and for Roger Elwood

PROLOGUE

WILLIAM ERIC SPRINGER: b. Pine Oaks, Illinois 7/4/10; educated in local public schools; B.S., University of Illinois 1932; LL.B., University of Virginia 1935; practiced law in Virginia, Kentucky, and Illinois 1935–40; Illinois State Legislature 1940; assistant minority leader 1944; elected Congress 1948; elected Senate 1950; majority whip 1954; reelected Senate 1956; majority leader 1960; reelected 1962, 1968, 1974. Elected president of the U.S. 1980; renominated and defeated 1984.

PERSONAL DATA: Married Eunice Constance Blake, 1938; Arthur Blake Springer b. 1940 (d. 1963). Married Hope Johnson 1958 (d. 1987). Author, *Years of Decision, Years of Hope* (1959); *The Power and the Vision, Memoirs of a President* (1987). Autobiography in progress, Residence: 1185 Park Avenue, NYC.

Don't think I can get a thing out today.

Not a thing, not a thing. Sensation of dim blockage not only of the mind but of the bowels; it is, then—and let me try to get this right—as if all of this rhetoric were choked within coils of possibility: too weak, distracted, dispirited even for simple recitation of the facts. Tomorrow, then, or perhaps the day after—the constant flickering of the light on this machine as I speak is a pain in the ass. Voice as light; the reduction of words to image. Incontinence beckons again.

Coming into Peoria there was music, five of the bands massed to greet me at the steps of the town hall, noise all around, color, return of native son in triumph after all these years. It must have hit me for the first time then—although again there might have been hints before then—a complete hint of disassociation. I did not know where I was. Suddenly all of it was flicking in and out of focus: one moment the town hall, the limousine, the noise, and the pressure against me on the seat (I thought, as I had a thousand times in open limousines, of Kennedy, leaning forward slightly to touch my shoetops with a glistening forefinger, which trembled only slightly out of the field of vision); and the next some dim, gray, open space in which I floated like a bottle bobbing in the sea, a *flick!* in the recession of consciousness— and then back into focus again, one high-school youth bleating madly through his sousaphone, dangling like an elevated prick into the car. But although I saw, I did not know where I was, literally could not place the segment for an instant: who was I? where was this? what was going on? And the panic began. Never had this hit me in public before. A few times perhaps in bed, once in a cabinet meeting—but those were moments instantly controlled. But this one went on, appallingly on. I could feel the sweat begin to come out of me in little ball-joints of excrescence, and I straightened, leaned against the seat, and opened my mouth, warning myself to take slow breaths. Slow breaths. Hope: "Bill, what is wrong? What's the matter, Bill?" Never could get a thing past that bitch—not that her knowledge ever did her any good either. "Bill, you're very white. Are you all right, Bill? All right?" shoving hip to thigh against me in the enclosure of the limousine then, and I could feel myself swinging perilously into alignment finally, a sense of history returning along with time and place, and I said, "Yes, Hope, I'm all right, everything is all right," forcing a trembling little wave above the door, the wind glancing off my palm, then another, and indeed I did feel better. Somewhere between the bleats of sousaphone and Hope's own kind, blurred words, I could feel assertiveness returning, a sensation that I had made some awful passage and was now coming out through the other end—all illusory perhaps but very comforting at the time. There is nothing like going briefly crazy and coming away from it to give you a shot of optimism, let me tell you. Let me tell you that, among other things. We welcome the president of the United States. Returned native son for the first time in so and so many years. Triumphant reelection campaign. First Lady too. She pressed my palm, gave me little glances dappled by the sun. You might have thought—even the local dignitaries and Secret Service might have thought—that we were lovers. Ah, well. Future of America within our grasp. Future of Americans also within our grasp. The end of the century approaching, crucial choices for the next two thousand years—the next *four thousand* years—and then, just as I was coming toward the end of it, one more image of Kennedy thrust into mind as if seen through rips in the mesh of consciousness, and falling, falling into her arms, their arms, the burning of the brain. ... That was a very difficult election.

Eggs with bacon on toast with a side order of hashed browns. Sounds of the road rising and filtering through all the sounds of the diner. A 1938 Packard Eight, straight cylinders with floor-shift and high cushions. Explosion of sun against the visors, the road falling.

Merrick is on duty during the days this week. He and Henry alternate, of course (I am very cunning and alert to everything that is going around me; this senility and now incontinence are merely by-products of my cunning; like the observant freak at the sideshow they permit me to watch the others without drawing attention to myself) so that Henry was my day-attendant last week and will again be next. But on the other hand, Merrick is the one with whom I have to contend *this* week, and I do not like him very much, although under all of the difficult circumstances attending this case, there is no particular reason why I should. Merrick is forty, or perhaps he is forty-two years old; he looks like a cabinet minister, at least in certain flashes and aspects of the light, but he is little more than a skilled male nurse—which is not to say that he is to be derogated on these grounds alone. I wonder why they will not allow me female nurses—but it is not mine to speculate. Perhaps they feel that I am at least potentially violent, but except for that one unfortunate situation, I have never been. Violent.

Tapes jamming in the recorder, the spool slamming to halt, and the tape exploding then in a filthy mess out of the machine and on the rug. It was necessary for me to call Merrick for assistance, my own old hands being insufficient to scoop the damned tape from the rug, untangle and feed it into the machine again. And in fury I bellowed for

Merrick, helpless tears coming into my helpless old eyes, my helpless old frame shuddering and shaking in its chair, the microphone falling away from my lips as I bellowed and bellowed for him … increasingly, I disgust myself. Self-revulsion may be the last identity of the aged, the last expression of the will which they are permitted. Merrick came in (I imagine that he is sitting in the outer room reading a newspaper, although this is pure sentiment; Merrick, I am convinced, can neither read nor write, undoubtedly he listens to my ravings with a disinterested ear, pausing now and then to take small, careful swallows from the pint bottle of gin which I can see bulging in his pocket) and saw the mess and stooped over to pick it up, shaking his head, his face carefully blank.

"Now, Mr. President," he said, "this is happening too often. This is the third time this week you've had an accident with the recorder, Mr. President. Don't you think that maybe you should rest for a while? Or at least you could use cassettes, now cassettes don't spill all over—"

"I'll do whatever I want," I said. Merrick does not bring out the best in me. "I don't want a cassette. I want something that I can feel. I want to see accumulation. Don't call me Mr. President."

"Why, Mr. President, you are the president, I mean you were. It's only proper—"

"Don't give me any of your shit," I said. Sometimes I enjoy using obscenity before Merrick merely to gauge his reaction. Henry never shrugs, is as likely to answer me scatologically as not, but Merrick underneath his shell of white has some lurking beast of Protestant ethic: obscenity disturbs him, even more when it comes from an ex-chief of state. "Clean up that filthy mess and go," I said.

He continued at his work, casting shy, careful glances over his shoulder. "All of the excitement," he said, "all of this excitement is not so good for you, Mr. President. Perhaps a nap—"

"I don't want a nap," I said. "I don't want to be told what to do. I don't have to take orders from you. Don't call me Mr. President."

A sudden roiling dust came up before my eyes; I realized that I was about to incur another spell of weakness. Not two hours before the machine, not three hours out of the bed, and I felt myself beginning to lurch and totter once more inside, all powers failing. I could not bear for him to see my disgrace. "Get out of here, Merrick," I said.

He stood there, strips of tape like ribbons of state filtering through his fingers, one spool dangling from his wrist like a scrotal sac. His eyes showed new alertness. "You're not well," he said.

"Get out of here."

"Upsy-daisy, Mr. President," Merrick said, laying the spools and tape carefully on the floor and coming over to extend an arm, pull me crumpling from the chair. "Now, we'll just take care of that later. We'll just clean that up a little later on this morning and have it nice for you when you're ready to come back. We'll have everything for you later. But it's time for a rest now; you don't look well. And also, some medicine will make you feel much better."

I could not resist him. Falling across him, riding his back like an insect, I could see the layers of white rising against my eyes, a field of white, becoming all perception. I struggled against him, flapped my hands like paper on the surfaces, but no good, no good. He carried me easily. He is 270 pounds. He used to be an amateur boxing champion, he once told me. There is no way in which I could resist him—and then again why should I? Without his presence, without the presence of the others in these rooms, how could I live? I would not trust myself to breathe.

"Come along, Mr. President," Merrick said, and we tottered and tumbled from the room. As we did this, I had a sudden jagged vision of the procession through the halls for the State of the Union and said to Merrick, "Yes, Mr. Speaker, yes," but he did not gauge the sense of this, having neither irony nor recollection, and after a time I did not gauge the sense of it either, being preoccupied with more immediate necessities. How can I continue the tapes if my health continues to flag? How will I finish my work?

Hovering above Eunice, Arthur's squalls from the next room mounting and mounting, it occurred to me that all I wanted to do was to finish, that lust or simple necessity had made me a beast and my concern was no longer for mutuality, for her pleasure, for the ethics of sex itself, but only to come and be done with it before the wretched screams became insuperable and she would have to rear from the bed, throw over the sheets, lumber off, sighing, into the next room to feed him. At the beginning I had performed with gentleness and fire, just as she had asked, but as the first blade of sound came from his bedroom, the rhythm of my purpose broke and I was suspended on flaming wire, merely trying to come into her before all of it was gone and once again I would have to dwindle into the gloom of self, ponder my losses while listening to the slobbering and sucks from the next room. Completely supplanted. Jabbing and jabbing away at her, all purpose concentrated into my organ, I thought for an instant that I could break through into the other side of her, force her to an excess of feeling that she had not known before. But then it all went away, and I was in the capitol with the two of them, the governor looking at me grimly, his eyes slanting toward knowledge, then away in contrived disinterest in that way of his, and I told him, "You haven't got the votes. That's all. They're not there."

"You're job isn't to tell me I don't have the votes," he said. "Your job is to get me the votes."

"We can't," Connors said, looking away from me. "We've been up and down the aisles on this one. The resistance is too strong; they're getting too much pressure downstate. It won't go through."

"Yes it will," the governor said. He jabbed Connors once in the chest, not too lightly, and reinforced that conviction which I had had from the first—that there was in the governor perhaps the desire to possess, but in Connors it was the need for possession, and this was the real, the operable relationship, Connors' pervasive need to be fucked, to literally be empty and dominated and overtaken. By that insight I turned away—it was too disgusting—and found myself in fact walking out of the office, and the governor said, "Bill, where the fuck are you going?"

"I'm going away," I said. "I have nothing else to say. There's nothing more to do here. We came to give you a message and now it's given. We haven't got the votes."

"Stay here," the governor said. "I want to talk—"

"No," I said. I do not know where that sudden conviction came from, but it came flaring from within; and it was as if I was seeing Connors, the governor himself through the other end of a very powerful telescope, dwindled figures revolving in statuary configuration like ruined stars whose light reflected the disasters of a hundred million years ago. "I can't stay and I can't talk. You say you're asking for information, but you're really not. You say you're here to listen, but you're only interested in telling. I can't go through with it anymore. Not under those terms."

"Come on, Bill," Connors said. There was a little wavering edge in his voice—or then again I may have merely constructed this out of my own disordered perceptions. "You can't walk away from this. We've all got to stay and figure—"

"No," I said again and opened the large door, shoving at it, pushing, grunting a little. "I won't stay. I won't participate in this anymore. You can't ram this through because they're on your ass, and if we try to, it's going to drag down all of us, including myself, and I won't have that— I'll take gas or something I've made up myself. But I'll make damned sure that it's mine and that it's worth the trouble and that a lot of people see me taking the pipe so that they'll remember what I did for them."

This statement simply came out of me. In retrospect it may have to be recorded as one of the Great Moments of Political Insight—in fact,

I trust that it will be. But moments of great insight never look like that at the time, all that they seem to be is a particularly appropriate response to a particularly grating stimulus.

"I mean that," I said, and even as Connors bellowed and whined behind me, the governor grumbling quietly, as was his habit, I walked out of the doors and through the padded surfaces of the statehouse, shaking my head. "Excuse me, excuse me," to servants, porters, legislative scribes, housekeepers, and so on, "I'll find my own way out."

In retrospect, it can be seen that I did indeed find my own way out, but at the time it was simply obvious to me that the Public Service Commissioner was a crook and was taking kickbacks from power and light—and anyone over the age of twelve with a passing glance at the newsstands could see this—so why get involved? And even if the commissioner was not a crook, even if he had been hung in the newspapers, as they say, well, the shadow is as good as the act, sometimes better in this trade, and what to say?

I felt my seed rising within me, little kernels shaking and shaking in the dim interior of myself, crying for issuance with their little separate voices, while far below me Eunice twirled and grunted on the spit of myself, her eyes closed, her fists coiled, her breasts seeming to shrivel and retract within. She was a good-hearted woman, had her points, never tried to take them away from her, but she retreated from sex, found it a descent rather than a rising. I do not believe that in the twelve years we had together I was able to bring her to orgasm more than once or twice—and those were accidents.

"Get it over with," she was saying, the screams pouring heavily from the next room, "for God's sake get it over with!" Not a pretty attitude, one must admit, from one's own wedded wife, but on the other hand that was my desire too, that was all that I was interested in doing— getting it over with. And finally, with squeals and small cries, I felt myself shuddering, beginning to move toward the edge—over which (I always had this fantasy) I might tumble fecklessly and never be heard from again—reaching forward, grasping her breasts, pulling out the nipples and two small stains of milk opening, and beginning to spread out from their flat, slippery surfaces as I poured into her.

"Well, are you done now?" she said, still sliding in and working her fissure. "Is it over?" Her eyes wide and moist, no intent to hurt there, I could see that, nor intent to insult; she simply did not know what was happening. At length I came off her in little, lofting stages, sliding first to belly, then flat to chest, and coming off her in a grumbling turn that sent my eyes ceilingward. "All right," she said, standing, taking her nightgown from the bottom of the bed, patting it into place around her, "all right, then," heading through the door. And I lay there, soaked by my own semen and the cries of my first-born, looking at the patterns which the cobwebs made on the ceiling—or maybe the spirals and network were merely in my eyes, filmed against the pupils, those cross-hatches through which I would have to perceive all of my life as I would know it, endless imperfection, perfect patterning.

Connors died of a heart attack on the floor six months after that while making a quorum call.

Going down to Joliet, the three of us in Mack's La Salle, beating off in the back seat early because (we were told) it would make us come slower with the whores, and Mack saying, "Nate Leopold went to this place, they still talk about him there." That was a shock, going to the whorehouse where Nate Leopold had been; for a moment, even in the midst of the pictures I was making in my head, a clear, bright image of the dead boy's eyes, staring—was there any collaboration between Babe and myself? Was anything welding us together other than the simple, sodden need to fuck, and at the same whorehouse?

"What the fuck does that matter?" Jim was saying beside me, "Everybody goes here, even he would, but I don't think he ever got it off." That was something to think about also.

"How about Loeb?" I asked them. "Did he ever go here too?" And they began to laugh. I could not quite understand the laughter for a moment, with the La Salle slamming along the state highway, hitting the rocks, making the curves perilously—and then at last I got it, could see the joke too.

"Oh," I said, "oh, I see—they could have saved the money, helped each other out." And that was it, Mack laughing and slamming the gearshift, Jim hitting me on the knee, thinking of the whores and their moist temples into which I would evacuate—then a long, singing blank space and into the whorehouse itself, a two-family on a sidestreet and slamming at last against the girl on the bed, her body long, my prick long, the two of us melding densely, surprising response from her, considering that she was a prostitute. But then again most of what I knew about them I knew only from books—there were many years before I understood that passion had to do with situation, not so much with role. And then at last, falling away from her, breathing pause on the bed, I asked, "Did Nate Leopold ever come in here?" and—oh, my God, the look on her face—oh, my Good Lord, how she looked at me. Then (I am beginning to drool into the microphone) she *hit* me— slobber all over the mike, my hands palsied and freckled, shaking against the wire, the spools overflowing, starting to foul again. Do not go gentle, my friends.

Inauguration: they needed something simple and straightforward, something at last which would cut through all that had happened and make sense of it for them. This is the key to political success, Henry, do not kid yourself. Are you listening, Henry? Of course you're not listening, sitting over there in the corner reading a newspaper, while I sputter and babble into this machine. *Henry*, you'd do far better listening to me than chasing those lies ... ah fuck yourself, you asshole, you want to read the newspaper, it's all right with me—just make sure that the urinal is strapped tight onto the leg, eh, Henry? No piss into your careful cupped palm for you.

Something simple and to the point, which would tell where we had been and where we were going, not that anyone knew where the fuck we had been—of course not—that anyone knew where we were going to go or why or for that matter there was any need to go *anywhere*, the need to go places having been deeply ingrained into the American psyche long before Springer, Bill Eric, first saw the mild continental light—but what is there to say? Ours not to reason why, Henry, ours merely to carry on the traditions of our forefathers. And so in this two hundred and fourth year of the republic, in this ninety and sixth year before the tricentennial, Springer, Bill Eric, endeavored to add his voice to all those who had preceded, beckoning all those who would follow.

No need to evoke images of the bicentennial, of course. That was better not discussed. No, this was a looking forward, not a looking back, soldering old enemies together, slaking old passions; and so it was resolved to give them a little of this, a little of that, a little of progress, and a little of eternity, a soupcon of dedication, and an earnest nod of or to tradition ... you know how it is, Henry. And so the speech grew and grew through the sheer and shaping hands of the assembled team; and at last, in the cold and blue weather of that Washington January (it was decided to keep the ceremonies in Washington, after all; it was important for morale, to keep up appearances; surely you recall all of that, Henry?), Springer, Bill Eric, was inaugurated as the thirty-*ninth* president of the United States. Do you recall that? Standing here in the place where others have stood, we pick up the standard which has fallen, countless times been raised, countless times knowing that in America this is the way it must always be and we are framed eternally between what we can and can never do ... but what we can never do today we will do tomorrow. Pick up the standard, let fall the standard, possibilities and promise, the awesome splendor of this great land as riven through its landscapes ... ah, well, compromise candidates arising from bitter national conventions must do the best they can. It is not to say how it might have been but only how much worse all could be spoken. Rhetoric will get you nowhere, Henry.

And then the Inaugural Ball, splendid procession of choices, seven of them in seven neighborhoods with seventeen hundred guests at each … seventeen hundred times seven to welcome the advent of the compromise choice. A bow here, nod there, dance at every one, and Hope beside me talking, talking, eternally talking; there was no end to the woman, no end to shutting her up, even then she must have been senile, although I put the best face on the matter that I could and simply tried to keep her under wraps as much as possible, her voice ringing the changes through the night, her gestures spasms as she danced, as she waved … the seven dances with her were horrors, particularly the last, where she lurched to a stop, and then simply fell, collapsed to the floor, her face constricted in that deathhead clown's mask which she had had for years. I cannot tell you for how long I had been seeing her face in only that aspect, all of the passion which I had felt for her parodied, inverted by the gross, coarse, and cruel lines of that face; but still in certain slashes and dashes of light, it was possible for me to think of her as attractive, if only as a perversion. But this last time, as she went sliding over, frantic pelting from the floor, and then the guards hauling her to her feet, leading her away, circling her protectively as I followed, all of us then swarmed over by the larger number of guards and into the limousine itself, Hope panting, wiping streaks from her forehead with a handkerchief in a gesture curiously masculine (I had never known a woman to wipe her forehead in just that way until I met Hope and saw her do it and considered it initially attractive; well, I learned better), and then whisked into the limousine into the night behind the stolid shoulders of the driver (I never knew their names, not once, not ever), turning to Hope then, I said, "There was no need for that, there was no need for that, Hope. You're fifty-seven years old."

"You old fool," she said, "you old fool, you're seventy."

And do you know, Henry, do you know something? Not until that very moment had it occurred to me that I was seventy years old. I mean, it was known, chronology cannot be ignored—and there was the question of it to cover in the election by presenting a vigorous image and calling upon after years of violent decadent youth and its convulsions, wisdom and statesmanship and a firm older hand on the helm of government—but until that instant, age had been nothing more than an administrative problem, having nothing doing with me in any personal sense or having to do either with the failing of powers. Looking at her then and seeing how her eyes caught mine, I realized for the first time that I was a very old man indeed. And the limousine, sheathed, sped through the night. What a bitch, Henry.

What a bitch.

"World government," he said to me, maybe he was twenty-five years old. This was the representative they had selected on their terms to visit me. An insult, but what could I do? What could any of us do? "World government, man, or we set off the piles."

I did not know what to say. Dolan in the corner twitched. "You filthy bastard," he said.

"Get him out of here," their representative said and twitched a finger at Dolan. "I don't care if he's the fucking secretary of state, I don't care if he's the fucking head of the Federal Bureau of Investigation, you get him out of here right now. This is man on man."

He was neither. He was the vice-president. It occurred to me that this man genuinely did not know who Dolan was and he did not care— that was the kind of people we were dealing with. "You'd better go, Harry," I said.

"And let that shit get away with this?" Dolan said, streaks on his forehead, a slam as he brought his palms together. He had been the governor of Nebraska, and a lousy one as far as I could gather (what do we know of the statehouses in the Senate? statehouses even our own, I mean). But he had the proper conservative appeal, and the polls showed that I ran better with no one than with anyone—and Dolan was as close to no one as we could get. "This is the president of the United States."

"Get him out, man," the representative said again. I never got his name. He never gave it. Of course, it would stand to reason that they have no names; what would they have needed names for? That meant identification, which was exactly what they did not need. Besides, they said, they were not individuals; they represented an irreplaceable element of strength, a group of power and efficiency where any individual could be replaced by any other. "Get that son of a bitch out."

"You bastard," Dolan said, standing, but I hit the buzzer on my desk and the service came in, and I said, "Get that man out of here!" pointing not to the representative, who they would have expected, but at Dolan. And before he could raise his arms to protest, the vice-president was being dragged out of the offices, the door closed, and I was alone again with the representative, without secretary or bodyguard. This was one of their conditions. "World government," he said again, looking at me, "we get a full field disarmament and the establishment through the United Nations of a world government, or we set it off. The whole thing. There won't be anything but ash here for a hundred billion years."

"You wouldn't do it," I said calmly, although of course they would do it—wasn't that precisely the point? They had gotten hold of the reactors at Oak Ridge and Park Intervale and a hundred other places in a coup the magnitude of which I could not even understand, and their ability to detonate was established. They had already set off an underground at Bismarck, North Dakota, for demonstration purposes, they said, and were ready to unload under a silo at some location in Kansas. One a day they told us, one a day until we capitulated and agreed to a unilateral disarmament under the terms of a world government. They claimed that they were doing the same thing in Russia, in China, in Israel, in France—but we had no evidence of this. Of course, they made it clear that one of their preconditions was a concealment from all intelligence sources so that each nation would have to deal with the situation on its own. Wasn't that true? Were we telling anyone? The situation, as the representative said, was quite clear-cut. For the first time in forty years, an American president was confronted with a clear set of choices. For our sake, of course, he hoped that we would make the right decision.

He reminded me of Arthur. Did I tell you that already, Merrick? Merrick is in this room, looking at me with his usual mixture of gloom and apprehension; unlike Henry, he is not a reader but rather a starer; looking at those fixated, glistening eyes, it is possible to believe that Merrick is looking deeply into me, is seeing, as it were, my very soul ... until I remind myself of the fact that neither Merrick nor Henry are of any capacity whatsoever; if they were, they would not be male nurses, day-shift, to a sniveling and senile ex-president locked up like a rat in the steaming, fuming quarters of his four-and-a-half-room prison on the eleventh floor of this very old-style residential building. Instead, Merrick and Henry would be out in the world writing instructions for injections and baths rather than merely administering them. They have satisfied the very minimum requirements of the board? Am I right, Merrick? Of course, the man is beyond taking offense; there is no way in which I could cause him to lose his temper, and if I did, it would merely result in his replacement. Merrick appreciates his position too much. There are only two living ex-presidents, and although one of them may be rightly considered to be as good as dead, the other one is not in the best of condition either. Merrick appreciates the honor and obligation of his position and would do nothing to sacrifice it. Isn't that right? Observe that stupid beam now, the slight lift of the eyebrows, that gleaming, steaming beam that both reveals and conceals feeling. You think that I'm a real son of a bitch, don't you, Merrick? I couldn't care less. I do not think well of you either. I think you are unequal to any challenge which I could pose. Stop staring—you're making me nervous now.

The man reminded me of Arthur. Stop staring; I might piss all over the floor, over this gleaming cuspidor locked in my thigh—and where would you be now? He was much younger than Arthur would be now, of course, and yet I could imagine Arthur, forty-four years old, wearing this outlandish garb, the highly stylized garb of what they called the resistance. I could even see that if Arthur had lived to this age—which he would have done and well beyond except for one tiny, genetic accident—he might have had this expression in his eyes, this bone of cynicism lanced through and just underlying the intentness of that face, the cast of the eyes in their fanatic glare undercut by the measured outlines of the skull beneath, the skull that knew all, touched and apprehended everything, and would soon enough assume its primary, the rest of the flesh tumbling into corruption. Oh, yes, looking at this man I might have been looking at Arthur, which is not to say that I was looking at him, which is not to say that my mind did not remain clear and alert through all of this, uncluttered by noisome speculations and sentimental lurches toward my deceased son, who it would be hard under the best of circumstances to see as a victim. But then, that one swinging glance past him to look out the window toward the parade grounds, what I had deliberately selected to give me inspiration (presidents, of course, can get away with anything, and now and then they try) at the enormous cost of shifting office quarters to the other side of the wing, at the cost of getting illuminated floodlights and one-way paneling in the window—and then my gaze swinging back, I confronted him and could see then, that he was serious, that he was absolutely serious, that he meant what he was saying. And up until that moment, I think I had been proceeding—all of us had been—on the assumption that there was an element of parody here, an element of outrage deliberately contrived so that at the last moment they could whip away the mask and laugh, having confronted us only with our own fears … but no, no, and no again. Looking at him I could see the strange, mooning cast of the fanatic, below the level of the chin, the tremble of the hands. "You have no time to think about this," he said, "nor will we negotiate. You are to give your response now."

"I don't know," I said. "I would have to discuss it with the cabinet. I would have to make a public statement of some sort. There is no way that what you want can be accomplished without—"

"Don't temporize, you fool," he said to the president of the United States. "We've lived with your rationalizations for forty years. We don't have to any more; we hold all the power. You must make your decision now. Dismantle or die."

"You don't understand," I said, "there are factors here that are beyond your comprehension, there are intricacies—"

"There are no intricacies. You merely create the idea of complexity to save your own skins, to maintain your totalitarian control. You resist change because change would undercut your own position, that's all. Well," he said, leaning forward, his eyes glazed with excitement, "it occurred to me that this was perhaps the key to any analysis of the situation." He was deeply excited, profoundly stirred—and why should he not have been? Under the circumstances, I would have been the same. "You must decide now. What will you do?"

And I sat there behind the desk in the East Wing, looking out at the parade grounds again, then back at him, swinging in vision, his luminescent face, the glowing of the grounds, before my reach the telephone with which I would communicate the orders; and there was no way to tell him, no way to tell him, Henry and Merrick, at all that he had misjudged the situation and that even if I were to use that telephone, it would make no difference. Dispersion. The fragmentation of power. There was no way in which I could do for him what he was asking, even if he had been Arthur himself and the appeal had been a restoration to life, an end to the stinking and eternal corruption of his flesh.

I can take a walk if I want to, Merrick. I can do anything I want to do; get me my overcoat and my cane, get me my little walker and stand close behind me, and you and I will go out onto Park Avenue like a pair of patients etherized upon a table, just you and I, stumbling and staggering down the length of the Avenue ... why, it would be a sensation—my first public appearance in what? two months? two years? It is difficult to recollect but certainly in a very long time anyway. And I think that I deserve to go out; it is high time that I took the air again. And you have no right to keep me prisoner in this apartment which, very cunningly, I know that you are doing. I know that you are merely representatives of interests in whose best judgment it would be a disaster if I were to see the street again, if I were consequently to be seen in public. Wild Bill. Wild Bill Springer. You are afraid of the walker, the cane, the overcoat, the canister taped to the thigh, and the slight, deadly stain of drool which would come from one corner of my mouth as thee and me went strolling down the Avenue. That is what you mean.

But I say that I have a perfect right to take a walk if I wish; I say that no one is more entitled than Wild Bill to a stroll down the Park

Avenue of his life and dreams. Remember old Harry Truman tapping his way down the Avenue in the sunset of his years, his cane cleaving out small, neat patterns on the concrete as he scurried ahead of the press and attendants in pursuit … is it possible that I am obsessed by old Harry, that I am trying myself to reconstruct old Harry in some conceived valley of the self so that it is not Wild Bill so much as Independent Harry that will be rolling down the Avenue? I do not know about that, Merrick. We ex-presidents, of course, are a very small and select group, our devices and motives not to be understood by the run of men; I am entitled, after all, to take my referent from my peer group—wouldn't you say so, Merrick? Bring me my paraphernalia!

Of course, this is impossible; I see it quite clearly now and you needn't stare at me in that way, Merrick. I am not at all stupid, despite the appurtenances of senility which you may observe in my psyche and on my person, my senility being carried around with me the way that a fat, elderly lady might tug on a suitcase chained to her and filled with her most necessary possessions; despite all of this, as you say, I am stimulatingly alert and cognizant of my situation, and the higher cerebral faculties remain clear and well preserved. I am extraordinarily lucid today, Merrick; even I can appreciate this lucidity, admit that there are not many mornings on which I share this balance of humor and insight … so let me tell you why I cannot walk out upon the Avenue. Let me make perfectly clear to you in the words of another ex-president, as they say, why I cannot go out tap-tapping upon the concrete of the Avenue, followed by faithful attendants and admiring press, gathering awe-stricken glances from passersby like flowers as I float down the avenue of the memory.

I am no fool, Merrick. My public appearance would be scandalous and embarrassing. I may not be the first president or ex-president to have fallen upon the appearances of senility, but I am the first to have done it at such an advanced age; and my appearance, as any fool can tell, is absolutely shocking. I can hardly believe myself on my occasional glances into reflective surfaces (all mirrors having been cunningly removed from these rooms), the extent of my deterioration. It would be a demoralizing and terrible thing for me to appear in public, far better to keep me here on a high floor under cover of male nurses, the tape recorder for sustenance and company, bleating whines from the sounds of the reversed tape as I dictate my memoirs … oh yes, I am working on my memoirs. That, at least, has been made known to the public and explains my seclusion over the last two years. The need for absolute privacy as I dictate my memoirs, bring them into organized format, the story of the eighties, the administration of Bill Eric Springer.

Although a healthy, hale, hearty, happy, hamstrung, and hellacious eighty years old, I have reached that stage of life where I realize that I must conserve my energies and turn inward if I am to make my last great contribution to the unborn generations of mankind. Of course, I can understand this and so can the press and my many admirers; it explains why no interviews can be given and why I have not been seen in public for so many years since that distressing incident of which we will not speak now. Perhaps later. Have I got it, Merrick? Do I understand the situation? You must have thought that I was a fool if you did not think I knew what was going on ... but as I said, I feel extraordinarily lucid today, little slants of sunlight pouring through latticework, casting mysterious patterns on the floor, little filigrees and filaments of the Presidential Seal I would imagine in my not-too-disordered consciousness ... oh, yes indeed, I feel today as if I could, if I really had to, control my situation.

Then too the death of my dear wife Hope, her sudden and unfortunate demise barely two years ago has turned me into something of a recluse. Everyone knows how much support and cheer I obtained from this devoted woman through the twenty-nine years of our marriage, how much of my late political career was the product of her guidance and patient counsel, how the bitch and I had a relationship which—magnified by our childlessness and the great and awful pressures of national politics—had as many secrets as a child's closet. ... Oh, yes indeed, the media have been very good on the question, standing aside respectfully at the funeral, honoring me more in the breach than the observance ... one could hardly tell from my stone-cold composure at the very private funeral how deeply shaken I was, and since then, of course, I have never been the same ... it is no small thing for a seventy-eight-year-old man to lose a devoted mate of twenty-nine years who was twenty years younger than he ... ah, yes, that would bring the thrust of mortality.

So no excuses have to be made for my failure to dodder out to Park Avenue and take the sun. On the other hand, excuses *would* have to be made if I were to do so; the effect upon so many of my devoted friends and one-time supporters would be extensive, ah, most astonishing: They would hardly know what to make of it.

So I understand quite well, Merrick, why it is impossible for me to go outside. It has been almost two years since I have stirred from these rooms given me by a grateful government along with the lavish attendances of two orderlies, similarly provided for day service and a group of night servants who I never see, being promptly anesthesized into torpor at 6 p.m. every day by your merciful needle and attentions.

... Really, gratitude oozes from every pore of me at this moment, so as others might be drenched by sweat so as I by gratitude ... it is not necessary for you to look at me in that way, Merrick. I am perfectly in control, perfectly in control of myself.

We want a world government and complete dismantling of the piles, or we are going to detonate. Ah, yes. That was a reasonable attitude suitable for calm dialogue and discussion. The line could have been delivered by you, Merrick. I think that you would have done it with even a flatter affect.

Thinking of Kennedy, the astonishing mortality rate of U.S. presidents, not only the twenty-year curse (which gave me ample pause, you may be sure—oh, yes indeed, there was a reason why that was a good year for a compromise candidate) but the succeeding administrations, one wrecked by assassination, the next by near-assassination and repudiation, the third broken from within, the fourth spectacularly its own victim ... oh, yes, it was, hard to ride straight in cars. Often, unconsciously, I would find myself curled over in the car in a *crouch*, my head moving kneeward, my knees moving headward, balled into a fetal posture, anticipating some Enormous Shock which would explode like a line of tracer fire from temple through skull through consciousness ... heaving over myself in the car until Hope, if she was with me, would tap me on the shoulder and say, "Bill, Bill, you've got to straighten up. Stop thinking, Bill." And I would turn toward her (always, always I would turn toward her) with that embarrassed smile and say, "Just thinking, just thinking," and she would say, "Bill, if we don't give them a good appearance, if we show fear, if we can't give them that appearance, then it's worse for them, worse for us," thinking as always of that place between the shadow and the act where all of the feeling began; and I would straighten up, guilty, mopping little beadlets of sweat from my brow, waving, waving until the urge to hunch over like some animal pulling threads in the viscera would come again and I would slump over to myself in the eave of the limousine, her own face impermeable in the light; she would give them nothing at all, not even at the end would she break—only that one time which came much later and had nothing to do with those rides.

Once, in Dayton, coming for a dedication of the Peace Center, someone took a shot at the car as we were coming out of it. It was strange, after living with the irreality, the conception of it for so many years, the actual occurrence seemed almost offhand, incidental; in fact, we did not know what had happened until we saw in the distance local police dragging off a screaming man waving and flaunting something gleaming in his hand. Only then did I manage to juxtapose the spang of shot off the car door and the picture of the man to realize that what had happened was an assassination attempt. But something known in dreams and conception over and over again is never the same, absolutely never the same in reality—like sex, which is all flesh, tugging and pain in the activity while not being at all like that in the mind— so assassination would have been the same way. It occurred to me then that it could have been in just that dull and unbelieving fashion with which the bullet could have struck home; lying on the stones and gravel, the blood running out of me, I would not have believed that what had happened could have occurred, because I had always conceived—even I, who should have known better—assassination as being an essentially glamorous business, something high about it, high and exalting, ringing epiphany as the shots struck the brain, a feeling of conclusion as one slumped toward one's wife or self in immolative glee ... but no, it would not have been anything like that at all. It was always a man in an undershirt, a crowd that did not know what was going on, flesh against flesh, heat and stones, and scuffle and annoyance; that was all that it was ever going to be, the damned *corporeality* of it, like sex, was blood and flowing. Well, that was how assassination would be, and no glow to it at all, not even in retrospect; in retrospect it would simply be death and nothing else. But still, even with that insight bubbling and bobbing around in the waters of the mind like a troll behind a fishing boat, it was still necessary to go through all the acts of ceremony which had brought us there ... the Peace Center, the steps, the library, the dedication, the speech exactly as laid out in the scheduling; only one corner of the mind exploded into lips mumbling and babbling to itself deep in the pocket of the brain about what had happened—but that never to reach outside, you can be sure. One must learn to be sealed off; one must do what one does without thought and on reflex, this being the key to politics and show biz. And certainly after thirty-five years, I was able to do so, miming the activities of interest while putting far into that corner of the brain that chewed and regurgitated death any considerations of what might have happened to me. Later, on the way to the airport, we got a report from the service: he had been taken to a police station ... he had collapsed ... he had been taken to a hospital ... he was in serious condition ... he had had a cerebral hemorrhage ... he was under artificial life-sustaining means ... he was an itinerant, a loner, a wanderer, an anonymous individual of no background ... the life-support mechanisms would bring him around, hopefully ... we might get the full story someday. ... Even then I knew he was going to die. We would know nothing. We would never know anything.

"He is going to die," I said to Hope on the plane. "He is going to die; all of them die; and we will know nothing at all right up until the very end."

"I don't know what you're talking about," she said. "Can't you forget this?" her own face blank, impermeable; the woman would show nothing. It was not until much, much later that I understood that this was because, most likely, there was nothing to show. "Can't you put this out of your mind? It doesn't mean anything." And I said again, "He is going to die," but not even thinking of him now, rather my attention distending, moving outward past the wing of the plane to the unimaginable land outside, striations brown and green beneath the clouds, structures slashed out of the wild, empty spaces: America.

"I saw it coming for a long time," Eunice said. "I knew it was going to happen—do you think I'm a fool? I won't give you a divorce; I'll ruin your career." (Perhaps I am compressing all of this a bit, but this is a license one is permitted when trying to dictate one's memoirs under vast and increasing time pressure—I might stroke out anytime—and certainly this was the evolving sense of it.) "You want to run for president someday; you certainly want to be reelected; you can't do it with a nasty divorce. I'll fight you, Bill. I'll make it miserable for you."

"Don't be ridiculous," I said. "It hasn't been a marriage for ten years, Eunice, you know that, ever since Arthur—"

"Don't you talk about Arthur. I never want you to mention Arthur's name again, do you understand that? That's an obscenity to me—to hear you mention Arthur's name. You have no right to say it now, you get away from me, you go back to your Senate Office Building, you—"

"Eunice," I said, "don't be ridiculous," I said again, "I'm just telling you this as a courtesy. You know there's no marriage—we haven't even lived together for years. You can't claim that—"

"You disgust me," she said, "you are filth. You are obscene. All of you are obscene and all of you are filth, but you disgust me more than any of them because I have been too close to you and I know your lies. You will never get a divorce." She was old and ugly. Always she had been old and ugly to me, even when she was young; but now I could see this. "Get away," she said again.

"Eunice," I said, "I'm trying to do the right thing here. I'm trying to tell you the truth, but you won't listen. If you listen, it will do us both a world of good, Eunice. There's nothing painful about the truth—"

"You bastard," she said. She was always swearing at me; she would curse me all of the time. Her body was a curse, framed in the pattern of obscenity on the bed. And entering her, moving low toward her open spaces, was to puncture the *u* in *fuck*. I never felt anything other than dirty when I was screwing her, but this, I want to emphasize, has nothing to do with my reasons for leaving her; simple guilt or doom would not be sufficient to leave that woman, not ever. I would need something far more concrete, more viable, something which would function as an alternative. But this is going back a long long way, and it is not really possible to talk of my mental state at that time, thirty-four years ago.

"You bastard," she was saying, "I'll make it hell for you." But my mind was already spinning off in some vague direction apart from her, likewise my body. I could feel myself filled with abstraction; and looking at me then, she must have realized that her time was past, there was no way that she could reach me, no way in which she could get through to me again—and this more than anything else is what must have broken her, caving her, kneeling into herself, her body a declension.

"Was it for nothing?" she said. "All of this then, was it for nothing?" And I wanted to say, "Eunice, you are getting upset over abstractions; Eunice, there are no issues here; Eunice, there is no concrete thing to which you can point and say this is what you will miss, this is what you will gain by not leaving me; there are no concretizations left in our marriage, everything is abstractions; we are fighting over abstractions; even this, my decision to leave you is an abstraction; I have decided to do it now, and I am telling you this at breakfast in the sunlit parlor of our five-room duplex, but then again I could have told you a year ago or two months from now in another parlor not floodlit as this one is; I could have done it at night in our bed or in the enclosure of a limousine … Eunice why won't you be sensible? It isn't me you are reacting to here but something, someone else, someone who you do not even know, emotions which you are supposed to feel, not the reality of the situation but merely the felt reality."

Oh, this was some monologue that I had stored up for her—and who is to say that it would not have worked, that I would not have somehow punctured through into the center of her and yanked her by the force of my rhetoric to a new apprehension. But I said nothing else to her at all, merely turned, merely moved away from there; there was nothing else to say and I simply wanted to leave. …

On our honeymoon, the first night in the New Yorker Hotel in Manhattan, the bridegroom tense and white-faced, the bride impermeable in the blues and browns into which she had changed right after the ceremony, sitting with her hands folded in the airplane, her head leaning against my shoulder, a silent and closed-in amusement on her face; and then in the hotel in the room as I had moved toward her, she had said, raising her hand, "We'll do exactly what we are supposed to do, but first I'm going to get some dinner." Seven hours in the plane and I moved away from her—who is not to say that I was not as relieved as disquieted, the responsibility of the wedding night suddenly awesome, although this is not to say that there had not been substantial playing around before the marriage, particularly in the last week before the ceremony, when she wanted to do it desperately but I held off from banging her for what I termed were moral reasons, but probably were just fear.

Looking across her at the table between us in the coffee shop, that closed-in aspect still on her mouth, that dance of amusement in her eyes, and just touching knees under the table, then all the way back up in the elevator, I hardly knew her; into the bedroom and she into the bathroom first—I did not know her at all then—in a pink nightgown I had never seen before filled with ribbons; back to the bed, and I into the bathroom into my clumsy pajamas, then back into the room which was suddenly dark; finding her in the bed that way I did not know her at all, but I was sure that I loved her; love would make everything work out, that was how we felt in those days … and then leaning above her in the darkness, poised on an elbow, saying, "The bridegroom is absolutely terrified, you know." And something had reached out of her, some bird vaulting in the room, hammering its pressure into my chest, and she had brought me murmuring against her, talking into my ear, biting it, filling my ear with confidences and lashings of her tongue, and I had begun to rise, sputtering beneath her, until suddenly that which was shapeless and without form in the void was no longer shapeless but had every purpose under the heaven and cold. Cold, I dug my way into her, feeling her yielding slowly, moving up further toward her center, then, feeling one small pocket of resistance caving easily under me as I wedged my way upward, and it was almost too easy (but she had warned me; hadn't she warned me already of a childhood accident which had caused a rupture? and I had no reason to disbelieve her, no reason at all), digging further and further, and suddenly feeling was all around me. She was crying underneath me. I was crying in rhythm too, and inch by inch I felt consummation being yanked out of me in what was pain and pleasure indistinguishable; and then, the orgasm having gone as quickly as it had overtaken, I collapsed across her, murmuring, feeling the bird of that orgasm depart with swoops and weird cries, now echoes in the room.

She kissed me on the cheek. "You see," she said, "you see?" and gave me a breast out of her nightgown. I opened my mouth, put my teeth on it, felt the nipple arc into mouth, and she gave me suck, then in the close spaces of the bed, and I took it deeply until the rising began again. "You see?" she said, "you see?" And I guess I did see. I must have come three or four times that night—no, it may only have been two—but it was constant. I was at her in those spaces for hours and hours and no sense of transition from one state to the next—

"You're crazy," she said, "you're all crazy. You believe your lies. You wouldn't know the difference between truth and lies if it were shown to you, because that's the kind of people you are."

You do not forget things like that.

Merrick and Henry, Merrick or Henry, whichever or both of you are on duty today (I have not looked up from this for several hours; I am filmed with sweat; it is pouring into my rheumy old eyes), you simply do not forget things like that under any circumstances.

Today the weekly visit from Doctor Goodenough. I do not know if it is weekly, my chronological sense having slipped along with so much else recently, but it *feels* weekly; the intervals of light and dark are consistent enough, and the rhythms of Doctor Goodenough working out their dark loose counterpoint to those of Merrick and Henry, and the unseen stalkers of the night appear to be consistent unto that cycle. I think that it is a week. Under Henry's observation, Goodenough gave me the standard fitness and reflex test, tapping me here and there, examining pupils with his concentrated light for incipient or progressive brain damage; slammed me in the stomach; felt thinly of a biceps; and then, with a gesture, ordered Henry out of the room—the bedroom, I should add, in which these examinations are always conducted. Henry was not pleased with this, remaining in position, his lips locked to sullenness.

"Please," Doctor Goodenough said, "I want to talk to the president alone."

"He's not supposed to be left alone at any time," Henry said, "the orders—"

"I make the orders. I make the orders here and I am telling you to leave."

Henry looked up at the ceiling, then in an odd gesture directly at me, as if looking for corroboration and support. "Isn't it true that I'm supposed to stay?" he said weakly, almost piteously—piteousness not being an element of the personality which I have ever associated with Henry—"isn't that clear?"

"You have been told to leave, Henry—"

"I take my orders from him—"

"No," Doctor Goodenough said, "you do not fake your orders from him, you take your orders from me," and with an exasperated gesture, slammed his little black bag closed, the report quite galvanizing in the little spaces of the room and quite discomfited by sitting like a suitcase opened for inspection on the bed, mute baggage.

I said, "All right, Henry, I am asking you to leave now. I'm ordering you to do so." Henry, standing, shaking his head. "I'm sure that the doctor is right," I said, surprised at my calmness and reflexive lucidity; really, it had been so long since I have given orders of any sort—little spiteful, senile outbursts not counting—that it was strange to see that I still had the power of command. The old, reasonable tone was in my voice, the steel and calm, the suspicion of threat, I sounded quite as well as I ever had before. A good day for me, and Henry, shaking his head, quit the bedroom instantly, mumbling to himself, snapping the door closed, leaving Goodenough and myself confronting one another in a posture on the bed that instantly converted itself to restlessness. Lying naked, I pulled the covers over me for some protection while Goodenough's gaze flicked politely away; then he said, "I might as well get right to the point. You know that your condition is not improving."

"Yes," I said. I have already said that this was a lucid day for me. I felt quite in focus and as a matter of fact able to discuss my condition, as if Wild Bill Springer were some unfortunate in the next room. I am aware of that.

"You still have your good periods, but they're coming further and further apart now, and it's almost impossible to regulate for them. You're out of control; it's not necessary to tell you that, is it? We can't really find a balance; it's hit or miss now. More and more we've just got to increase the dosages, but that's no good either, your tolerance levels are just moving way up. I don't think that we can promise any sort of control at all, and the periods between lucidity are going to be greater and greater."

Goodenough is in his fifties, I imagine; he comports himself with a strange youthfulness. And underneath the sagging outlines of his face, the corruption of the flesh, one can see a wasted, eager youth, which he indeed must have been in 1960 or thereabouts, but this illusion has never comforted me. He is what he is and what he symbolizes is dreadful. Nevertheless, feeling that I understand him as I do, there is a kind of control. I know nothing whatsoever of his personal life. I know nothing of his professional background either; to be quite honest, he was merely assigned to me. Nevertheless I have no reason to believe that he is anything other than competent, although he has a clumsy hand with an injection, a real shudder on the needle, which more than once or twice has brought foaming blood to the surface when he has slipped the controlling drugs into the pathways.

"We might have to face the question of institutionalization again," he said to me quite seriously.

"I have faced it."

"I'm willing to discuss this with you. As a matter of fact, Mr. President, I have demanded from the first the right to discuss all of this with you objectively. I have too much respect—"

"Institutionalization is out," I said. "We have already decided that. They have already decided that."

"It could be done very quietly," Goodenough said. "We originally, all of us, feared that it might become public knowledge, but things have changed a good deal in the last six months. There's much less interest and attention than there has been in the past. In fact, you're practically forgotten. In fact," he said excitedly, "in fact, it could be said that it would be possible to arrange it with a minimum of publicity and in an institutional framework—"

"I don't want to be institutionalized," I said. It was like telling a child that despite the logic of his arguments, he *still* could not fly. Goodenough settled back in position, the flickering little activity within subsiding. It occurred to me that he was not a bad person and that in many ways he was a creditable individual, and therefore it was not his fault, not strictly speaking his fault at all that I hated him. He did not want to be this way any more than I wanted to be in my own position, but on the other hand questions of role dominate. They always must dominate.

"It's just a matter of going day by day then," Goodenough said. "I'm being quite frank with you here. What I'm doing is not professional at all." A disturbed look flicked once again across his face. "I could get in very serious trouble for talking this way with you. I'm just supposed to administer and that's that."

"I do understand. I do appreciate that."

"But I feel that you're capable of understanding your own situation and of reaching a decision. Of making decisions on it."

"How long do I have?" I said.

"Before what?"

"Before I won't be able to function at all. Before the periods of lucidity are gone. Before I'm not capable of thinking."

He shook his head. "There's no way of determining that," he said, "no one can make judgments like that. We can try, keep on trying to hit a balance. It's possible that we may find some combination—"

"But you haven't yet."

"No."

"And you think that there's going to be a steady decline. That you won't be able to hit this balance because you haven't already."

"Yes," he said, "yes, that's pretty much the way I see it. Of course, it's possible that you may find the balance on your *own*. The metabolism is a very subtle and tricky thing. We're trying all kinds of combinations and possibilities, and at some level the body itself may find an accord."

"But you doubt it."

"Yes," he said, "I doubt it very much." He leaned over and picked up his bag, dangled it from his wrist in that curiously effeminate fashion. "It wouldn't be that bad," he said, "I mean, you could find a situation in an institutional framework where you'd be able to do as much as you're doing here, maybe even more. There wouldn't be any more restriction of your activities, and you'd have advantages—"

"No," I said. "I will not do that. That is one thing which is absolutely clear. The president of the United States is not going to be institutionalized."

"I didn't say you had to be," Goodenough said with a rather sullen expression. "I've tried to avoid it from the first. That's the reason I'm here. But there is much less public attention now than you might think, and it would be possible—"

"That is all," I said. My fingers began to coil and uncoil. An image hit me broadside; I could leap from my posture, spring on Goodenough and attempt to strangle him, dig my long and graceless fingers into his throatline and start to throttle him, watch the blood drain out of his head, his face becoming a bulbous white in the light of the room, his floppings and thrashings as he fell before me like a fish on the carpet, dribbling out his life on the rug ... but no, no. It would not work. If I had had the strength to have done this, I would not have been in this position to begin with, but instead would have been in an entirely different position sitting *ex-partum* in the Senate, giving wise and mellow, only slightly ironic, dictums on the state of the nation, offering my wise and distant counsel to those who would gather around me, perhaps acting as the moderator of my own internationally acclaimed television presentation.

Yes, any number of things could have happened, but none of them did, because a funny thing happened on the way toward senescence, and just like that I found myself beginning to lurch out of control. It was Peoria all over again, except that Peoria had been merely a symbol, a metaphor for everything that was to follow—sliding, sliding out of contact, my eyes drooling their way down Goodenough's lapels and down to his pants legs, my mouth falling open to slackness.

What a disgusting old fool you are, disgusting. The elements of my revulsion were so interesting that I felt myself dwindling into a little place in which one by one I picked out all the pieces of my persona that repelled me the most, all of the reasons why I was despicable, evil, weak, repulsive ... and in that eave of self, after some passage of time,

I tumbled and tumbled, coming out of it to find that Goodenough was gone and that faithful Merrick had returned to the room.

"Do you want to do some more work today, Mr. President?" he said— I thought that he was laughing at me—"or would you prefer to rest?" Surely he was laughing at me; he knew of my condition; he and Goodenough had consultations all the time, explicit instructions delivered.

"No," I said, "no, I do not want to do any more work today; no there is no more work today; no there is nothing more at all today." In a way I blame Goodenough for everything and in a way for nothing at all. "No more work today, Merrick, I must stay in the bed and close my eyes and disgust myself."

Now the question of the curse was clear, no one could avoid it anymore. Now the question was, was it a hundred-year curse, terminating out on the point of 1960? Or was it merely to go on and on, presidents elected in years ending with *0* dying and dying in office? First Lincoln, then Arthur, then McKinley and Wilson, Roosevelt stroking out in a garden, and Kennedy of course, which had added a whole new element to the situation, more McKinley than McKinley himself. But what the mystics (who were very active that year) wanted to decide was whether it was merely a hundred-year cycle or whether more likely it would go on and on, this curse, on the presidency, and every twenty years on the dot the proud inauguree would have to juggle thoughts of pride and power with blacker images of fire or water, pestilence or disease while working his way through the ritual ironies of his address. Hope raised the issue herself years before, but of course I was not thinking of it at that time, my own modest ambitions secreted below the level of purpose, being largely invisible even to myself in those benign years, and the incumbent being apparently well settled into his eight-year course. But when the incumbent announced that he would not run for a second term late in '79 and did it in a fashion which seemed to block off any forced renomination, little tender shoots and flowers of purpose began to gather in my mind for the first time, and in the strangely lacklustre field of candidates that emerged at that time, I seemed to have as good a chance as any.

"You know why nobody really wants it," Hope said. "They're thinking of the curse."

"The curse?" I said. I had not even thought of it until that time. "What curse?"

"The twenty-year curse," she said and went on to explain. And of course once she did, it all came reeling back—or should I say exploding—into consciousness.

"Well," I said, "that certainly has nothing to do with me."

"It has everything to do with you; it means that if you really want it, you can get it," she said. "You don't think that anyone really wants this now, do you? When you come right down to it, you'll have a clear field. Anyone who announces early and campaigns hard for this can have it. Everyone will get out of your way. No one really wants it, but you should be aware of it." Hope had none of Eunice's problems. Second wives in politics rarely do; they know exactly what they are getting and are, in fact, titillated by it. This is one of my generalizations.

"It's just a silly coincidence," I said, "it's just happenstance." I was then in what I like to recollect as my rational period: rational possibilities, rational solutions, a Johnsonian precision in the cultivated majority leader who did not believe in myths, dreads, phantoms, spirits, or the onslaught of the uncontrollable, except as it might have affected him in his fantasy life or in certain vagrant impulses of sexuality. I don't think that anyone takes this seriously at all.

"No?" she said. "You don't think so? Have you ever heard of a president retiring in mid-term, announcing that he wouldn't run again?"

"Coolidge," I said, "Coolidge announced that."

"What does Coolidge have to do with it?" she said, "Coolidge was no president, he was a man who inherited. He ran again because he didn't even know what he was getting into, but once he did—when he did— he found that he didn't like it. He never campaigned for the nomination; it never interested him. We're talking about a man who dedicated his life to the presidency, who won, who gave it four years—"

"It's ridiculous," I said again. "I don't even think that he knows about it. I can't imagine—"

She gave me that look. Hope always had a way of giving me a look— in certain aspects of light, in certain ways, a look which undercut me completely, which turned a situation around and wheeled me back upon myself. At one time I thought that this was an affectionate gesture, that it came out of affection and understanding and a kind of deep subterranean closeness which is exhibited in only the very best of marriages; but later on I learned that this was not so and that the look was always the same, what it had been for twenty-nine years, annihilative. But of course as age burned her flesh and attractiveness away, duplicity was harder to come by and her purposes franker. She said, "A man like this? *This* president? Do you really think he doesn't know exactly what he's doing and why he's doing it? It could only be that. He's aware of it."

"That's ridiculous," I said again, "that's absolutely ridiculous. Why, a president of the United States! A man doesn't abandon national office because of a superstition, because of a bunch of mystical nonsense." But later on, as the season progressed, I began to make the slow, cautious changes in cloakroom and party. (There are ways to put a nomination together which are too subtle even for the refined mechanism of these tapes.)

You don't think that I'm really going to give you information like this, do you Henry? Why, you could use it and run for president yourself someday—not that this would necessarily be a bad thing, I mean, there *have* been presidents worse than you would make, Henry. At least your reach would not exceed your grasp; and you know that in your heart you are a very stupid man, although a very competent male nurse. To be sure. To be sure, Henry, you are a competent male nurse.

Putting together the filaments of possibility slowly—Georgetown here, consultation at the statehouse there, discreet meeting with contributors over in that corner, conferences on the floor of the Senate, working the press and milking the media for the little bit which was due me—I could see that what Hope had said was right, that what she had constructed was not indeed of whole cloth but had some basis, because I could see that the curse—I began to think of it in a very feminine way, masculine curse of the presidency, feminine curse of the month—the curse was very much on everyone's mind. And instead of what we could have expected—eager scurrying and jockeying of candidates—there was a vast sighing reluctance from anyone to emerge from the corners, even those who would have been felt most likely.

As you note, Henry, I am keeping the use of proper names to a minimum here—I do not think that the transcribed tapes of an ex-Chief of State should be a place to exchange old gossip or pay off old personal debts and animosities. But rather I like to think that it is the twenty-first century nearly upon us for which I am dictating, and these memoirs will have far more value if personalities are suppressed and vague descriptions are inserted for names ... of course, I am perfectly aware, Henry, there being no nonfool like a senile nonfool, that I may be accused, as other presidents have been in their authorized memoirs, of concealing personalities and descriptions for their own sake—out of cowardice, that is to say—and the desire to paint a nice image even if retrospectively. Not so, Henry. Not so at all. Between this excellent microphone and my own lips, there is a complete collaboration, one of utter understanding; I can say anything to it, it (it knows me) will absorb. There is nothing holding me back from the dissemination of names, events, dates, places but my own sense of decorum—that and advancing arteriosclerosis, of course. My recall is not what it should be.

But what's-his-name did not seem to want the nomination; and the young fool from Kansas stuck to fund-raising only in his own state, for his own reelection campaign; and the boob from New York, who is to this date in the Senate, did not as expected come out but rather stayed to his own bovine mutterings; and the closet case from the Midwest, Governor of one of our more populous states, did not himself show the proper inclination to make that gesture—fusing courage, the moment, and the man in that great lunge toward the turn of the century (I am quoting him here; I am not incapable of creating such rhetoric). And as we scurried down toward July, the field of us, it became increasingly apparent that the field was *me*, that of all of us, that is to say, the only one whose efforts were at all serious and whose conviction seemed to match his possibility was the distinguished majority leader of the U.S. Senate himself. Not even the president wanted it.

I think at heart all of us thought that he did. All of us convinced ourselves, I think, that he was merely waiting for the Right Psychological Moment to reverse himself, to declare that he could no longer withstand the cries of a grateful and devoted citizenry and that he would, after all, accept the renomination. It might have been the specter of that, a sitting president and our reluctance to offend him, to seem too much like sniffers of carrion which held down efforts at the nomination; on the other hand, his sincerity, as we staggered into the homestretch, even seemed to increase. He had pulled out of all the primaries; and somewhat reluctantly I made the rounds from New Hampshire to South Dakota to Oregon, finding to my own astonishment that opposition was lackadaisical; and by two months before convention time, with only a minimum of attention to the campaign, meanwhile spending my time in the Senate building a Working Image, I was the leading candidate for the nomination by default. It is best to pick one's spots in the primaries cautiously, Henry, it is not possible to win them all, no mortal man can do that, but by carefully preselecting and concentrating efforts, it is possible to win all those that one enters, and this gives an impression of invulnerability. I hope you are paying close attention to this course in practical politics.

Finally, not three weeks before the convention was to convene—it was in Las Vegas that year, if you recall—I was summoned to the White House, not with the rest of the leadership but *in flagrante, in solitaro* (to reach for the little bit of Latin; not too hard, it comes back), and there I met the president alone for the first time in several years— or since a notable, rather drunken incident which I will not discuss and which had occurred in 1970 in circumstances different for each of us. It was the first time I had seen him alone since then, ten years almost to the date, and I was surprised to find how little the office had touched him. Always in the Congressional conferences or at state occasions, it had been at a distant remove under conditions favorable to him, but here in the Oval Office, seeing him face to face and without benefit of lighting or assistants, he still looked surprisingly youthful, although of course there was a rather sullen cast to his face and his jowls sagged. Still, what is there to say? None of us get any younger ever, and he was a man close to fifty years; but next to my rather careworn seventy, he looked as youthful as ever, if not more so.

I sat before him rather restlessly, my hands folded in a strange and unaccustomed primness and tried to keep the anticipation out of my gestures as I leaned toward him.

"I suppose you wonder why I asked you to come here alone, Bill," he said to me.

"Well no," I said, "not exactly. I imagine that you wanted to tell me first that you have decided to take renomination after all, and as a courtesy to me, you're telling me this directly."

He shook his head. "No, that isn't so. My withdrawal, Bill, was absolute, and I'm not reconsidering under any circumstances. If you want the nomination, you can have it. You're certainly in front; you've done a good job here, and I wouldn't do anything to stop you. I don't think that anyone would."

"You're not going to run," I said. "It's true, it's really true; you're going to retire."

"Not retire," he said with that famous and well-beloved smile, which at close range was all props and greasepaint, like actors observed in dress rehearsal under poor lighting from the first row orchestra. "No, I think I'll write my memoirs or something. I've asked you to come, Bill, to find out if you really want this job. You can have it if you want it, you know. The nomination is pretty much in the bag, and I've done a fairly good job of holding the party together. If I make the nomination speech for you—I probably will—and if you play your cards right and I do a little campaigning mostly by staying here and out of your way, I think you should win this by about sixty-forty or at least fifty-five forty-five. The point is, do you want it?"

I had never thought about it. This is true; until that moment it had never occurred to me to think whether or not I had wanted it. I had never thought about the majority leadership, about the House, about the state senate. I had thought about nothing. All of politics is tropism; you go where you can, that is the key. One moves toward vacancy. Metaphysics has never been my strong point. It was a strangely disquieting question. I should say that metaphysics had up until *then* not been my strong point—now, along with urinary behavior, it is clearly one of my obsessions.

"I don't know," I said looking at him, "it's an opportunity, isn't it? I mean, I guess I want it."

"You've never thought about it."

"Not seriously. I never thought that I'd be president, so why worry about it? It never occurred to me that you wouldn't want to run again, and by that time, I'd be seventy-four years old. Even now, I'm seventy. What's a seventy-year-old man doing, running for the presidency? It's ridiculous," I said quite frankly. "But no one else was there, so I did it."

"Don't worry about seventy. Geriatric science is wonderful. They can keep you going, Bill, until you're eighty or ninety. You'll have less trouble being president than you would have being retired. But do you really want it?"

"I don't know," I said, "I guess so. I guess if you gave me time to think about it, I'd decide that I wanted it—yes. I mean, it's just about as far as you can go, isn't it?"

"You'd be surprised."

"It's nothing that I couldn't handle."

"There are problems, Bill," the president said vaguely.

"I'm aware of the problems. I know what's happening. But the Algerian situation is pretty quiet now, I think we've made good strides on Syria, and the monetary situation is working out. Domestically it's no good, but when has it ever been good? We're always going to be dealing with vigilantism—but even there we're making strides."

"This isn't a civics lecture, Bill," the president said, and. stood, stretched, looked out his window toward the monument. "I'm sure that you're quite capable, and of course most of our problems are insolvable, they just take on different names as we go along." He paused and looked at me. "Have you thought of the curse?" he said.

I shifted in my seat, looked up at him mildly, "Curse?"

"Don't be a fool. It's just the two of us here and I'm not taping. There haven't been any tapes here for five years, Bill. Nothing will be held against you. You have thought about it, haven't you?"

"I've thought about it," I said.

"Well? What do you think of it?"

"I don't think anything," I said. "It's a historical accident. If it isn't a historical accident, *I* can't change it. Who can? How can any of us? What can we do, not have a president? Not have an election?"

"People were thinking of that," he said lightly, cracking his knuckles above his head. "That was one of the alternatives which was raised. Seriously," he continued, looking at me, "in '77 we saw all of this coming along. We had conferences about it. We decided that nothing could be done, that almost anything would look like a meddling with the process or a coup d'etat; and after what we had been through with Nixon, we couldn't afford stuff like that anymore. But it was discussed, of course. Putting the election off a year or even calling for a referendum on the question. Getting a caretaker in or resigning and appointing the vice-president."

"That's ridiculous," I said.

"It was my idea, Bill," he said, "I was the one who saw this coming. Do you think it's a coincidence that we can't really get a candidate, that a seventy-year-old senator looks like he's getting it by default? It's even worse with the opposition. They've got a couple of governors, and both of them are trying to back out in favor of the other one. It's really an embarrassing situation, both of them trying to jump. I have good intelligence. Of course, I always knew this office was good for something."

"Are you afraid of the curse?" I said. "Is that the reason you're withdrawing?"

"What do you think?" he said, and then sat down abruptly and leaned over the desk. "If I really was, do you think I'd tell you? Of course not," he said after a pause, "that's all mysticism, superstition, and nonsense. How could a president of the United States be influenced by garbage like that? It would make a terrible impression on the populace. I don't even read the INTELLIGENCER."

"So you are," I said, rather wonderingly I might add. There must have been rather a youthful disillusionment in my aged voice. "You're really influenced—"

"I didn't say that," he said, much more sharply, sitting abruptly, moving in his seat to command an imposing view of the monument, giving me a view equally imposing of his shoulder blades. He wheeled back to me then. "I didn't say that at all and that isn't what I called you here for. If you are going to be president—and at this point you seem to be as likely a candidate as we have—then you might as well be apprised of certain situations you'll be facing that you might not be aware of. That was the reason for this."

"I'm the majority leader," I said. "Don't you think that your own majority leader—"

"I'm my own majority leader," he said, "nobody is responsible for that but myself. Do you think you're told everything, Bill?"

"No," I said, feeling constraint now, the whole situation reeling around, I did not like the situation; I liked none of it—the sullenness of his manner, the puffiness of his face, the strange, glazed expression of his eyes, a certain arrogance in his manner, the threat in his bearing, the hint that matters had been held back from me—and it was as if I could see pouring out of him some aura, some veritable, palpable haze of fear. It must have been the aura of fear itself in the room to which I was reacting, which was contributing to the hostility of his manner.

"There are things about the nuclear situation that we've pretty well managed to keep hidden Bill," he said. "I don't think the press has gotten hold of any of this, at least the national press; there might be a few here and there in Washington who have sources and have gotten a leak, but not the nationals. It would be a disaster if they got it, but I don't think they will. There are problems with the nuclears, Bill. We've lost control of a couple of the plants."

"What?" I said. "I don't know what you're talking about." Nobody thought about nuclears anymore. The strategic arms limitation along with what China and Russia had been doing to one another in the late '70's had pretty well taken any consciousness of nuclears away from us. We just didn't think about them in those gentle days, Henry. If one generation had grown up thinking about nuclear holocaust, then another one was utterly unconscious even of its definition. And I admit that when he started talking about *nuclears*, it was necessary for me to send my mind momentarily skittering back ten to fifteen years in plane of reference, simply so that I knew what he was talking about. I didn't know what he was talking about.

"I've got to tell you something very serious now Bill," the president said. "It's a situation with which I've been living for some time. It's something you're going to be living with too, and if you really want to campaign for the presidency, if you want this office, you're entitled to know exactly what you're heading into. You won't like it Bill—I don't think that anyone would like it. But you've got to know."

"I still don't know what this is," I said, but some chill—or maybe the word is apprehension—had brushed me as with a bird's wing for the first time; then I felt that I was moving close or closer into understanding. "Why don't you tell me?"

"We've lost control of two of the piles, Bill," the president said. "They've been taken over; the entire installation has been taken over in both cases. And they've fallen out of our control for the moment. It's a stalemate because they don't want any publicity and we can't go in and get them. But they're just waiting, I think; they're just waiting for the proper time, and then they're going to hold us up."

"Hold us up? Hold us up for what?"

"You still don't understand, Bill," the president said. "I never would have thought that—I mean we've had our disagreements and so on—

but I never would have thought that you would simply miss the point like this. They've got hold of two nuclear installations, atomic power plants—don't you understand? And they—"

"Who are *they?*"

He waved me off. "Don't worry about who they are right now," he said. "If I gave you one name or I gave you another, would it make any difference? They give themselves a name, do you think that the name means anything? We know who they are too, but that's just biography; it doesn't solve anything; it doesn't make us any more likely to deal with the situation considering what they've got. They're just biding their time and then—"

"Blackmail?" I said, making the leap, "Is that it? They're going to hold us up—"

"The whole planet," the president said, nodding at me encouragingly, his eyes very bright and deep in his face, "the whole fucking planet. Do you see what I mean, Bill? It isn't the curse. I mean, *this* is the curse."

We sat there for a while.

I didn't know sex (I mean, I did know sex, of course, I did in the clinical, or academic sense of the word), but I really didn't know it or had forgotten what it was (take your pick) until Hope came along. It had been so long—oh, my God—it had been so very long, and I had not even thought of it, what with the responsibilities and distractions of my office.

"Don't be a pig," Eunice had said, "you're forty-two years old. Isn't it time you grew up? That kind of thing isn't for us anymore, we had all of that; we had our time, and now our time is past; and I won't tolerate it. Separate bedrooms, please."

I was naive, of course. I should have understood what it meant, that this was not normal, that it is impossible for a marriage to shut off sex unless something is deeply, tragically wrong with the marriage at the heart and that something has been lost forever. As a matter of fact I *did* know it, but what was the difference? I didn't find her that attractive anymore myself; she was ugly, as a matter of fact, all the ugliness to the surface.

And then there were the random adulteries. Don't look so shocked, Merrick; I didn't say that I had no sexual outlet—of course I did, everybody in Washington does somewhere, somehow. There are secretaries, speechwriters, PR gals, teachers at colleges, newspaperwomen, conventions … it is impossible for a U.S. Senator not to have a satisfactory sex life unless he is a eunuch, in which case he can certainly find himself a pimp or set of them catering exclusively to the needs and desires of eunuchs, whatever they may be. I was a

U.S. Senator, Merrick; I was a powerful U.S. Senator—the majority leader—and reasonably attractive, considering all of the cosmetic benefits which can be heaped upon one who has access to the corridors of power. I am not speaking of the routine adulteries—now they meant nothing. I thought they were entirely satisfactory, and in their own way, they were. They certainly kept me away from Eunice's door—a consummation devoutly to be wished by the two of us—and greatly lowered the level of tension in our dying marriage.

It is true—nothing will keep a dying marriage going any longer or any better than casual adultery. I would feel much better about Eunice in the aftermath of my fucking, in and out, three pumps and come, fall drooling to one feminine shoulder or the next and the arc of breast under my stomach; the dead motions of my flaccid tool against her in the act of withdrawal would convince me that Eunice was right—there was something ridiculous to sex; at the very best it was trivial, a custom really, a series of twitches and tropisms not unlike the tropism of politicians toward higher and higher office. If this was all she was denying me, then she was denying me very little. Of course, I am talking about the aftermath—of aftermaths there were many. But for every aftermath, there is of course an anticipation, a conjugation; I would not think this way at the point of entrance, but instead all fire in my fucking would move to fuck and come as quickly as possible ... not to disgrace Eunice, of course. If I would do it quickly, I would not disgrace her. I want you to know that I am talking about the constancy of my life here for years and years, no compression (although through the miracle of tape and incontinent babblings, it is possible to compress a great deal into a very little), but rather a condition which went on and on—it must have been this way for seven years, seven or eight of not too careful, not too joyous but always sufficient fucking. And it might have gone on and on—in fact it *did* go on and on, until Hope changed all of that by showing me something that I had clearly forgotten, perhaps because I had chosen not to recollect it, perhaps because it had seemed worth the forgetting: she showed me the power of the flesh. The entwinement of connection or perhaps it is confection I am thinking of connection/confection oh the words are very hard sometimes to disassociate enjambment in the mind being as it is in the progressively senile but then again the sounds are pretty, the sense is in the sounds as was once pointed out about political rhetoric and oh my God the collisions we had, the small and terrible explosions of the flesh, flowering, flowering.

I must concede the point; I must approach the truth; I think in certain angles that my second wife was a piece of ass the cunt. Even I could think of it; she was able to do certain things in her own bedroom, contrive certain angles of light, resistance, costumes, makeup (which as the light-show developed would make her seem beautiful). And it was many, many years and only at a different stage of my life when I realized that she was not beautiful, that everyone was right and I was wrong; that it was not her special beauty I was seeing but merely the same raddled face and complexion that she had worn before her thirtieth birthday, and which everyone else knew. Nevertheless, I was entranced. We are not talking about an adolescent now, we are talking about a forty-three-year-old man in the flower of his manhood—and my, oh my, how I flowered!

How I flowered underneath and above her making all of the changes in her room. (It was always her room in the hotel; it was the best and most discreet place, she said; she wouldn't risk anything by going elsewhere, and only in Washington could I absolutely control my schedule and my companions; she was very thoughtful and protective even from the first—I thought it was altruism; it was only later on that I realized how entirely clever she had been.)

Going into her was entering knowledge itself, her yielding, springing past the initial softness into a resistance harder than any I had ever known; push harder and open her up a bit more, meet more stone, push harder and inch so a little further. I never knew a woman it was harder to fuck or whom the entering took longer. But finally, inch by inch, I would get into her small, gutted cluster of a hole, her breasts crowding all around me, huge hard flowers reeking of the hothouse … and pounding in and out of her, I would then feel that accomplishing penetration was of a more profound nature than anything which I might accomplish on the floor, never was anything so worthwhile in my life or so worthy of pride (if there had only been someone to brag to) than actually getting inside this woman.

"Oh, my," she had said in the confessional of sex time and again, "oh, my, that's wonderful. There's never been anyone who was ever able to get all the way inside me. I've been to doctors and all that and they say that there's nothing wrong, but I've always been afraid that there *was* something wrong. Isn't it wonderful? Isn't it a wonderful thing to know after all of this time that there *isn't*! But it would take a man, it would take a real, real man, to be able to do that Bill; oh, you're wonderful," putting an enormous breast in my mouth while I sucked and banged away, still imprisoned within her (she was as difficult to leave as she was to enter, but who in God's name would want to leave something like that?) and working myself toward another peak—and if you don't think this was heady stuff, you are quite seriously wrong.

You are wrong indeed to misjudge off the page on which you will read this—assuming transcription will be accomplished. But somehow I wonder if they will actually permit a typist to get hold of these tapes and do the job; but one tiling is sure—I am not going to. I can barely hold my fingers out straight, let alone consider transcription. If you don't think that was something I needed badly at the time, exactly what I needed, as a matter of fact; and although out of the boudoir the language of sex may seem silly and rather naive, you would be equally naive not to understand context and situation. What works here would not work there; what works within the boudoir—while not quite passing for a Nobel Peace Prize acceptance speech—can do things in those confines that the laureate's mumblings could never do.

Not to be mistaken about this, I tumbled within her again and again, past excitement, past all rationalization, merely sensation and that rising pressure, that engorgement sliding past level and level of her, the walls of her breaking and opening within me ... and all of the time, every night of It, returning to my own quarters at some disastrous hour of the morning because the majority leader could not risk any scandal in his personal life. It is one thing to make inching and drastic entrance into a passionate woman at midnight; it is quite another to come staggering home at three in the morning, a certain burning shame overwhelming retrospection.... Merrick or Henry, it must be understood, there are certain contradictions possible in one's personal life which cannot be annealed, which cannot be covered over in any way, which simply exist and must be lived with; and this irony, this tension, this gap between the expected and the actual behavior can be said to function as that emptiness from which all true acts of statesmanship may begin.

I may exaggerate. Hyperbole is not unknown to the political act, and there is a certain tendency to overstate. One can attract more attention through overstatement, of course, but it must be said that the politician's overstatement may come only from his need to set larger and larger shocks to the psyche, which enable him to move past reflex to feeling ... only lying will give him feeling, and the lies must become more and more preposterous as time goes on. Furthermore, since he is fundamentally an honest man (it is in search of his honesty that he has sought politics), the politician, or at least the majority leader, tends to believe his own lies—so there is no longer a question of duplicity here but rather one of psychopathology.

Politicians are not liars. I was not a liar. I have never been a liar. I took myself to be passionately linked with Hope Johnson; I was truly and deeply in love with her ... if this were not so, why would I skulk to her apartment night after night, risking more and more, increasingly careless of my responsibilities or notoriety, simply to plumb those depths once again, to feel the oozing release of her cunt as I wedged myself in there, gasping? She was never any easier to penetrate. She remained tight from beginning to end. I thought at the outset that it was titillating; it was only much later that I came to understand that the woman was absolutely impenetrable. I was not dealing with her cunt but with her personality.

Honesty commended me to make a full statement of the situation to Eunice. Nothing else could be done in the circumstances. I felt that she was entitled to know what I wanted. It never occurred to me for an instant not to divorce her and to marry Hope Johnson immediately. I would have had it no other way. Politicians, from an excess of promoting convention, are the most conventional of people. My life itself is testament to this.

"It is all finished, Eunice," I said to her in that recollected conversation. "Eunice, it is all over. I must be permitted to leave. It will be better for both of us if you permit me."

"I won't," she said, "you are filth. You are lies. You are deceit and moral waste," and so on and so forth. I will not repeat already transcribed material; I have a good recollection of what I have and have not put down on these tapes, my recollection being much better than I am given credit for possessing.

"I will make it hell for you," she said, "I will tie you up in the courts and take it to the newspapers and make statements as to exactly what kind of person you are—and by the time that I am done with you, you would not be electable even for the Illinois lower house again. That's what I'll do to you."

"Be reasonable, Eunice," I said, "be reasonable. I'm going to do it no matter what you say."

"You'd give up your political career? You wouldn't know what to do without it—"

"I will give up my political career," I said. "I will give up everything. I am trying to be honest, Eunice. This is more important to me than anything else."

"You are a liar."

"I am not a liar. I am going to do it in any case. I am going to do exactly what I want and be damned; and if you understand that, you can make it easier for both of us, Eunice." I had not called her *Eunice* in many years. I had not used her name for more time than I could remember. Perhaps that was part of the difficulty; I had lost any sense of her as a person. She was merely a device, an obstacle. One cannot say. That was part of it, but there might have been another part as well.

"You think you're the Duke of fucking Windsor," she said, "marrying the woman you love. That's what you're going to try; you'll make a radio speech—"

"No," I said, "no more. I cannot take this anymore." I stood. "I am going to leave, Eunice. I am not going to come back. I will take out what I can take out now and the rest I will send for."

"You can do whatever you want. If you disgrace me, I'll ruin you forever, that's all. Do you understand that?"

"I'm leaving," I said again. There was nothing else to say. One reaches a point stock-still in the center in which there is nothing, absolutely nothing to be done; even the devices of further movement seem fruitless.

It was with an effort that I turned away from her. "I'm very sorry," I said. "I didn't want it to be this way. I didn't intend it to happen, but it just did, Eunice. People don't remain the same. Everything changes around them and they aren't what they were when they started. It has nothing to do with you."

"Yes it does," she said shockingly. "Look at me," and I looked at her, saw the bleaking, aging, ruined stones of her face. "You blame me for Arthur," she said, "that's always been it."

I gasped. I could not believe it—the audacity. There are certain things so improbable that it is impossible to find any attitude of confrontation leading perhaps to some explication of the popular effects of the assassination. I am only guessing. I claim no expertise in this area. "That's ridiculous," I said finally. "Eunice, that's ridiculous."

"You've always held it against me. You've felt it was my fault from the first."

I shook my head, staring at her. "Eunice," I said, "Arthur died of cancer. There was nothing to be done. No one can be blamed for this; it was simply something in the genes—"

"That's what I mean," she said, "in the genes. You blame me. You think that he inherited it from me."

I did not know what to say. You go through the convolutions and movements of life for a long time, decades perhaps, living within that shell of mortality which is (I will swear this) as liberating as constricting, and something comes then which completely punctures and makes you understand that all of the time you have lived under a misapprehension. That the shell was not cover but mere translucence for something unimaginable outside of it.

"That's crazy, Eunice," I finally settled for. "That's absolutely crazy. Arthur died of leukemia. It could have happened to anyone. It happened to our son. It's a rare but not at all unknown disease of late adolescence, hemolytic leukemia, and it happened to him. It has nothing to do with heredity."

"I know that," she said. "The doctors knew it. Arthur knew it too. But you don't. You didn't then and you still don't. You blame me."

"You're crazy, Eunice," I said again, not as gently. "You're crazy if you believe that I think that."

"First Arthur's gone and now you want to get rid of me. Then you won't remember anything. Then you can start again, as if none of this ever happened."

"I'm leaving," I said. "I am leaving. I cannot listen to this anymore, Eunice. You have got this impossibly wrong, but I can't deal with it. I can't make you see any differently." I was already through the door. "It has nothing to do with Arthur," I said.

"Then you deny your son?"

"What? What is that now?"

"You're just going to leave? You're walking out of here and cutting this off from you, and your son means nothing to you at all. It's like you were never here, like he didn't exist? Do you think you can bury him, Bill, only in this way?"

I did not know what to say. There was nothing to say. "I'll kill myself if you leave, Bill," she said, "do you hear that?"

"But why? Why?" I instinctively took her seriously. I believed her; there was no doubt in my mind at that moment that she would. That was how far she had taken me. It did not occur to me to disbelieve her. If positions were reversed, I might have done the same.

"Because you're leaving me nothing but shame. You're making me look like a fool."

"First you said you'll ruin my career and now you say you'll kill yourself. Which will it be, Eunice? Which do you want to do? Couldn't you try at least for a little consistency?"

"Both," she said, "I'll kill myself and that will ruin your career. I can have it both ways. I'm not inconsistent at all. I've never told anything but the truth. I've been consistent in my own fashion from the first. You're the one who lies. You're the one who changes position."

I saw the humor. Let it be known that I saw the humor. "All right, Eunice," I said at the door, "all right then. You'll kill yourself, and that way you'll ruin my career. You're perfectly consistent. You haven't deviated from your position for a moment. Only I have. You'll have to do it, Eunice," I said.

I could not believe that the woman was serious. Someone who you have lived with for twenty years must be as well known to you as yourself—if not, then you have no insight whatsoever, because there is a fusion, the two of you are the same person after a while, the only separation in anger; and I thought that I knew her well enough.

"You can't be stopped from doing something like that," I said. "You know that if you're serious, I could stay here and argue with you all day, and you still would do it. And if you're not, then it's pointless for me to stay here. And if it's just a threat to hold me, it won't work. It can't possibly work because I'm not going to stay. Not for any reason. It's too late."

I went out of there.

I did not think she was serious, and I think now that she did not think she was serious either. But there are levels and mysteries to motives, which are beyond us; we are the response, the motives, the stimulus; and somewhere in that great synapse of the Twitch, something may happen which we cannot understand ... but my judgment was absolute, she could not do it. She could not possibly do it.

If she had—if she had been capable, that was—it would have meant that I had misjudged everything and that the life I had lived was fraudulent. I did not think that there was so much conviction in her. I did not think that there was that level of sincerity; and if there had been, then everything, always, had been wrong, then she would have been a different woman entirely ... and I should not have left her.

Open on emptiness and pan the sky; move down to the peanut-shell of the limousine in which the Gadget Man sits, his tentacles like a spider's, hunched in one corner surrounded by the white bugs that protect him. Gadget Man is old and cold, bold and mold, lolled rolling into the cache of the limousine, above the dazzling sun, beneath the concrete, and sealed deep into his conviction, Now they come upon him in little waves and ripples of color, disguised as birds fluttering down from the sky, the wavelets of birds rolling over the limousine in which Gadget Man lolled. But he is too bold and cold for them, sees their purpose and knows their cunning; with a cunning of his own extracted from the tomb of himself, Gadget Man reaches inside, the white bugs to his left and right fleeing as he seizes upon the weapon ... and then he shoots the birds with his fiery gadget concealed within his armor. The birds break, their colors fall away, and they no longer have the form of birds but instead the form of insects. Seeing this, Gadget Man understands something, he understands that birds and guards are the same thing, and what he took to be the protectors are merely another form of that which he must be protected against.

This insight—not to say, the way it registers upon him—drives Gadget

Man quite insane. He has not been in the best and most vigorous of health for years; indeed he has been traveling precipitately along the edge, skirting merrily, his limbs crackling with energy as he holds the line between center and disaster. But now, as the birds/insects come upon him, their wings beating like hearts, he is quite mad—oh, indeed, he is quite sufficiently mad—his weapon drooping within his hand, no firearm—not even a clout—but merely a wet, pendulous affliction coming out of the ridges of the hand.

He hits them once! They scurry away; and rising in the seat of the limousine, he hits them twice! And they have reconnoitered; and as he tries to strike them a third time, they have worked out their vicious, cunning, and destructive plan. So they close in upon him, battering and battering.

Despite his bravery, Gadget Man's great heart begins to give out. He feels weakness overtaking him. Looking through some aperture in the attack, he sees the slick web of sky pressing upon him, wheeling his glance left and right, little patches of city; but these are merely interruptions in the panorama of white bodies which press upon him, the limousine picking up speed now, the winds of acceleration transformed to winds of ascension as, tiny gnome pressed against the cushions dwindling in size, the white bugs and birds pressing around him, he becomes at that moment *one of them* and in some coiling and uncoiling of time joins them wheeling in the air. Of course, he sees the Gadget Man himself, Hail Chief, riding to the city.

Spools fouling in the fucking machine; all sense of grasp and control lost; the reels snarling through the loops; loops exploding like confetti; fucking tape all over; surrounded by tape, some of it imprinted, some of it not, the place where it is imprinted covered with streaks submicroscopic—I think the place where it is blank merely blank small streaks—the only trace of what I have left; all matter reduced then to filaments and streaks; everything come down to little marks. Who was it? Beckett? Krapp? Old man in old room talking about life. Am I Krapp? No, am the president of the United States. Repeat that, sir. The president of the United States of America, one hundred and eleventh State of the Union message to the assembled Congress joint houses, great challenges, great years ahead, the American destiny unfurled before us, low taxations, baby boom, strike, manifest, splinter groups, disjointed youth, hungry elders senior power, rage of the aged, increased benefits, lower taxation, loyal opposition, harmony and balance, equality and justice for all Americans under the law, egalitarianism, the New Dream, the Old Dream, the Old Frontier, the New Frontier, the New Deal, the Fair Deal, the Square Deal, the

Nothing Deal, the fouled deal, the fucked up deal, the fucked up, the fucked, the tape, the spittle coming out all over sons of bitches now …

"Let me think about it," I said. "You can't come in here, confront me with something like this, expect me to make a decision. I've got to consider, to—"

"That's the same old shit, dads," the representative said. He lit a cigarette with manifest casualness. I could admire what he was doing (fucking Hope was never like fucking Eunice, but in the end it was the same). "You are going to make that decision now. You are not going to go behind closed doors and figure it out with your advisors and give us the same old temporizing shit; you are going to come up right against it now. That's the point. That's the whole point, dads, president or not," and he flipped a match to the carpet always came fast in the first enjambment. "You are going to live in the world just like the rest of us poor fuckers and take your chances."

"It's impossible," I said, "you can't blackmail a whole country. You can't hold up a nation for ransom—"

"Why not?" he said. He puffed on the cigarette. (I always liked to get blown, but how many women can you find who know how to do it? really get it in there and work on it patiently?) "It's working fine so far."

"This is insane," I said—I think I was saying I was insane. "This is madness."

"We'll take it to the media. They're all outside; we'll put the case to them." I looked at him and realized that he was crazy. Not fanaticism, nothing political, this was clear, clinical insanity, and I could measure the effect it was having upon me: it was making me crazy too. The two of us were crazy. Both of us there in the East Wing were madder, but I was madder than he because I was supposed to run the country and I could not get my mind off fucking. All I could think about was fucking. This is impossible for a seventy-three-year-old man, the act of fucking— that is to say, it is almost impossible—but it is very possible to think about; and that was what was on my mind. "Are you listening to me?" he said.

I looked up at him; my eyes must have been quite bleak and staring, watery, as if floating in soup. "What's that?" I said, "what did you say?"

"You crazy old fuck, you're supposed to be the president of the United States. What kind of horseshit is this? We knew you were old, we knew you were sick, but we didn't expect to find someone here lying in a senile stupor, for Christ's sake! What's wrong with you?"

"I'm thinking," I said. "I'm thinking of your offer. The terms and conditions, that is. Didn't you want me to think it over? Isn't that what you said?"

"We asked you to think, not to dream, you crazy old fuck! Hey, what's wrong with you, dads? You cracked or something like that? I mean, you freaking out?"

I stood shuffling my limbs, like canes handled in the wind by a very old man. "I've made my decision," I said. "I think I've made it now."

He backed off. For the first time, there was something hinting at yield in his position. "Okay," he said, "what is it?"

"In due time," I said. "In due time." I walked deliberately away from the desk, went to the windows, looked out at the monument, behind it the spires of the mountains. Once, Hope and I had driven out to a motel there and fucked in view of the Washington Monument. She said that mine felt bigger. (This is the kind of thing you tend to hold on to as you get older and the juices dry out.)

"Not so fast," I said. "I'm an old man, remember? I'm a senile old fuck. We senile old fucks have to think slower, act slower, perform slower than you younger people, so you will forgive me if I take my time. After all, you've got all the time in the world. It's going to be your world."

I had no belief in an afterlife. Despite the appearances of religiosity incumbent upon the office, I have not believed in God or a religious construct for more than fifty years. This makes this taping somewhat easier; in any event I know that it is *finis*, and I will never have to listen to these spools again under any circumstance, which gives me a nice, tight sense of completion—not even to say an ironic impact of some sort. One must take one's ironies where one can get them at eighty years of age. One must take them where one can get them, as a matter of fact, at seventy-three years of age. Ironies for the aged are not unlike orgasms for the young—this is an aphorism which may as well be noted.

Will you note that, Doctor Goodenough? I am glad to see you, as always; yes, things seem a little better today. Let me finish just this little bit of reel here, and I shall be right with you. I had a little trouble with the reels yesterday, but Henry was very helpful and everything is in order today. As a matter of fact, I feel distinctly better. One must take one's ironies where one can get them.

"What do you want?" I said to him.

"You know what we want. We want world government or—"

I made a dismissive gesture. "No," I said, "that's the cover, the rhetoric. Let's get to the substance. What do you *really* want out of this?"

He shrugged, but his eyes held me close, fastening into me like threads. "Don't worry about that, you son of a bitch," he said, "just worry about yourself."

"But I do," I said. "I worry about myself, and I have to worry about the country too; after all that's the president's role, isn't it? To worry about the country? And I've got to assess your motives in order to be able to assess my own and approach a proper and judicious balance."

"You say you've reached a decision."

"But have *you*?" I said and looked at him levelly. Oh, you would have been proud of me then, doctor—what a man I was. "Have you reached a decision? Do you know what you really want? I don't think that you do."

"You're not talking to an individual. I'm merely a representative. If I leave, there will be another. There is no individual but merely a group whose purposes we enact. There is no decision to be made. The decision has already been made." He was sweating.

"Nonsense," I said quietly, "you are not a representative; you are a person. It is not a group in this room; it is merely you. You are the only one I see. I see no one else. What is your decision?"

"My decision," he said, "my decision, you crazy old fuck, is to walk right out of here now and tell them that you won't negotiate, so we'll have to go ahead. That's my decision." He moved toward the door.

"Is it?" I said, and he held up. "Go on, walk through the door. Walk out. Tell them that nothing has worked, and you've come out with an ultimatum to destroy because you wouldn't let me talk. Tell them that. Tell your group that. Will they send in another with the same orders?"

"You can't bluff me," he said, "there's no one to bluff. You're dealing with a revolutionary instrument—"

"There are no instruments. There are only people. We talk of institutions and great movements, but at the bottom it is merely sweat and blowing. Don't you understand that, son? Don't you realize that you've got to accept the fact of your humanity?"

"Don't call me son. Don't—"

"You know that you must," I said. "They won't help you on the outside. They're not an instrument, but you are. You are only an instrument to them. They are using you, and they will use someone else in your place. You are in the grip of forces you cannot deny. You had better begin to think and act for yourself, son. They won't help you. They simply don't care what happens to you."

He stood by the door. "You're daring me to leave," he said, "you're really serious about this."

"I am not. I am not doing anything of the sort. I said I had reached a decision. But it is reciprocal. All decisions are reciprocal, and now you must make yours. You must decide what you want to do. I know what

I want; have you decided what you—"

"Bastard," he said, "bastard."

"It's your decision," I said, "you see that now. And it always was. From the first. It will never leave your hands; it's your life and you must deal with it."

"Bastard," he said, "dirty bastard."

"Now," I said, "what do you want? Tell me what you want and touch yourself for the first time."

All right, doctor.

In the night the witch's kiss of sheets surrounding my chin, cutting into the undersurfaces like a blade and opening my eyes, I think I see his hand for just a moment tucking those sheets into my neck: the night attendant. I have never seen him whole, nor the unknown substitute who fills in for him on his mandatory time out, but the sensation of being wrapped in coils of ice by this unseen but benign hand is comforting, it reminds me as it were of the other part of life, the unknown underside into which I descend for twelve hours, half of my life now lying deep in the darkness tended by those unseen, my heart pounding away at its faithful old rhythms, the blood still roiling in the veins, only the light of consciousness extinguished—but the world, dark and mysterious, holding and protecting me, going on.

So it will be when I am no more; so it will be when I am dead. The unseen hands will tuck the sheets around my neck, the presences will float in and out of the grave chambers of the self, and what I know and touch for twelve hours a day now I will touch forever ... that does not sound so bad now, does it?

On the way back I said, "That whore I fucked, that whore fucked Nathan Leopold. Do you know, that?"

"You're crazy," Jim said and giggled. "Maybe you're not crazy, it's possible."

"I'm telling you," I said, "I'm telling you it's the truth. I asked her and she did."

"She said she did?"

I put my hand to my cheek. "No," I said, "she hit me here when I asked her."

And up in the front, giggles, and he said, "Hitting isn't agreeing, hitting is for getting mad. Maybe she didn't like you asking if she fucked Leopold."

"She did, I tell you," I said, "she did. I don't give a damn either way, it doesn't matter to me, but I know that she did and that it did matter." This was a lie, knowing that I had rested in the same place where the Babe had, knowing that the Babe's prick, the prick of a murderer, had churned in the same tunnels that had mine was exciting, no question about this; we had performed the same motions against the same body, and what did that make us? Did it give me any further understanding of his motives? If Leopold could do the same things that I had done in the same way to the same woman, did that mean we were the same? That was what excited me—knowing that we could have been in some way.

But there was no way to carry forth the message before they would question me more closely and possibly think me crazy, so I kept quiet, the car speeding, rubbing my jaw, little darts of pain spreading from the jaw down the chinline and becoming filaments deep in the flesh. And not another word, not another word all the way to Urbana. I never went to a whore again, and that was the only time. Somehow it wouldn't have been the same.

Big, fat sousaphone jabbing like a prick into the car, missing my head by inches, fat red-faced man behind the sousaphone, staggering, bleating, apologizing as they grabbed him by the arms, voice shrieking, eyes tearing, "I didn't mean it, I'm sorry, I didn't mean to do anything." And they whisked him out of sight. I wanted to give him a smile, a nod, some remission. But before I could do so, he was gone. Impossible to make contact, although I certainly tried. One cannot say that I did not try—that is what is known as having in politics the common touch.

"The taping is going to have to stop," Goodenough said, "or at least you're going to have to cut down."

"I can't do that," I said, "this is my whole life now, getting my memoirs down on tape. What else would you leave me? It's got to be done."

He held my wrist, watched my pulse solemnly, "It's taking too much out of you," he said. "I don't like the gross modal signs and the kind of tension under which you're working. You could have a cerebral blowout at any time. You can see that I'm being frank with you. I'm not holding back, The excitement is disastrous."

"I can't stop," I said. "I just can't do that. It's got to be done. This is my mission."

"You're having trouble with the machine," he said. "I understand that you're having trouble more and more operating it. You're spilling tape out of the canisters and getting it fouled in the recorders."

"That always happened. I'm not mechanically minded."

"At least we should get you a cassette operation of some sort. You could just put a disc into the machine and begin to talk. Cassettes can hold up to ten hours transcription, which is more than reels, no matter how slow the IPS you've got."

"I will not do it," I said. He dropped my wrist; it clattered against my knee. "Bone to bone and to dust we shall returneth. I will not use a cassette. I want to talk into something that I can see. I want to see it mount up. I want to see that I am having an effect. In some ways, I am very old fashioned."

Goodenough smiled, except that he did not smile. "I don't like the signs," he said. "More and more I'm beginning to think that deciding not to institutionalize you was taking too big a risk. That it would have been better to have gone ahead and done it with whatever risk that entailed. This is not safe for you."

"You forget one thing," I said. "I did not want to be institutionalized."

"And now?"

"No," I said, "I do not want to be. I am perfectly content here. I have Merrick. I have Henry; and you. I have my tapes and my memoirs and they're all building very nicely. I'm finding some very keen new insights. There are things that I never understood about my two marriages and my administration until I actually got down and started in on this. I feel in many ways that I'm growing as a person."

He smiled at that. I had expected him to. For Goodenough there would only be irony, but for me it was something much closer to insight. It is possible to change. It is possible to grow. Life can and does begin at eighty, as I recall from the radio show of my youth; and besides that, how can anyone elect a point of termination? The underground did and we see where it got them.

"I am doing fine," I said again. "I have no complaints. Now and then I get bitter and depressed. I have my bad days, but don't we all? More and more I feel that I'm being taken care of. I'm getting along. Everything will be all right."

"You don't understand the risks," Goodenough said.

"Of course I do. You've told me."

"And the deterioration," he said grimly. "I told you. I've never lied to you. You're deteriorating rapidly. Yesterday when I was here, it was necessary to triple-dose just to bring you to this point."

"But I feel pretty good now."

"How long do you think it will last?"

"I don't know," I said. Nothing would break the shell of my optimism; I was resolved that this was indeed going to be one of the good days, in fact the very best. Nothing would fracture my calm. "I'm sure that I'll manage. You can keep on triple-dosing me."

"And then quadruple-dosing and then quintuple. But with every rise, the risk increases. The pressure on the cerebral hemispheres. That's where the risk of stroke comes in."

"You have told me that."

"There's no way that we can strike a balance. At least not when you're at a level of such constant excitement, which these tapes seem to be doing to you. If we could get you into a quieter, more controlled—"

"No," I said, "No, I won't go. That's definite."

"All right," Goodenough said. He leaned over, hitched his pants, sucked in his stomach rather self-consciously. "No one can force you to do anything, that's well understood. That was understood from the first. If you want to continue this way, you may. But I warn you," he said, "we may be forced to measure this situation not in months, or even weeks but in days. It's perilous."

"I don't think anything different. I'm eighty years old. It would be ridiculous for even a healthy eighty year old to measure out things in months, wouldn't it?"

"I like your philosophy," Doctor Goodenough said. "I admire it. It shows courage and strength. Unfortunately I don't believe it. It's merely the product of drug therapy, and we're getting a very temporary release, a very temporary balance. Fraudulent, I might say. I would like to have the opportunity to listen to some of those tapes. I understand that there are very interesting things. I'm sure that from a medical standpoint, it would be helpful—"

"No," I said, "nobody listens to the tapes." I patted the key in my pocket. There is a key to the study in my pocket, and as far as I know it is the only one. It is possible that Merrick or Henry have a duplicate and that they have in turn handed the duplicate to the unknown night attendants, who open up the study and in the darkside of my life listen to all of the tapes; but I prefer not to believe that this is so. The confidentiality of my memoirs is the key to my sanity at this time. If I did not believe that they were uniquely mine and that no one but myself had access to them as I chose, then it would be impossible to maintain any illusion of self-worth, my tenuous hold on reality would probably collapse, and I would be no good for anyone at all, least of all myself. "I will not let you listen to the tapes, doctor," I said.

"All right."

"When they are finished and transcribed and published, everyone will have access to them. But fright now they must be mine and mine alone."

"That is your decision," Goodenough said. He suddenly seemed seized with awkwardness, his hands fluttering on his knees. "Do you want anything else?"

"Anything what?"

"Anything at all?"

"I have everything I need," I said. "I can't imagine that you could give me anything at all; I mean what I need, you can't give, isn't that what you're saying? I need six more months, is what I need. Enough time to finish the tapes."

"I can't promise that," Goodenough said. "I can't offer you that. That is entirely out of my hands. If you go on this way, however, I do not think that you will have it."

Nothing else.

"Do you want me to stay?"

"To stay? To what?"

"To move in," Goodenough said. "Perhaps you would feel better if I were on the premises all the time. There is no reason why this could not be arranged. I could have a room—"

"You have other patients."

"Not any more."

"None?"

"Not for the time being. My sole role is to render you patient care. You are my only patient."

"You must think that I'm going to die soon," I said, "if you're willing to move in. You would only do that if you thought the end was near."

"I have never denied that," Goodenough said solemnly enough. "I have never tried to hold back from you the true facts of your condition,"

"So you think the end is near?"

"At this rate, it is," he said.

"I'll fool you," I said. "I'll fool all of you. You're all waiting for me to die, but you're going to get a hell of a surprise. You're going to get a surprise like you've never had before in your life, because I am going to live and live. I am going to live for twelve or fifteen more years and bury all of you."

"Not if you keep on going this way."

"Get out," I said, "I don't want to talk to you anymore." I felt rage coursing through me, carried by the blood, rage palpitating the small and ruined cells of the heart. "I want you out of here now."

"Emotional liability," Goodenough said, standing. "These sudden switches, these inversions of mood are characteristic of the condition, that's all. Don't you understand, Mr. President? You simply are no longer in control of yourself. This isn't you, it's the drugs talking. But it's too radical. It can't go on this way."

"Get out, you sanctimonious fuck," I said. "You sanctimonious old fuck and fool, get out of here. Get out of here now." I stood—quite a difficult operation, let me assure you. I will not describe it. It disgusts me to describe it. "Get out of here," I said.

Nothing resistant—he has never defied me in any form, way, shape or manner—Goodenough lumbered tangle-footed away from me, his bland features spreading open like a ripped heart, exposing the interior, softer, more dangerous flesh. "All right," he said, "I'll do that. I'll cooperate with you as I have from the first. But it's not working, don't you understand that? It's simply not working."

"I agree with you," I said, and of course I did. "I agree with you on that, but what's the alternative?" And he went out of there, leaving me alone with much to think about, I can assure you, except that thinking did not seem to be quite the course of action that I was looking for at the time. I went to the spools. Do not go gentle into those good spools but rage against the flickering of the recorder light.

Eunice died in 1981. It was a difficult occasion, of course; the question was, whether or not to go to the funeral. Although the divorce had been almost no issue at all during the campaign, had been pretty well covered over, as a matter of fact, by other issues, her death received pretty good play, and there was no question of sneaking into the funeral in a quiet and composed way. She died in the nursing home in which she had been bedridden for many years. She was only sixty-six years old, but from all the reports I was able to gather—and a President has fairly good intelligence when he puts his mind to it—she looked and acted much older; in fact, she had as advanced a case of senile dementia as a sixty-six-year-old woman is capable of having. The obituaries, however, cut off any discussion of her life after 1970, discreetly saying that she had retired from public activities. Her work in social welfare up until that time, however, had been well known. Eunice was always dedicated to social welfare, no more so than after I had left her.

"You're going to have to go," Hope said to me. One thing that lady could do was seize an issue. "It's going to be bad if you go, but it's going to be worse if you don't. So you might as well."

"She's no longer my wife," I said. She hadn't been my wife for almost a quarter of a century.

"That doesn't matter. You were married for almost eighteen years, you had a child, she was beside you all throughout your early career. You can't deny that kind of thing, Bill."

"I'm not denying it," I said, I thought reasonably enough, "there's nothing to deny. It just seems that it would force a feeling, a relationship that wasn't there."

"Bill," she said, "you're going to have to go because anything else would be worse"—she was right—"and the only way to make the best of it," she added, "is for me to go with you. If the two of us go, it will be somehow less personal, it will merely be a thoughtful, sincere gesture in which the two of us can join; whereas if you fail to go, or you go by yourself, everything may be raked up again. We couldn't have that, Bill."

What was there to say about the woman? Always her judgments were superior to mine, right up until the very end, when it could be said—although many may disagree—that her judgment was so great that it looked only like an enormous miscalculation, its true implications far removed from those like myself with more ordinary minds.

"All right," I said, "we'll handle it that way, even though it's going to turn it into something of a circus, don't you know that? Can't you see all of that coming?"

And if she was right about the one thing, then I was very distinctly right about the other; it was a circus—an affair of state is a more proper way to describe it. Eunice was buried in Omaha, where the nursing home was; there was no reason for her to be buried anywhere else. There was no other family, no one to particularly choose a site; the occasion created my going.

In the presidential jet we went there, with full presidential paraphernalia, five hundred at the funeral, all that could be admitted into the chapel, and another five thousand outside looking for a glance of the prince—the Prince of State if not the Prince of Sleep, that was. And looking at the bier, the closed coffin, I felt almost a lurch of feeling, something close to rage and loss intermingled in a way that had been very private to our relationship and which I had not thought of for twenty years—what the woman could evoke in me, what the woman could do to me. Hope must have seen this, the way I was locked into a small, silent, removed place far away from her.

At the end of the prayer and the brief eulogy by the head of the nursing home, telling about Eunice's great spirit and great optimism in her last days, I could really believe it I felt myself, unbidden, lurching out of my feet, concerned servicemen snatching at my elbows. I waved them all away and staggered down the aisle, flashbulbs going off in funerary precision as I crossed the altar, leaned over and then past the coffin and ascended the stairs, then stood next to the head of the nursing home, who backed away from me, his eyes like that of a porpoise, and I said, "I would like to say a few words, if I might."

The minister said, "Surely." Some obscure Baptist on obscure assignment through the funeral home, they are a very special breed, these ministers.

"Just a few words," I said, as the minister, panicked, back-pedaled his way all the way off the podium and nearly into a pew, and gripped onto the lectern found myself regarding the mourners with an almost professorial stare, which was a horrible way to look at the situation. I could see the irony of it.

"I lived with this woman for many years," I said, "I was married to this woman. I have never denied her impact on my personality—her grace, her influence, the way in which she made almost every achievement of mine possible. This woman has suffered. She suffered two losses, a son in the flower of his youth to a terrible disease and the loss of a husband not many years later to something that she could only think of as another kind of terrible disease. And the two might have been interrelated; which is to say, how may one work on the other? But despite these two terrible shocks, this lady was able to go on, to live bravely and well, to move beyond her great and initial contributions to a different stage of life altogether in which her contributions were magnified and altered by being given to an ever larger body of people. As she had given to the one, so gave she to the many ... and with those characteristics of grace, vision, and sacrifice which had been hers from the start."

It was a stirring speech, not the least bit affected by the fact that it was not so much felt as willed; I knew that she deserved better than she had gotten and this was an attempt, however weak, at reparations of some sort. The channels of the mind are devious and convoluted indeed if I thought that this constituted reparations; at any moment I could have swung my gaze into the open coffin where Eunice's eyes, dim and moist, cocked to alertness behind their half-closed lids, would have confronted me, could have looked, up and down the angles of the corpse's body and felt an almost personal sense of revulsion for what had happened.

But I did not look at the open coffin, being very opposed to this kind of thing on principle, having already left the most explicit instructions in my own case that the coffin is to be closed at once and that discretion will abound throughout my own funeral. The deterioration of the aged in the flesh is quite enough; they are entitled to some privacy in their passage; age, senescence, corruption are public enough, the exhibition of enough shame ... let the lid be closed.

I said good-bye to Eunice in the most regretful and yet impersonal sense and stepped away from the podium to a great hush—it was a daring thing, of course, for a president (they said) to make a gesture of this sort and to rake over the ashes of a relationship which had long been thought to have been dangerous to his popularity. But then again (they said), he had long since been elected and had nothing to lose.

Leaving the chapel was the same panic as its entrance; for a moment I thought that I was going to be overwhelmed. This sensation was overtaking me more and more that year, that there was something uncontrollable about crowds and the nature of the public event, and that I would be whipped into a confrontation that I could not bear. … But we managed to get inside the limousine, the closed top one which Omaha had provided; and on the way to the airport, behind the shielding, Hope said, "You didn't feel a thing, did you?"

"I don't know," I said. "It had to be done."

"You didn't feel a thing," she said decisively, and her head nodded as if she were an auditor. "It was just something that you felt you ought to do."

"That's as good as feeling," I said. "If you do something because it ought to be done, and you do it right, what's the difference? The only thing that matters is the act."

"That's a very presidential statement."

"But it's true," I said, "isn't it true? Of course it's true; don't consider feelings, consider accomplishments. You want to know what happened, not how people felt when it was going on."

She shook her head. More and more that year she was moving away from me; I could not understand her. I had always found her accessible and comprehensible even if others did not, but since the election she had transmogrified into something else—was it First Ladyship itself that sat uneasily upon her? "I just hope you do better for me," she said, "I hope that you feel more."

"What? What's that?"

"I said, at my funeral I hope you have more feeling than you did at this one," she said, and then she said nothing at all. It was the first time she had ever done this to me—of course there were many other times as well, but one tends to remember the first—and as we whisked our way to the airport, it was with a feeling of all time coalescing, past and future telescoped into that one burning pass of her eyes as she looked at me, looked away from me, and left me there, hanging suspended by the threads of the thought of Eunice who was dead; and that was not the only death that year—oh, my, yes.

Inheriting the total cabinet, I thought it best to make the transition as inconspicuously as possible, to make as little of an alteration; but that was probably a serious mistake. Easy to know that now, but hard then, one's judgments always being superior in retrospect—this being part of the condition of being human. But it seemed best to retain the cabinet, to say nothing of the general structure of the executive branch, because my hold was so tenuous … or at least I thought it was tenuous. Like good Pope John I had been elected to tread water and to die. I think that many of them expected me to die in office, what with the curse; and with the question of age, it would have been the most equitable means of satisfying the curse, tossing the corpus into its maw, so to speak. Half-accepting that myself—the proposition, that is, that I would die in office (but quietly, not violently, something mild and exhilarating like a stroke that would black me out and send me on, spinning vault immediately), I hesitated to deal with the superstructure of the situation. It was simply better to go along—or so I thought.

Dolan could have helped me at that time, but Dolan had his own problems, suspended in a constant state of disbelief, vice-presidents not a species like thee and me but a special, private, sullen breed who can find communion perhaps only with one another. If I had worked with Dolan, there might have been more control; but Dolan, of course, was simply waiting for me to die in office along with the rest of them; and there was little possibility of connection, not that I wanted it. Everybody expected me to die in office. I should have known that the news magazines filled with speculations and hint; not a story I ever read in which my age was not mentioned first paragraph, last paragraph, and middle. And yet I went on, on and on with consummate stubbornness and grace; the aging or aged president of the United States went on—and what a surprise to them; what a surprise to Dolan as well as it seemed that I would, impossibly, beat all of the historical and mystical odds. But then again—and this was well remembered too—the curse applied to a second term as well. There was no reason why I should die in the first term. Lincoln hadn't; it was after reelection that he had been assassinated. It only held that presidents who were elected for the first time in years ending with zero would die in office, which gave me plenty of leeway; and there was the possibility, always the chance then, that I could beat it by standing aside at the last moment for reelection, resigning even ... I do not mean to imply that I was obsessed by this. Do not get the wrong impression.

Most of the time there was little thought given to it. A president can be a very busy man, after all, if he puts his mind to it; he can also be a very idle man—it all depends upon his personality. Johnson was busy, but Nixon did nothing; Kennedy was vigorous, but on the other hand my predecessor went off for long trapshooting sessions in the wilds of Tennessee and would not be heard of for weeks at a time—although a stream of releases, of course, gave an impression of vigor and dedication. This kind of thing can be arranged. The office has great potential for evasion of all sorts; one can evade as easily as one can confront, depending upon style—and certainly I did my evasions. But I did my confrontations as well, didn't I, doctor? Nothing ever was so far out of touch that I could not touch it; but then again nothing was ever near enough that I could not get away. The capacity of the office granted the occupant to move in and out alternately of situations is marvelous; it is almost sexual, wouldn't you say that, doctor? Oh, doctor, of course, it would be sexual—moving in and out, out and in of situations, pumping them, milking them, exploding finally through them with a great dense fire …

Goodenough says that more radical action must be taken, but Goodenough does not truly understand the situation. I think Henry called him in; I think Henry and Goodenough are in collaboration to drive me insane. It was not time for his visit for a week and yet here he is, Goodenough, bag dangling from his wrists. "I warned you," he said, "I warned you that the effects would be increasingly temporary. You had a breakdown yesterday."

"I am going to finish," I said. "I am going to finish this project." My blood bubbled with steroids and radical cortisone therapy. I just learned that this morning, isn't that interesting? Radical and dangerous cortisone therapy, Goodenough perched way out on a limb not only for cause of his patient but for medical science as well. Steroids sang in my blood, bobbed up and down, bathed and laved one another, the effect of coming back into focus after having been out was almost orgasmic—not that anything down there is working at all; do not think that I have a dirty mind, doctor. "I will finish this project," I said, "my last great project. I am going to leave my memoirs, the true and final statement of my position. I am entitled to do this, and I will not stop as long as I have breath."

"You're going to kill yourself," Goodenough said to me. His face seemed translucent; I could see the carving of bone in some witchery of the light. "You are going to blow out with a hemorrhagic stroke." He stopped to take a deep breath, which neatly empurpled his complexion, and said, as if with great pride, "You nearly did yesterday, you know."

"Was that it? Was that what happened?"

Goodenough seemed to be beaming with some enormous secret inflating within him. "I won't go into it," he said. "There is no need to go into details of the situation. You know what is happening as well as I do. You were warned."

"I must finish," I said. I swung my aged, feeble gaze over the room, noticed that matters seemed out of perspective. I seemed to be peering as if from a reservoir. Looking around I could see enormous, swollen limbs rising. "You've got me strapped in!" I shrieked.

"Not at all," said Goodenough. My feathery struggles verified this; I was able to move from the waist up. "We've elevated your feet."

"What have you done to me?"

"We're trying to induce an opening up of the oxygen supply to the brain," Goodenough said. "Your feet are above your head." I could see that they were indeed suspended on massive pillows, seemingly floating. "It's a temporary prophylaxis. All of this is."

"I've got to finish," I said, allowing my feet to remain in their position. "Don't you understand? I've got to finish now."

"You're not doing very well," Goodenough said, "it can't go on this way. Don't you understand? You're full of *cortisones* and *steroids* ... this is a *very dangerous therapy*. And still you're not responding seriously. Your blood pressure is 280 over 120."

"You did this to me," I said. I felt possessed with mad conviction. The last throes of the aged are burlesque, all farce with pillows and tumbling. It is impossible not to see the humor of it, even the humor of what Goodenough has done to me, but the absence of dignity is insuperable. "I've got to finish, don't you see that?" My eyes must have been glaring madly. "Where's Merrick?" I said.

"Who?"

"Merrick. Isn't he on duty today?

Goodenough's eyes showed a faint understanding. "Oh," he said, "your attendant, you mean. He's off duty today."

"Where's Henry?

"Don't worry about that now."

"I want to talk to him."

"You're not in any condition to talk to anyone. You'd better lay back right now." Goodenough seemed to be oozing excitement or then again maybe it was only perspiration. "Everything's failed," he said, as if he was announcing some profound medical discovery, "And the risk factor is too great. I think we're going to have to institutionalize."

"No," I said.

"You intend to go on this way?"

"Then move in with me. If that's the only answer, then you can do that. I'll let you stay."

Goodenough shook his head. "You misunderstand. You've always misunderstood. I don't want to move in with you. I offered it before as a last resort. But you didn't want it. You rejected it then and I think that you're right to reject it now. It's too far advanced."

"No," I said. It seemed to be the only word left in vocabulary, or then again perhaps in the manner of the aged I had made the negative affirmative. It is not easy to say. Everything is irretrievably complex. "I must finish. I only have a little further to go."

"What is the point of this?" Goodenough said. "What does it matter whether or not you get these down?"

"It matters to me. Don't you understand that? What could be more important? These are the true and final recollections of my administration."

"It is my duty to regard this only from the medical standpoint. From the medical standpoint, this cannot be considered within the elements of acceptable risk. Cortisones and steroids have unimaginable side effects, and the further we go in trying to strike a balance, the more radical the symptomatology. Haven't you seen that?"

"Increase the dosage."

"You're on massive doses already. We've already exceeded all tolerable limits."

"Increase them," I said. I waved my feet in the air, the wriggling of the toes like beacons from another aspect of space. "Increase them all you want. Move in with me. Give me a constant monitor."

"This is insane," Goodenough said, but he shook his head, and from his eyes a little perceptive light gleamed. He must have seen it as a great and final challenge, the great and final challenge of his life, just as I did. We find our purposes, our great accomplishments in the strangest places. "It increases the risk factor unacceptably, I told you. God, how far could we push it?"

"Try."

"It would be impossible."

"You could write a paper," I said. "You'd be famous. You're famous already, the president's physician. Think of that abstract in preparation. Think of what it would mean if you could test the limits of the treatment."

"My obligation is to keep my patient alive. It is not to see how far I can go to kill a patient."

"That's my decision."

"Why do you want to die?" Goodenough said, and I looked back at him. There was no need really to say anything; and to his credit, his face softened from its inquisitive glare. "All right," he said, "no one can stop you. If you want to do this, you could find someone easily enough who would help you if I refused. So it might as well be someone who has your interests at heart."

"Right. That's right."

"You'll have to keep your feet elevated all the time. That increases the blood supply to the brain."

"I like to talk and move about at the same time. I think better when I'm moving about."

"We can give you some elastic stockings. Tight elastic stockings. They will constrict the blood vessels below and increase the supply of oxygenated blood to the brain. But they're going to be very painful."

"Old women wear elastic stockings."

"You're asking me to help you," Goodenough said. "I'll try to help you. But you must follow instruction. We're not considering the cosmetic aspects here."

"I was just joking."

"If we can keep your feet elevated and have heavy constriction and increase the cortisones and steroids a little further because of the immobilization, we might buy a little time. The end is going to be catastrophic, however."

"The end is always catastrophic. Tell me when it is not a disaster. When was death ever otherwise?"

"I'm being very frank with you. I hope you appreciate that I'm being honest with you. I've never tried to conceal—"

"I know, doctor," I said. "You've told me that before. It's very much appreciated. I can't tell you how much I appreciate your frankness and medical honesty," I said and peered at him through the little aperture of self, the thin line of sight that was permitted me in this position, and saw him in a way that I never had before, his face riven by emotion—or then again I only may have been imagining this— some cast of feeling to the face which I would never have apprehended before. It was too much for me—oh, too much for me indeed—cortisones and steroids roiled sickeningly in the ruined circulation, blown through the diminishing pump of self. And I felt myself falling away from there through some dilating tunnel of sensation, but knew as always before that I could never fall so far away but that I would not be back there again, see the light again, cut my way through those ruined spokes of light once more—and those broken spokes were America itself.

"I've made my decision," I said to him. "The question is, have you made yours?"

"Talk, you old fart," he said, "you old son of a bitch, do you want to blow up—"

"But yes," I said, "don't you understand that?" I turned toward him. I missed Dolan at that moment; it would have been a good thing to have had an audience. I would have appreciated an audience if only to measure the reactions, because they were too profound and complex to be wasted on one person—me, who was himself a participant. "I want you to tell me how it feels. What it's like to have on your conscience what you're going to do? Because I'm going to call the bluff," I said. "I'm going to let you people go ahead and have your cities. Your demands are impossible. They are, as a matter of fact, suicidal." I went to the intercom and picked up the phone. I ordered the Secret Service in and hung up the phone "We're going to put you under arrest."

"You'll never get away with this. You'll never—"

"The situation can't be saved," I said. "You've already blown up two installations. You've given us no room for maneuver at all, you see. Maybe the next time, you'll learn something about politics, something that any state assemblyman could have told you. Don't box your opponent in. Don't spring your worst before you've even given him a chance to negotiate. Once you do that, once you carry out your threat without giving the threat itself a chance to work, then you've left your opponent with no room at all because you've offered him nothing. You've already done the worst. You could have worked something out, you were in a very good position; the infiltration was cleverly arranged, you've planned this for a year, and the takeover was excellent. You caught us flat-footed. It was inconceivable that these plants would be overtaken by saboteurs. But you've left us with nothing, and you've left yourself with nothing. Two installations gone is so bad that you might as well go three and four."

"Man," he said, "man, you're crazy." His eyes were wild. I mean his eyes were rolling and flickering within his face; I had never seen them so out of control in a human being. At the end, leaning over Arthur's bedside, seeing what the drugs were doing to him, seeing the creeping patterns in the network of the blood as they had rolled and surfaced to his eyes, I might have seen something like this; but what lay shrouded behind Arthur's pupils was different from what I saw here. The man began to convulse. His body slammed against one of the walls, he jackknifed, moved in against himself, collapsed to the floor. I thought it was an epileptic fit. The Service was in the room. They looked at him on the floor. He coiled and uncoiled as if to mark the passage of electricity.

"Get him out of here," I said. They looked at me wonderingly. "Arrest him." Are you sure you want to do this? their glances said. "Get him out of here," I said, "put him through the legal processes; I'll have nothing more to do with him." Have you considered the consequences? their expressions said. "I've considered everything. I don't care." He was still writhing on the floor. "Get him out of here before he vomits," I said, and they dragged him out. Presidential orders are presidential orders, regardless of the condition of the executive, Nixon having proved that; and in the office, again alone, I had to think very little before I issued the orders that had to be—and then there was nothing to do but wait.

They threatened to tear up Boulder, but nothing happened. The militia went into that plant and got them all without a struggle. In Cleveland they surrendered at White Sands; there was a little bit of a fire fight, but nothing explosive. After White Sands the rest of them came out voluntarily. Fallout was contained within the narrowest perimeter; they had worked out clean fusion.

The situation was saved. I was a national hero. What a great outpouring of love! It was only Hope who knew, and how could it have been concealed from her? How did I think she would not know, that I had done all of it from weakness? They had left me simply nothing else to do at all.

I had not been lying to the man.

They had simply left us without any room at all for negotiation. If they had, I would have capitulated. I would have given up the office itself if there had been room for maneuver. But there was none at all. I struck out, cornered, in terror.

Lying here, the elasticity of the stockings binding tightly around ankles and calves, sending (Goodenough insists) revivifying little jolts of blood to the brain, I have encountered an entirely new way of looking at reality or that simulacrum of reality which is my operating terrain these days; there is no question but that on the one hand, as Goodenough has predicted, the cortisone and steroids, along with the elasticity and elevation, have put me back into relative contact. I feel far more lucid and able to rake through the garden of the past patiently than I have for quite a time, and it is possible closing my eyes at times to find such an astonishment of recall, such a pinpoint precision of recollection that I can describe every object in the room ... this is not the action of an eighty-year-old man.

I feel revivified, a hoarse, hysterical seventy at least, seventy-five anyway ... but on the other hand, staring at existence through supp-hose socks, as spied through the lump made by the canister strapped to my thigh, my head some three feet below the level of the feet on this very strange contrivance they have rigged for me, this parody of a bed ... this is no picnic at all. I feel that I have lost that fundamental control over the situation which was always the key to my ability to confront reality—that I could control it. Lying back here in swooning ease, babbling my reminiscences into this microphone held not two inches from my lips, little flecks of phlegm and drool mingling on the holes so that now and then I must put out an indolent thumb, wipe them away, this is not contrived to give one that internal sense of dignity from which placidity and true, reasoned recall must issue.

Then too I have lost Merrick, for reasons that cannot be explained— not Henry, Henry remains with me, although of a rather more mournful temper; it must be his friend that he is missing. But Merrick is gone from me and has been replaced by a lady in a white uniform who tells me that she is to be called Margaret and that she will tend to me. She and Doctor Goodenough are in the closest of consultation, and what he tells her and she in turn tells me can be considered direct orders. Margaret will brook little or no nonsense; she is a shapeless woman defined merely by the uniform but to see her merely in her role as a trained nurse—I suspect that this is what she is, a trained nurse— would be to misunderstand the situation; she is every bit as much of a personality as the departed Merrick, the sullen Henry, and her interest in me is not at all clinical—is that not right, Margaret? She has just come into the room. The woman will not leave me alone, unlike Merrick or Henry, who would disappear for long convivial periods in the pantry or the adjacent rooms, doubtless drinking and exchanging reminiscences of other patients—they have known famous and obscure—unlike these two gentlemen, who combined forbearance with inarticulateness, with understanding, in a way which reminded me of a postmaster general in those dear, departed days before the office had been abolished ... unlike those people, Margaret is dedicated to her work—isn't that right, Margaret? She takes it seriously and personally and is constantly fluffing, pulling, arranging, supporting, kneading, rubbing, administering, whispering; the woman is driving me out my fucking mind—not that I realize it is for the best, my dear—and she has never interrupted me. Yet even when I say the most shocking and disgusting fucking shitty motherfucking shitty phallic things into this microphone, does she even give me a twitch of an eyelash. You are a miracle, Margaret.

A miracle, Margaret, you remind me of my first wife, you old cunt. Have I told you about my first wife? Well, it is all on the tape now. Supporting my back on pillows, thrusting up and into her, I would feel as she came down in counterweight that it was not so much the activity as the sheer *weight* of her which would destroy me, not that she was a heavy woman, but the expression of disapproval, her breasts flying like pillows, the dry, hard, metallic sheath of her cunt colliding against me as she would move up and down, everything poised as it were toward a revulsion so profound that it was private, immutable ... all of this, Margaret, gave me the feeling that with every downward thrust, every bitter curve in her mouth, she was willing me toward annihilation. She made me feel so *guilty*—that is what I am trying to say.

Back in those days, in the twenties, I mean, we were hardly raised to regard sex as if it were the most guiltless of passions; but even for that era, Eunice was something remarkable. I don't think the woman enjoyed it once. I can never recall her showing any sensation other than forbearance, and she would never out of the bed refer to it—not once in retrospect. She would not even admit that it existed between us; it was just something dirty and subterranean which occurred in that tiny enclosure of the sheets, and was otherwise negligible, beneath negligibility; it was something that was an object of revulsion, except that revulsion demanded thought, and she did not have any of that either. Am I making this clear?

I think then that she blamed herself for Arthur—Arthur's cancer, that is. She had a theory that the way the child was conceived was the key to the personality and physique of the child; that if a child were conceived in love, the child would be a strong, loving individual; but if it were conceived in hatred or in indifference, those limitations would show within the child's very expression, the life which it adopted. ... You are asking me, Margaret, I am sure, how she could reconcile this theory with her own hatred for sex. And I can only tell you that in her own mind, she surely believed that she loved me very much; and if she had not, she would not have been able to participate in sex at all—that was her rationalization. ... But when Arthur got the first diagnosis, all of that fell away, and I saw her face as it had been in the bed twenty-two years before, desperate, caved in, the eyes hollow and bleak, staring outward, staring inward, fixated on nothing whatsoever.

He died eight months after the final diagnosis; that is remarkable, I understand—usually they go in four or five months, and the most heroic efforts rarely get them beyond six. But he held on for a full eight months and twelve days, dwindling within himself all of the time but in contact until the very end. And as his body became more and more compressed, so did it seem to shrink into a point of hardness; there was less of the flesh, but the spirit remained the same, so as the corpus sprang tighter around Arthur, there was more of him peeping out inertly through the windows of his entrapment; and all of the time as he shrank and dwindled, so did his intensity increase. At the very end he was all purpose, concentrated, bleak, and staring on the bed. If I went up, Arthur came down—or so I thought in those days, but my thinking was not characterized by any unusual lucidity.

It was difficult enough to deal with Eunice, who I had not seen at all in five years but whose relationship I had to painfully reconstruct over and over again in the times when I went to the hospital (which was often enough, but not enough to suit me). She blamed me for everything, of course. If I had not left her, Arthur would not have gotten leukemia. If our marriage had lasted, our son would have lasted. If there had not been something corrupt, rotten, and sick about our marriage, then our son would have been strong, healthy, and wise.

He served in the Peace Corps in Uganda, you know; I think it was the only thing in life that he ever wanted to do, the only time that he was actually doing something which was his, rather than contrived for him; but that ended pretty fast. They sent him home sick, and he went to the hospital immediately. At least Eunice never blamed Kennedy or the Peace Corps for that. It would have opened up fascinating levels of material—perhaps more than I could have handled—if she had taken that aspect on it, but she never did.

Finally he died. He died three days before Kennedy was killed, and although the collision of events was momentarily shocking, it was probably the best thing that could have happened to Eunice or myself— not that I want to turn that dreadful public event into anything reflecting personal gain—but it did … Arthur died; Kennedy was killed; Oswald was killed. It became apparent that we were living in a universe whose insanity was not circumscribed but which rather leached over into the lives and circumstances of others, so one could not conceive of a personal or malevolent destiny; it was general. The insanity was malignant, all right, but at least it could be said that it was not particular; it chose no favorites; it got all of us. I think it was this knowledge that wheeled Eunice around.

Certainly there was no extended period of mourning. For me, there was enough to do in those days after the assassination to make the thought of personal loss somehow irrelevant—great tasks, great deeds, we were putting a nation together … I did not think of the curse then. It was only some months later that talk about the curse began to filter its way into the circuits of discussion, and then only in an idle and abstract way. It was generally thought that the Kennedys had such particular bad luck that they did not need the curse to explain what had happened to them. Nevertheless, over the years I thought about it. Certainly all of us did. It was one of those undercurrents washing the national psyche, along with so much else.

Arthur died. He had not been conceived in love, but this is not to say that he was conceived merely in lust either; he was conceived the way most people are, that is to say, out of a kind of tropism. I believe that I am going to vomit, Margaret. This is something that has not happened before. You had better get this microphone out of my hand before I do something …

The Hope Diamond, curse and all, has been the property of the United States of America, courtesy of the Smithsonian Institution, since sometime in the late 1950s. I wonder if anybody has ever considered this.

"I don't want to run again," I told Hope, "I think this decision is irrevocable."

"Don't be ridiculous," she said, "we've had this discussion before. There hasn't been a morning since the election when you haven't complained and complained, but you know perfectly well that you're going to do it; this is your obligation, and furthermore you've never been happier. You're going to be renominated and reelected and serve four more years and finish your work."

"What work?" I asked. "What work are you talking about? There is no work. It is merely a matter of filling in time. And if I do it this way, the way you suggest, I'll be seventy-eight years old in my last year of office. Seventy-eight years old—that's ridiculous. That's no age for a president. And what kind of retirement can I look forward to? No, I really don't want to run. I am quite serious about this. I think I am going to make a statement next week."

"You're not going to make any statement," she said. She liked being First Lady more than I liked being president. This is not an exceptional observation, of course; it would apply to almost all First Ladies and every president. "You are going to be renominated and reelected because you are the best man for the job and you owe it to the country."

"Seventy-eight years old? I'm going to be seventy-eight years old in the last year and I owe this to the country."

"De Gaulle was seventy-eight years old and still premier," she said. "Churchill was seventy-eight years old."

"And look what happened to them."

"You think it makes any difference?" she said. "Everybody gets old and senile, everybody dies. It's a question of how you spend your life."

"I don't want to spend my life this way," I said. "There must be some other way to spend my life. I want to go fishing."

Both of my wives were very determined women. Both of my wives knew exactly what was the best thing for me to do, the most moral and courageous action; the fact that it just happened to be to their best advantage as well was merely coincidence. They would not have thought for the moment of doing anything that was not for my best interests. If I had reconstructed Eunice with Hope, then perhaps I had anticipated Hope with Eunice.

Is the future a reenactment of the past? Or can we say that what we are merely comes from the dark anticipation of what we will be? This is a question which I meant to ponder sometime before the very end, but it is obviously too late for that now, and it might be better to stick to the main topic of discussion. I did not want to run again.

"Who's going to try and stop you?" Hope said. "Why, it's impossible for anyone to win this election for the party except you, and you owe it to the party." And then she walked away from me. She was always doing that you know, preparing incisive, devastating lines and then deserting a conversation. Maybe the lines were not so incisive or devastating, but there is nothing like a quick exit to give them color and density beyond perhaps what they really deserve. Owe it to the party! Why, I did not! Owe it to myself; I had no obligation whatsoever.

But the struggle over the nuclear power plants was still holding a year later. The outburst of popularity and love for my "courage" and "forbearance" and "strength" showed no signs of declining. Why, from the way it looked on the charts, you would have thought those two cities that were half-pulverized were filled with saboteurs instead of citizens and that in essentially being party to their ruin (for I was nothing else), I had been a martyr.

It is impossible to figure the complexities of politics. Mostly I left it to staff. After Nixon it was easy to leave it with staff, I mean, although I was never so much above the battle as I pretended to be. No president is, to be sure. "Above the battle." "Pretended to be." Hobbling and limping, stumbling and scurrying, canister banging on my thigh, I will make my way yet into the plains of cliché before Goodenough, his steroids, and their cortisones are done with me. Cliché is irresistible. We could hardly live without it framing all of the dimensions of our lives.

The situation was good and the charts encouraging; however, I would hardly have walked away from it without ample consideration. No one but a fool walks away from that; most of us have to be carried, even at the mandatory end, out of it—consider Johnson. Still as that smudged and equivocal year of 1984 staggered on, as my luck held, as the curse stayed in abeyance, that small blooming shoot of a thought which had been little more than an apprehension years before poked its irresistible way under the surfaces of the brain more and more the semaphore of consciousness: by God, I might just get away with it. I had much less than a year to go. If I refused renomination and actually managed to see a successor inaugurated, then I would have the curse beaten and at the age of seventy-four, would be able to enjoy the fullness and opportunities of life available to a seventy-four year old.

I would have gotten out of it clean, which is something that could not be said of any of us after Eisenhower—and how clean can Eisenhower be said to have been? I knew that dark old man a little bit in the middle years of his retirement, and all of his equanimity can be said to have been ceremonial. This would have been something new for me then, if I had been able to bring it off, but there were so many pressures—pressures not only from Hope (who was unofficial cultural affairs commissioner and who loved her work) but from the party itself. Doddering as I might have been, I was still washed by national approbation and was, to be sure, the only absolute winner that the party could nominate.

Also, I must concede myself, that there are pleasant aspects to the presidency of the United States: one is insulated at all levels from woe or worry; one has any number of personal prerogatives satisfied; and for one who does not travel—as was my policy never to go out of the country, dedicating my administration to the recognition and solution of painful national problems—it can be considered to be an extended if rather pressured vacation at the highest levels of luxury.... Any President who tells you that it is not essentially fun is lying; all of Johnson's crabbing and bitching about loneliness and decision-making was so that they wouldn't get wise to him and throw him out. It is one of those offices, in short, from which it is almost impossible to resign; one must be thrown out—or as in the case of constitutional guarantees, mandated out.

As we plunged toward the summer of '84, insulated as I was, I felt the pressures mounting, balanced off against that the little frail shoot of a flower of possibility was as nothing, only fit to be trampled ... and yet within me a secret was buzzing greedily, for all of it was counterfeit. I knew this; everything had been contrived on a single misapprehension underlying the nuclear blackmail, and no one understood this. I did not want it to be understood, of course, but on the other hand, it is not pleasant living a basic deceit—oh, you can understand my conflicts, my pain, my doubt, my indecision. Conflict may be the most important element of the satisfactory novel and by implication may also be the key to the success of these memoirs, the second serial rights to which I hope to sell to all of the important newspapers via the press syndicates to say nothing of the movie rights (there is certainly a hell of a movie in my life, is there not?) and I have contrived them toward that end. The conflict was within, not without: I knew something which none of them knew and which I would not dare to tell, cannot tell at this moment, the real reason why I stood up to the blackmailers and dared them to annihilate the millions. Oh the burning of the brain, folks, the merry, tarry burning of the brain, small drops of the horrid jelly dripping, dripping like scepters in the night of the light of the skull.

"Here," she says. "Here is today's therapy." Goodenough stands behind her, beaming. He has never looked better. He is carrying equipment and a smile lightly; aglow and alert within his responsibility. "Do take it," she says, extending her hand on which I see a light, bright pill.

"No," I say. The pill casts back colors that I have never seen before. "I do not want to."

"You must."

"I will not," I say. "I am entitled to the integrity of my prophylaxis. Besides, I am getting stronger. Every day in every way and my memoirs are coming along."

"If you do not take it," she says, her hand steady, giving me what must be even to her internal monitors a rather horrid smile. Every given expression of her is a rather horrid smile, "If you don't take it, we're going to have to go to more radical theory."

"What is it?" I say,

"This is a vasal dilator," Goodenough says. "It will open up certain passageways and reduce arterial blockage."

"I've never seen a pill like that," I said. I had swallowed unthinkingly everything that had been placed before me, had rotated myself benignly for every shot in anal or deltoid area, had turned myself upon the spit of a circumstance; like a patient, overpaid whore, I had accepted everything that was given unto me, but something about the size of the pill made me resist. It was orange. And as I peered closely, I could see upon it the shadow outlines of imprinting, some marks as if in another tongue, which for all I knew might have been obscenities. It would have been all the same. I did not know. "No," I said. I dug my old, gnarled hands into the smooth and slippery surfaces of the couch on which I was reclining heavily, retracted my head like a passenger slinking back into the receptors of an automobile. "No," I said again.

Goodenough held the pill, Margaret closing ground behind him, holding a glass of water, the two of them staring at me as if they were parents in some hideous parody of the primal scene, the pill objectification of that subtle exchange working between them. They could have been my mother and father, I thought, and of course the likelihood of the image sprung into my mind. It was proper that I would think of them that way because senility is the true and final passage, the absolute circularity of life, closing the gap, so they had become my parents. I was completely enthralled to them; they could do anything that they wanted to me, little stabs of paranoia like illness flickering up and down.

"No," I said again; it was the first resistance I had ever shown any of their medications. I was surprised myself at the force of my denial; I would not have thought that there was so much revulsion in me. "No, I won't take that. You can't do it to me."

And with a lurch Goodenough came toward me, closing the space, his palm opened like a priest's, dispensing blessing, and the pill fell into my mouth like a wafer, glowing briefly in the drop, then falling between teeth and tongue, my mouth still hanging open in protest, and I choked. Goodenough smiled; a beam came from one side of his face to the other in a transfigurative way, and he moved aside as Margaret took the cup of water, inserted it in my mouth, and forced me to take choking swallows—it was either that or inhale the water. I felt pill and water sealing together in some obscure way within the cave of self, and then, as if it were music, I felt a slow, murmuring, billowing within. I inhaled slowly, trying to pace out the breaths. The sensations were excruciating.

"I told you this would help," Goodenough said.

"Don't you feel better now?" said Margaret.

"This is going to oxygenate you; it's going to give you some of that oxygen which the constriction has cut off. You'll be able to think again. You'll find that your mental processes return toward alertness."

"You'll think much better," Margaret said. "This is good for you; it's going to make everything seem so much easier—"

"Of course, the effect is temporary," Goodenough said. "All of the effects are always temporary. But there's reason to be exceedingly optimistic about this."

"Don't you feel better?" Margaret said and put a hand on my palpating, twitching brow. "Of course you feel better; I think that fever's going already. You're getting a nice, nourishing supply—"

"And of course those memoirs will go along fine now," Goodenough said. "You'll find that your energy levels are much higher, that you'll be able to concentrate for longer periods, and that they won't get away from you the way that you might have been afraid they were doing. I think that this is the right step."

"Oh, definitely," Margaret said, "definitely this is the right step." Her hand did not desist nor did her pressure upon my brow. "You go right ahead, Mr. President, you go right ahead now and work."

"I warned you of the risk factor," Goodenough said. "We were always very honest to you, but within the risk factor—"

"Oh, yes," Margaret said, "oh, yes, there's always risk; life is risk, isn't that the truth, sweetie? But you're doing much better, you're doing so much better—"

And falling back on the couch then, I saw another aspect of the truth or as close to the truth as I might come; that at the end it would be as the beginning, and that these furies chanting over me were neither priests nor predators, neither fiends nor salvation but only those versions of the primal scene which I had myself glimpsed—and as I came, so I would return, all of the sounds coming over me for the first time in years. I felt growing above the place where the canister was set a palpable erection, not quite an exclamation point but a comma, at least some little breathing strophe in the rivers which plunged toward darkness.

But difficult to concentrate, focus, they were right, the mind churning in wild activity, so many thoughts—I have never had so many *thoughts*. But the microphone is holding me down, my hand is holding me down, my voice is holding me down, the sheer need for language to sit here patiently and speak into the microphone chains me, I do not have the patience to sit and talk, rather I want to run wildly over the room.

Closing my eyes I can see my actions run at one-and-one-quarter speed, like the old films; clownishly I race through the room, toppling unsettling things, materials falling in slow motion just as I move in quicktime. I want to explode with activity, move chattering out of these rooms in search of companions or auditors. I could make a campaign speech in this mood or some declaration of conscience for the nation; impossible to lie here, my huge clownish feet suspended above me; all I need is buttons on the shoes and bell-bottoms, a red and glaring nose, wink and cast in the eye.

I could hurl this microphone across the room and catch it on the fly—but am locked here in place. Damn it! Straps here, straps there, huge pillows propping up the feet, and the shoulders way down in the couch impossible to move, cannot even roll; they have put me in position where I cannot move but the mind raving and wandering free.

Is it possible that they are preparing me for exhibition? I could see that. I could see the doors flicking open at a certain point and the press pouring in, all of them, first interview the president has given in two years, first time the president has made public appearance since the last inauguration. How are you, Mr. President? Oh, yes, I could see that. Answering from the muffled depths of my pillow, I'm just fine. Do you have any statement, Mr. President? Not at the present time. How has your retirement been? How have your memoirs been progressing? Well, it is very difficult to answer that in a sentence satisfactorily, I suppose. A picture, Mr. President? No, I'd prefer that no pictures be taken. Don't be modest, sir, and the explosion of light in the room, the pictures coming out the next day … I would have to confront my own appearance, something which I have not had to do in a considerable length of time. I do not think that I am ready for this; I do not think that I have reached the point where I am really able to look at a photograph of myself, much less deal with a public appearance. But they are undoubtedly preparing me for that.

Paranoia now streaks in coloration; I am positive that they are out to get me. They would be utter fools if they were not. I am sure that if I were in Goodenough's position, I would do the same. I would sell out to the press. I would take advantage of my position.

Still spewing out my memoirs, trying to make some sense of it, the reels stacked up one by one on the shelf above me to the right near the door; and it is only faith that all of those memoirs lie stacked up here. First Merrick, then Henry, now Margaret pick up the completed spools from the recorder and they add them to the shelf. But there is no way of knowing when I am sleeping in the unseen enclosure of the night whether or not they may not be playing with these reels, feeding them through the recorder, mapping out my laborious reminiscences ... how do I know that they are not listening to them, playing with them, making sport of this my life's work, perhaps even sending out the reels to an anxious set of institutions and substituting them with blanks?

I have thought of this from time to time. I am taking so much on faith; the confidentiality of my babblings is something in which I must believe in order to maintain that essential sense of control which enables the great work to go on, and yet there is no basis on which I can be sure of this. I know nothing. I have no assurance whatsoever that what I think is on that shelf is truly lying there. I know the recorder works because occasionally I engage in playback listening to the (always shocking, I did not know I sounded that bad) sounds of my voice; but as far as the project itself ... I have no assurance. None whatsoever. Still, what is the difference? At all costs I must go on; it would make no difference whether or not there was integrity to the reels; I would continue. What else do I have? Besides, when I get the full and final explication down on tape, I know that I could die in peace—which would be the only framing point and purpose to all of this, the only referent I can possess ... if these memoirs cannot be punctuated by death, what veracity will they have? Obviously it is that rounding and final symbol which I desire.

But I do not know; I do not know about the integrity of the project. I dream sometimes in the clinging night that they are sitting there, Goodenough, Henry, Margaret, the unseen attendants of the night, and that they are listening to these reels, the playback of a day's ravings. Sometimes Margaret twitches or coughs; she is instantly motioned to silence by a furious Goodenough, who is bent over the machine, his features contorted with concentration. Sometimes Henry sneezes, a long, riffling bark of sound, the sneeze trailing off into a whimper, the way that the cries of orgasm are likely to do; and Goodenough turns that furious gaze upon him again, the eyes bland and bovine in the face, curiously expressionless even as he urges Henry to silence. Now and then one of the attendants giggles as something obscene comes off the tapes, instantly silencing himself; Margaret bends forward, lets out a fart like the sound from a cannon; Goodenough pokes a finger into his ear, begins to wring out wax and fluids while with his other hand he continues to take desperate notes, the pen rattling across the paper, while all of them suck on cigarettes, devour drinks, whisper to one another hurriedly in the pauses. But all through this the tapes drone on. Nothing can stop them but that they are heard through to the end; with fascination, my grisly little set of auditors incline their heads toward them. Buried on those tapes they feel is some fragment of knowledge, some delicate epiphany which will yank them around and frame the entire sense of their lives. No less than me, they are looking for some meaning to come out of those tapes, and they dare not miss a word lest they miss epiphany … but though they hush one another, though they pass notes back and forth, though Goodenough distends his mouth to great yawns of speculation now and then, they hear nothing. The tapes do not give them what they want.

Disappointed in the dawn's early light, the last shrinking spool clattering tape out of its twin, they are in the task of cleaning up. No one must know how they have spent their night. I must not deduce their purposes; if I did, I would feel constraint in my dictation, possibly would cease in my conversation, and where would they be then? Well, they would be nowhere at all; that is the answer. They would be unable to continue their search. So with hushes and cautions uttered through pursed lips, they begin the laborious task of cleaning up so that the room is in the same state of filth and disorder that it was when I left it: here an empty glass, there a discarded bottle, little strips of toilet tissue replaced, boxes in which the stockings came strewn throughout the room … not for a moment would I know that anyone had been there, that my tapes were being casually, carefully audited in the night. They are careful about this, there is nothing lackadaisical about their efforts to leave everything as it was. But despite their cleverness, despite all of their admonitions, I can tell; and come night after night, barking and yapping from the kennel of sleep, snaffling like a dog into the pillow … deep in dreams I must know all of this, must be one of the auditors in that room, my kindly, ponderous spirit lurking around them, my great, bearlike head nodding its own rhythms of assent; my spirit is truly then and all around them. And by the time I am taken from the bed, assisted through the task of dressing like a child, led into the bathroom to evacuate the remnants of my bowels, and plopped into the couch in my state of risen feet, I am already exhausted, not so much from the efforts of the morning, which are grim enough, but from all of the attentions squandered through the night.... I have missed none of it; I am on both shifts; I am dictating during the day and listening at night, just as they are listening through the night and administering to me during the day, an exhausting and pointless cycle for all of us. I wish that it could stop ... but that would mean the taping itself would have to stop, and this is obviously impossible. I will not hear of it.

Campaigning: from Fargo to New Orleans to Mobile to Dallas within twelve hours, seeing nothing but the interiors of the plane, the limousine, the hotel rooms, and the television studios into which I am guided. To campaign is no longer to see the country—that is understood—but only to see the interior of various enclosures; pointless to attend a rally which attracts ten thousand people, several of whom might be potential assassins, when for one-half the cost and one-tenth the effort, one can make a taping in a local studio which will be shown on the metropolitan network reaching two million base audience on the six o'clock news; pointless to shake hands, whatever mystical strength may be drawn from the crowd, the hand squeezed to pulp when one can instead meet a selected group of citizens at an informal cocktail gathering, all of it being filmed for the eleven o'clock, a bank of local and national reporters tracking all of this. The travel then is merely for the effects, the brief splices on the newscast showing one disembarking or embarking once again, the personal appeal, that is to say, but the only personal appeal is into the eye of that cranking camera.

And deep into the summer of 1980, the polls indicating that it was going to hold, the slender consensus was going to hold and unless I did something disastrous I would be president. I said to Hope, "We are not seeing the country. We are not dealing with the people. We are merely going from room to room. We came not to listen but to talk."

"What's wrong with that?" she said. She was optimistic until the last. She really loved politics; that must be understood. I will give her credit for that. "It's what people want."

"But we're just talking; we're not listening," I said. "I don't think anyone's listened for years. That may be the reason for most of the real trouble in the country—nobody knows what's going on. I don't know what's going on, and I'm running for president."

She shook her head. "I can never stand you when you become idealistic or ironic or cynical or groping," she said. "There's nothing more boring than a politician talking about metaphysics. For God's sake, you know you love it, you know that this is what you do best. Why do you have to make yourself hate it? There's nothing wrong with any of this. Let's have sex," she said. She put herself down on the bed and hitched her skirt up.

"Sex now?" I said. "For God's sake, the press is supposed to be up here in five minutes and there's a conference—"

"Right now," she said. I do not know if her look was mischievous or passionate—maybe a little of both, maybe neither. I could never tell. I could never tell with her; her moods were always veiled. She was always coming at me on at least two levels, so at no point, even in the most intimate or perilous moments, did I know how she was feeling, what was the constituent of her thought. Even her cries in orgasm seemed to have a willed quality, but then again it is difficult to say exactly what she was willing.

"It's ridiculous," I said, and yet my seventy-year-old prick was already squirming within my seven-day-old suit. It is a shameful thing for me to remember how I used to be sexually, right up until 1986—or maybe it was seven; I was always able to do *something*. I could even give myself erections just thinking about it and—fool that I was—thought this was somehow shameful or disgraceful, certainly not presidential. Of course, she was twenty years younger than me, this must be remembered. It is something to keep up with a younger woman; it will either kill you or revive you. In my case it did both.

"Come on," she said, her elegant face appearing at angle between her legs. With the skirt pulled all the way up, her face was now peering at me through her crotch. The juxtaposition of pubic hair glinting through her panties and the cool, graciousness of her face was exciting—like looking through a peephole in a Victorian bathroom to see a Princess diddling herself. "Come on," she said again, yanking down her panties, "you don't have to undress or anything, just unzipper and take it out."

"Ridiculous," I said, "what if they find us?"

"Isn't the door locked?" she asked.

"Well," I said, "it's locked but even so—"

"Then what?" she said. "What's the difference; what can happen if they come in the middle? *You* can come in the middle. Will you stop manufacturing excuses, Bill?"

It was madness. This was New Orleans (I believe in one of the Sheratons), not that there was any sense of place that summer, but for the record it was New Orleans. I got on top of her, a few fragile pumps and I was able to make an insertion and connection, then rocking easily above her, running my hands over the cloth of her dress.

"You are a pretty agile seventy year old," she said. Even then she had begun mocking me about my age. All of that had started somewhere in the previous year; until then she had never mentioned it, never mentioned the gap. "For a seventy-year-old man you are fantastic," she added, her cunt like a hand gripping me then and beginning to yank me forward. "Oh, Mr. President," she said, "give it to me, fuck the shit out of me." And with yelp and hammer I was beginning to; with fire and tongs I sat in the saddle, hauling myself through the deep fires underneath, plenty of juice there—fifty-one years old or not—pulling myself slowly up the long mountain; and then the quick slide beginning, around the slick crevice on the bobsled and down toward the chasm, yanking and pulling, riding her like a mountain climber now zooming down the opposite slope; and just at the timorous peak, of course, I heard the slamming and shouts at the door.

"Bill!" Brick was shouting, "Bill, open up in there. What's going on?" And I looked at her, trapped in some cartoon of astonishment, to see that she was already over the edge, pulling, sucking me in, her hands like webs on my shoulder.

"Don't stop," she said, "for God's sake, don't stop," the pounding on the door accelerating. But what was there to do? One cannot displease a lady; a lady's wrath is terrible (I am in a position to know of this) when denied that which has been wrung with such difficulty from them. "Don't stop," she said, increasing her movements; and like a butterfly pinioned in her grasp, I kept on swooping and fluttering, wondering vaguely at the storm-center of the motions if this is how heart attacks were induced in overaged, overexcited men—this would be no way for the campaign to end.

Sucked in, clambering within her, I felt myself suspended between the urgency of the cries outside, the signals of an advancing and demonic press, and the other, more immediate signals from my wife underneath me. Some state of suspension this was, to be sure, on the one hand stay and finish and risk disgrace, discovery, stories which would circulate through the press rooms for years; on the other, seal her up in the midst of her own slow ascension, meaning that similarly for years or at least months afterward I would bear the burden of her anger, Hope being slow to forget anything that ever happened to her. The fact that my own orgasm had not occurred was almost incidental, peripheral to this more immediate issue; at the moment my own satisfaction meant nothing; my own satisfaction indeed would have been my disgrace, because how (I could see her asking), how could I be beast enough to satisfy myself while leaving her suspended!

Oh, my dilemma was awful, and you can understand that I have painfully here, brick by brick, mortar of the most painful substance, constructed a metaphor, a metaphor for all the political dilemmas of our times. The personal or the professional? The incessantly internal or the more generalized demands of those who seize upon us? Are we men or machines, are we devices or artifacts? Do we hunger for the populace's approval because we have no approval of ourselves, or rather is it some eternal self-image which we are trying to dredge out of the circumstances of our struggles over and over again?

Well, I do not know. Although putting the question, as they say, is in itself at least half of the answer; the question can *be* the answer, and I have put it as forcefully as I can, not even altering the facts and difficult circumstances of my life in order to do so…. But it was the cunningly planted question of my own averted orgasm which was the solution to this dilemma, because I was failing and failing against her, even as I twitched in her grasp; so I was failing, the diminished flesh falling, and I could not sustain after a short time even the substance of entry. She gave me a look of such disgust that you will never know; I cannot possibly explain that look—it was the first time I had ever seen that expression on her face.

"Go on," she said, "get off, you disgust me." And with some surprising agility, more strength in her thighs than I would have conceived, she tossed me off. I rebounded from the bed nearly falling to the floor, and she as she lurched up from the bed, a rather furious expression on her face, fury clotting all of the arteries, pressing color through all the opping and disintegrating vessels underneath the skin, I understood that her rage in many ways went beyond my own and as was her rage magnified, so was her pain … pain at insufficiency, which I had never before understood. Putting it another way, she felt fifty-one to be more terrible than I did seventy.

"You'd better get the door," she said. I was already lumbering toward it, my discombobulated, detumescent little organ bobbling like sacrifice within the urn of my pants. "You want to make all of your appointments," she said. "You wouldn't want to miss anything, after all; we know what's important in this world, don't we?"

That was the last time I think that she ever showed passion in sex; we had a good deal of sex together, but it was automatic, reflexive; feeling seemed to be squeezed out of it. And soon enough I saw the fundamental ridiculousness of a man in his seventies trying to have sex; you can kill yourself doing that kind of thing. It all fell away shortly after Eunice's funeral; it just would have been obscene to have tried to rekindle any of that anyway. That is campaigning. You are here and you are there, but it is always in and out of the same dark corridors until you are spilled free forever.

"I've never been offered a bribe before," I said. "I can't believe your audacity. Go away and I'll make believe that this never happened. Go away and I'll put this out of your mind."

"Don't be a fool, senator," he said, "this isn't a bribe; this is a contribution. Anyway, what do you care? What are you talking about with that law firm—"

"Get out of my office," I said. He was a fat old man and there was no subtlety in him. "Get out of this office right now or I'll turn you in."

He stood—he was quite graceful for all of that bulk—and laughed at me. "You're a fool, senator," he said, "you're a fool because you think that *we're* fools. But you can't get away with this kind of thing forever; sooner or later you're just going to have to face up to what you are. We have. Everybody in the world has got to, and you'll have to do it too. You just don't like the approach," he said laughing, "because you're not sure of your ground. Believe me, I wouldn't be here if it wasn't all right; you know it's all right, senator, don't you?" As I got to my feet, he laughed at me, laughed and laughed. I looked at that face and the face of course was myself; and the dialogue must have been in the sheets at night.

"Eunice," I said, coming out of it, "Eunice, this is ridiculous. I can't take it anymore. Please hold me." And she held me, of course; she always did; she was very good that way. I was never able to separate dreams and reality sufficiently in my mind, but I am glad to say that I kept them straight on the business end of things.

What do you think? he said to me. You think we're a pack of bums? You think this is a two-bit cheap-jack operation? You don't give me that bullshit, buddy, you just come right off it; you're dealing with the top here. When you're dealing with the attorney general of the United States; you're dealing with credibility and power and honor gilt-edged. If you're going to deal with the attorney general you're going to deal with a man who can deliver. We're not asking anything that we can't follow through on. At these kind of prices, we demand and get the best. And frankly I'm appalled at your attitude. You can take your business and money elsewhere if you're going to insult us like that, insult the attorney general like that. What do you think? Don't you realize that you're not dealing with two-bit crooks here, you're talking about the attorney general of the United States, and he delivers.

To say nothing of the commerce secretary.

Bitch, I said to her, although of course I said it silently; there was no need to say it to her face. Bitch, you can't do this to me. You're twenty years younger; you're not going to die. You're going to live past me by at least thirty, you bitch. You knew it; you were counting on it. So was I. How can you tell me you're going to die? First Arthur, then Eunice, now you. I tell you I won't take it anymore. I won't take this horseshit; now tell me you're all right, tell me this, is all crap.

Leaning over, thinking this but saying nothing—oh, God, she looked terrible against the pillow, white against a denser white, her eyes bleak, and the doctors saying you've got to get out of here, you can't tire her anymore, she only has so much strength … it was inoperable of course, things like that are always inoperable. I knew a good deal about cancer by that time—I should. The face was halfway toward ash now bone, but I could see the fierce, glinting determination in her eyes; talk about not going gentle, she wasn't going gentle, not Hope, she would hold onto herself toward the end; she had always reacted toward illness that way—colds, menopause, viral pneumonia—it was a personal insult, an explosion of the body against the psyche which she simply would not tolerate. That is what she thought, but it was no good—I knew that too. It was impossible to see bravery in it or conviction, metaphor, or strength; it was merely death, that was all.

But this was impossible … the woman was fifty-seven years old. People do not die at fifty-seven. I didn't. In my fifty-seventh year, my primary difficulty was in finding an acceptable position on the war issue that would not clash with the positions I had arrived at before, but at the same time would establish that I was moving more to the left.… Nothing as personal as death ever got between me and the war issue. How could this be?

I found myself wondering if I gave cancer. I understand that this kind of guilt is often present subconsciously with close relatives of the cancer patient, the fear of contagion turned around and projected into an exaggerated guilt for being the carrier … but in my case it was more personal. First Arthur, then Eunice, now Hope, the same disease, even the same symptoms early on—weakness, loss of weight, the enlargement of the eyes in the shrinking skull.… Was it possible that I was giving it to them? Clearly I could not be; and yet the common denominator in all three lives was my presence, my kiss planted upon them, my touch, my hope, my closeness.… I had fondled Arthur often as a baby, in later years I had not fondled him at all. This would have been abnormal, but could that dark kiss of the cells been then implanted? I did not know. Nothing was to be known.

But thinking about it, being obsessed with the possibility kept me from thinking about more painful and direct things, like how I was going to survive without Hope, how I was for that matter even going to get through the funeral … oh, it was too much for me, too much by far; and yet had I not always known at the root that she would die before me? Everybody would die before me; it was with that sublime conviction that I had entered politics, a profession in which advancement is only possible as those senior perish. To be convinced of one's political success is to be convinced only of one's long-delayed mortality. So I must have known it.

Then toward the end I was unable to function at all, weeping around the hospital. The press was into it, of course; there was no way they could be avoided, and my posturing frame was always good for a third- or fourth-page picture on the slow days, although out of discretion they would get me coming or going, chatting busily with "aides"— never pounding the walls or rubbing at my eyes.

And then the obligatory death scene, nicely timed, managed to the absolute, as only Hope could have done it; first the summons from the room where she lay surrounded by equipment and nurses, half-propped on the bed, her eyes brighter than they had ever been before; and at the center of them this deep rage.

"Bill," she said, "Bill, this is the end. I cannot survive this."

"Oh, Hope, you will—"

"No," she said, "this is my decision. I'm going to let it end now. I want to die. I'm ready to die. This is good-bye, Bill."

What a woman! What a scene! The strength of it was incredible. It was hard to believe that the woman could manage it with such finesse, such a powerful control of circumstances. It was only later that I understood that she had only been trying to manipulate factors out of the belief that if she were able to manipulate them right up to the end, she could similarly manipulate away death … elect to spring from the bed at the last moment, her last victory of scheduling, and greet me in the corridors. I know the syndrome well, now. I am engaged in it myself. I cannot possibly die until I finish these tapes, the true and real story of my life revealing factors hitherto unknown, passions never unrevealed …

But it did not work for Hope, as it will not work for me, as it will not for any of us. She died near dawn the next morning—which is when most of them die, I understand—a willed death too, with the body at the lowest ebb … she must have expected that if she carried it through to the end, she would spring through the ceilings for sunrise. But no such thing happened. The news was carried out by messenger, and I received it with no surprise whatsoever, not even surprise that she had not wanted me at her bedside at the end. Hope's gestures were always accomplished best in privacy; she would take her sex straight but with her eyes closed, her limbs opened but her face locked. People take their death in the same manner that they take their sex, and Hope always took hers neat with just a little shot of pain on the side.

It was at about that time that I began to feel that great and grievous sense of isolation which, to be sure, has controlled the impulses underlying so many of my later acts.

Here I lie, feet to the ceiling, babbling. The vasal dilators—or whatever they are called—which Goodenough now administers to me at the rate of three or four a day, the vasal dilators are having a little effect upon me, even I can see this. My thinking seems to be a little more straight-line, a little more lucid … although the ponderous depression which has now settled over me as a side effect of the drugs is hardly pleasant. It is not a pleasant thing to see oneself as a worthless, piteous object, but then again this may be not a side effect of the drugs but merely the outcome of my clearer thinking, my new perspective on the situation as aided by the drugs. … One can hardly say that my outlook is hopeful. What is there to look forward to? What exactly could be said to be my prospects? But I do not wish to complain. I have never tried to be a complaining sort.

You remind me of my son, Arthur; this is what I should have said to the man in my office. He would have been just about your age, but of course I do not think that he would have been as bitter as you. Arthur had all of the advantages. It was not my fault that he failed to take advantage of them; certainly they were there. And even though there was some profound failure in the boy, some inability to confront possibility, still he would never have hurt people. That is your trouble; you are hurting people—don't you understand that they are not abstractions? That in detonating power plants you are killing people? Don't *people* matter to you, or is it all a question of causes? Well, I did not ask that, and good thing, because the answer surely would have depressed me out of all proportion to the manageable.

We're trying to save the human race. Shit, he would have said, when you're dealing with the human race what do a few *people* matter?

Hope didn't matter dying—she was already an abstraction, that to be retained in memory, that which I would look back upon at a different time with an entirely firm and certain feeling. She would be objectified in memory. Hurry up and *die*, I was thinking in the hospital; the sooner you die, the sooner I'll be able to remember you with pain and horror, pity and astonishment … what the hell good are you to anyone lying in the bed preparing to die? It must have been the same with the man in my office; come on and capitulate so that I can relish. He was not even confronting me. And of course back in the early days with girls, I couldn't wait sometimes for a date to finish, for the petting and necking and fucking to be done so that I could go back to my room and begin to cherish it.

Maybe I should have served in the army; a commission was ready and waiting, it would have been easy. But politicians were exempt, of course, and I was thirty-one years old; besides, I thought I would do the war effort more good by staying in the statehouse and keeping an eye on the profiteers … sure, I did. This was my rationalization, anyway. And what with a year-old son and a wife who depended on me for everything, what business did I have going into the army? Anyone who says that I saw the war coming and picked up the assembly race to stay out of the draft will be instantly dragged out of here and burned by presidential fiat—oh, yes indeed. You bet.

"I've never had an injection like that," I said. The vial was filled with orange fluid, viscous, deadly orange fluid. "I won't take it."

"Yes, you will," Margaret said, "it's for your own good. It's a palliative. You'll find that it relieves—"

"You're trying to kill me," I said. The insight came upon me suddenly, and all the events of the last week swung into place. Merrick gone; Henry no longer near me at all except for certain vagrant clean-up details; my contacts restricted to Margaret; Goodenough having moved in. I should have seen it from the first. "You want to kill me," I said.

"Honey, don't be ridiculous—"

"Don't call me honey," I said. "I'm the president of the United States, no bitch nurse calls me honey. It's all a plot; you're here to kill me. I know too much and I'm saying too much, and now you want to kill me. You're all spies from the administration."

She hovered near me, the needle in view. The fluid swirled sickeningly like blood in the phial; I imagined that I could smell it. She shook her head. "Look sweetie," she said, "I know you're not feeling too well, it's common; this will make you feel a lot better. We're all here to help you—"

"Help me?" I said. "You're not here to help me, you're the angel of death. You were put on this job to kill me, you and Goodenough worked the whole thing out." I found myself literally babbling with terror. Hoisted up, compressed into the stockings, squeezed like a gnome into helplessness, I saw the terrible needle closing in on me and realized what they had done. Step by step I had been led to this from the moment that Hope had died and they had put me in isolation, then filling me with drugs so that my condition deteriorated, administering deadly, painful drugs to me under the guise that I was ill and that they were curing my illness … it was the drugs that were making me sick! "You bitch!" I screamed, thrashing around, trying to rise—but it was hopeless. I was helplessly pinned. "Get away from me. Get away from me with that!"

Her face swung before me, moonlike, enormous, pendulous, that face suspended like a hanging tear from the panel of her forehead. "Mr. President—" she said.

"No!" I said, "no!" and bellowed then so loudly that I must have terrified her; if nothing else, I still have power in my voice, I have the habit of command. A president is still a president, no matter what they do to him, what drugs they fill him with to make him weak. And she backed away from me, the needle shaking. I saw everything. I saw everything then—how cunningly I had been led step by step to exactly this position, what they had done to me, what they were planning to do. "Bitch!" I screamed again and with a mighty effort thrashed free of my confinements. I fell in a half-roll to the floor, the two-foot drop shattering; it was as if every bone within the body took the shock, the muscles spavining; and I lay there then looking at her with hatred.

"You fell," she said. She reached toward me, putting the needle horrifyingly *between her teeth* as she leaned forward like some grotesque animal then, shades of light washing her face.

How I bellowed and thrashed! This next presidential wail must have cut its way through all of the chambers and pockets of 1185. I squirmed like a rodent under this fury, my body literally melding with the floor. I had never had this sensation before, that there was no differentiation between the body and the surfaces on which I slithered—a snake must feel this way, the crawling and dreadful things in the unseen forest, half creatures of the slime, half of corruption. And winding underneath her that way, everything came into focus as it never had before! I realized that from the very first they had been out to kill me and that they had used my obsession with my memoirs as a means of distracting my attention from their purposes.

"Old cunt!" I screamed, lying there, "I know what you are. I know what you're doing!" And she started to come forward with that needle again; but sly, sly in my weakness, I rolled again.

"You'll get yours," I said, "you'll get yours, all right. I'll put everything down on tape. I have already. I know what you've been trying to do, and I've put down the most explicit details. It's all there for the police."

This was a lie, of course, I had put down no details at all. But it was enough to make her think. I could see connivance and dismay mingle in her eyes, and at that moment Goodenough came into the room.

"What is this?" he said. I could see him looming huge by the doorway. "What is going on here?"

"She's trying to kill me," I said. "She's trying to kill me with that thing. You are too; you've been planning this from the first." If nothing else, I was always very free and frank with my public announcements.

There was no duplicity in me at any level; I would always say what was on my mind. After decades of lies, they appreciated me as straight-talking Bill. "You've been planning this from the first," I said.

He knelt by me. His face too was pendulous, but rather than glistening like a tear, it was dull, dull. "Bill," he said, reaching toward me, "Bill, you can't—"

"Don't touch me, you murderer!" I shrieked, pivoting on the floor; but he was after me in a flash, scuttling on hands and knees, and he laid his strong, calm hands on me and yanked me to a halt. "Murderer!" I shouted, "you've touched me!"—and then let my body go limp in his grasp. I would not give him the satisfaction, I would not permit him the satisfaction of weakness or pleading but rather would become completely submissive. I would disappear within his grasp. I felt myself being lifted then, whisked levels and levels, as if in skyscraper by elevator; and with moans and little hisses of effort, I was placed down on the couch again, where I lay at my swooning ease, the canister tucked into place, again the stockings tightened, my feet hoisted high, high over my head, my head pushed down firmly into the matting. Still I kept my eyes closed; if I kept them closed, there was nothing they could do to me, no way they could reach me—like being young again and under the covers, where no nightmare could get me. "I want you to listen to me," he said, yanking at my hands, pulling at the fingers. "I want you to listen to me now."

"Nothing. I won't listen to you."

"This is very serious now. Your condition is too far advanced. If you don't listen to me, we're going to have to institutionalize right away. I'll call an ambulance. I'll notify the press too, so they'll all be here to take pictures when they carry you out."

That brought me into alertness. Slowly I unsealed my eyes, zipped them open. "Don't even think of that," I said. "I have a right to do as I see fit. I have a right to protect myself."

"Get out of here, Margaret," Goodenough said, "I want to talk to him alone."

"I'll get out of here," she said. "I am leaving this house. I am never coming back. He has accused me of trying to murder him. I don't care if he's the ex-president of the United States. In forty years of practice—"

"Forget it, Margaret," Goodenough said, "I don't want to listen to your nonsense now. Get out of here."

She left, her needle with orange phial still in her hand. Obviously she had forgotten that she was still holding it. I did nothing to remind her.

"Listen to me," Goodenough said when she was out the door, "I think we've carried this as far as possible now. I don't think we can go this way anymore. You're going to have to be institutionalized."

"No," I said. "I know you're trying to kill me," I added. "I know you've always been thinking of it. You had me fooled for a long time, but now I'm onto you."

His eyes flicked, he tapped his knees. "Then you should be happy," he said patiently. "If you think that we're trying to kill you, then obviously you're unsafe here; you'd be better off in a place where you would be watched all of the time, where you wouldn't have to be fearful."

"Fuck off," I said. "It's my life, I can do anything I want with it. I want you out of here with your lousy nurse in an hour, that's what I want."

"I'm sorry," Goodenough said, shaking his head, "if no one can take the responsibility, then it falls to me. I have no choice. I didn't want it to be this way. But the paranoia is starting now. When the paranoid syndrome begins, it means that you're entering an area of potential clot, and if you get a clot, you could bow out …"

"What do you mean, paranoia?" I said sullenly. "You mean you're not really planning to kill me, that this is just something I've imagined?"

"Exactly," said Goodenough. "It's a very predictable part of the syndrome, but I hoped that we could avoid—"

"Get out of here," I said. "Murderer! Assassin! I managed to survive the curse, and if I can do that, I can survive you! I won't permit you to have me, even though you've been stalking me since the day I was inaugurated. I cheated you fair and square; you couldn't catch up with me, and you're not going to have me now. You'll have to live with the knowledge of your defeat. Fair's fair; if you couldn't get me when it was open season, then you can't get me now!"

"You don't understand," Goodenough said, "you're a very sick man."

"I'm not that sick. I'm not so sick that I don't know what you're trying to do to me. I'm going to outlive you," I said. "I'm going to outlive all of you. William Eric Springer will live to the age of ninety-five in the year 2005 and will bury all of you."

"I can't be responsible," Goodenough said. "I've done everything within my power to keep you going. But now I'm going to have to call in other parties. I can't take the responsibility alone anymore."

"Don't you threaten me," I said. "I'm not afraid of you."

"It was my responsibility up until now," Goodenough said. He began to move toward the door in sidewise scuttle, his motions awkward and yet somehow graceful in the way that Margaret's had been. These people are clever; they live on levels; it is impossible to see any consistency within them. Only I have been consistent; and up until the absolute end, that is how I will remain. Consistent. True to myself.

He stopped at the door, hanging over it like some ghastly ornament. "Will you cooperate?" he said. "This is your last chance."

"How should I cooperate?"

"Follow medical procedures," he said, "follow medical advice. And the dictation will have to stop. It's too dangerous. You're becoming overly excited—"

"I am going to finish my memoirs," I said. "I am going to make my true and final statement, No one can stop me."

"It will kill you," Goodenough said. "You've built yourself up to a peak …"

"You've been listening to them. You've been spying on me."

"No one's been listening to you," he said. "No one's been spying on you. You've constructed all of this in your mind. You've created a set of fantasies that cannot be punctured. This is part of the arteriosclerotic pattern."

"Fuck you, you son of a bitch," I said. "Go get laid."

"This is all my fault," Goodenough said vaguely. "I did this. It did not have to be this way. It could have been different."

"Leave me alone."

"I admit that I identified with you. Your struggles to get it all down, to recapitulate your life. It was unprecedented. It was something that had never been done before. I thought it could be a valuable contribution to history. I thought it could be an important part of the historical record. It was vanity. I wanted to share in it vicariously."

My stockings were pinching. "Leave me alone," I said, waving the microphone at him. "I've got everything down on tape, you son of a bitch. Everything that you've been saying, all of your plans and plots. Wait until the courts get hold of this. You'll be jailed for manslaughter."

"I'm sorry," he said, "I'm very sorry." He left the room, leaving the door to sway in the abscess, like a gigantic ear torn from a dismembered body, the breezes from the corridors causing it to twitch to and fro in its vague way, like a misplaced synapse. I felt an assumed control. Holding the microphone, I had the feeling that I had once again taken over some control of my life. They could not get away with this. They would not. All of it was on the record. All of the time, always, they were out to get me, but I was too cunning for them, and even at the end I had the power. I have the tape. I have the memoirs. I have the absolute consistency from first to last of my own position.

"What's a senator, daddy?" Arthur said. "What does a senator do?"

"That's hard to explain," I said. "A senator is a member of the highest legislative body in the United States."

"What's a legislative body?" he asked. He was only nine years old, fourth grade, I had to keep on remembering that.

"A legislative body is a group of men who make and uphold the laws of this country and also represent the opinions of the people."

"All the people?" he said

"The people who elect them," I said, "the people who vote for senators, two from every state. If you get more votes than the person running against you, then you become a senator and it's your duty to act as the people who voted for you would. To let their wishes be known to the whole country."

"Mommy says that this is going to mean you'll be away from home a lot," Arthur said. "I don't want you to be away. You're away too much already. Will you ever be home if you're a senator?"

"Oh, yes," I said. He was always able to get through to me emotionally in a way that Eunice could not; no one could reach me as Arthur did. This may be some betrayal of tragic weakness—I am not looking for sentimental response now, being far beyond that—I really believe that this is a flaw in me that he was able to reach me so deeply on an easy, superficial level of connection, when the fact is, that at the bottom he did not care for me at all, nor I for him; we were merely linked genetically, that was all. "Yes, I'll be home, don't you worry about that."

"No, you won't," he said, "you'll never be at home. You don't like to be at home."

"Who said that?" I asked. "Who said that?"

"I said it myself," he said, and then he turned, ran down the panel of beach, blue bathing trunks against the white of him, against the brown of the sand, the sea coming in. I heaved myself from my back and pursued him slowly, limping, running down that streak of beach after him, out of breath, weak from having risen suddenly, the absolutely first intimation of mortality that must have been at nearly thirty, the realization that, not even I was going to live forever. But I wanted to catch up with him, the beach house in the background, the sun falling away over my shoulder as I pursued him; and he waited for me, his run slowing to a lope. I caught up with him, reached out, touched a shoulder, and turned him around.

"You should never say that," I said. "You should never say that I don't want to be home; you should never believe that."

"But it's true," he said, his boy's face bleak, the absence of expression of the imprint of experience upon that face, giving him oddly a sense of greater corruption—as if the maximum corruption, I thought, might be no experience at all, like the smooth and blasted faces of the old in nursing homes.

"It's true, isn't it? You always said to tell the truth in this world, and

I am. The truth is that you don't want to be home."

And what could I say? There was nothing to say. I reached toward him, meaning only to comfort him, to stroke his arms, to lift him into the air against me; but he must have taken something in this gesture for threat, for he turned and was running down the beach again, faster this time; he was running in something which could have been real fear, his legs pumping, eyes and head fixated, arms moving steadily and slowly. And as he ran away from me, as I watched him dwindle and diminish, I knew that I should have pursued him. This was something that I definitely should have done; I should not have let him run away alone. But I did not know what to do, did not know what could have been said; and turned instead, let him go away from me, began to walk slowly back toward the house where Eunice was waiting, hands on hips, the sun glinting off her head like glass an explosion of light around her head.

I should have followed him, but I did not; instead I went back to her. Tropism. That was the nature of my life; it was always tropism until the greatest one of all came to take me ... and then I refused to realize what had happened, and instead called it bad luck.

Politicians.

Even when we have learned, we know no better.

It was only a thousand dead, twelve hundred at the most in the two detonations before the blackmailing demand was made; the next would have escalated, however, and then beyond that, and there was no question in anyone's mind but that at least forty or fifty thousand Americans were being risked by my refusal to negotiate. We would have broken the ring; there were only twenty of them altogether— twenty: Unbelievable. But it would have taken time, and in the meanwhile there would have been forty or fifty thousand dead, maybe much more than that if a chain reaction had been set off by any of the explosions. Later on we realized that this had been a real possibility. But even forty or fifty thousand was considerable; it would have been the greatest national disaster of its type in history, as many dead as in the Vietnam war.

I was asked, as I inevitably would be, at one of the press conferences whether the stakes had ever crossed my mind ... that is, if I had ever for a moment doubted the wisdom of my actions, if I had not held back from the consequences. This was still early after the incident, when I was running, so to speak, on a floodtide of national approval and sympathy; and if the question were ever to be asked, this was the time to take an honest answer ... but I found myself astonished to realize at the time that it was being phrased that I had literally never thought of it. I had just never thought of it at all. I had never doubted for a moment that the only way to handle the situation was to deny all demands. Their desires were untenable and were in no sense negotiable; to have capitulated would have brought even greater disaster. It never occurred to me to give in to them. This was the answer, as a matter of fact, that I gave.

"Yes," the reporter said, "yes, I understand that. Would you say this was the same kind of thinking that lay behind Truman's decision to use the atomic bomb? The decision to save more lives by risking some. Or Johnson's decision on Vietnam?"

I had never thought of that either. I did not like the equation between this and Vietnam, and I said so. "Vietnam was a policy misjudgment," I said. "Everybody knows that now. Vietnam was not acceptable risk for the returns."

"And Hiroshima? What would you say about Hiroshima?"

"I don't know," I said honestly. "I just don't know. I was barely in the Congress then. I was thirty-five years old. What part could I play in it?"

"But surely you've given it some thought. I mean, in all the years that have followed, Mr. President, you must have, as all American presidents have done, pondered this and thought what your own response might have been in this situation. Surely you can't tell us that you never thought of it."

"But I didn't," I said, and I was telling the truth. It was not my decision to make and never could have been, and it never occurred to me for a moment to wonder about what I might have done. Every situation is unique and different.

"Then you're not prepared to say that that decision was right."

"What decision? The decision to bomb Hiroshima? That was almost thirty-eight years ago; there's no way that we can go back and consider that situation. No, I won't second-guess another American president. In my own decision, it seemed that I had no options. Anything else would have been worse."

"Even knowing that forty or fifty thousand—"

"Even knowing," I said, furious, "even knowing that," and pointed for the next question. But this kept on revolving in my brain, just the way the bastard, undoubtedly, had meant it to; it was a setup. In the months to follow, I realized that I had never thought of this—the forty or fifty thousand, that is—they simply did not figure into the equation. All that mattered was on a cost-plus-risk basis, and seen that way, I could not lose by challenging him. The other way was intolerable; they would have taken any sign of weakness for fiat to extend the blackmail, and they had twenty, thirty, maybe forty plants (we simply did not know) under their control. How could I risk it? The greatest good for the greatest number, that was the democratic theorem; but I simply had not thought of that forty or fifty thousand that would have gone in the explosions if they had not been the ones to show compassion.

The reason that I had come out of it so well, I understood finally, was not because of myself, but through them. If they had not been incapable of killing on that scale, I would have been a murderer, because *I* was. All of the time I had been—I had been a murderer looking for an occasion. That was all. I was led to see it. It was the same principle that had underlay the Kennedy heroism in Cuba, the Kissinger settlement in Vietnam. The enemy had simply shown more regard for human life than we had. Then *I* had.

Of course, I never discussed any of this with Hope. There are certain things both in and out of this world which cannot possibly be shared.

I do think, though, that this was one of the reasons for the loss of the election; not because the opposition picked up on it—because they did not—but because somewhere in the lurking subconscious of a good proportion of the electorate was the suspicion that their president was a man who would not hesitate to risk any or all of them for principle's sake; and they did not like this.

I could not say that I blamed them.

The ability to convert people into abstractions is given unprecedented assistance by the technological devices of the late twentieth century, but abstract as we will, there is no similar technological means for the alleviation of pain, as—all of the murderous Goodenough's ministration to the contrary—I am now beginning to understand.

"Come on," she said, "fuck me. Even a senator can fuck, can't he? Unless everything I've been reading is true, and the only person you fellows can get off on is yourself." She was a little heavy in the hips, but a good fuck. Banging away at her, I thought that Eunice would somehow understand; this is what is known as statesmanship.

Merrick had the answer; so did Henry. See it all, listen, retain nothing, forget everything; if you don't know that it's happening, then nothing is happening at all; if a gigantic tree falls in a forest and there is no one within miles around to hear the tree, then it makes no sound. Merrick and Henry know that without understanding there is no pain, without damned knowledge there is no culpability, without insight there is no guilt. I wish I could have been them and downing the pills one, two, three, the neat red-and-white little pills offered me from those open, glinting palms. It was the feeling that I was taking in not only them but the essence of these spirits themselves, the faithful nurses, my comforters and attendants. I was more than their charge; there was a personal interest. But of course they knew nothing. This is the key to survival in the world. I am not so out of it to know nothing.

If there is an afterlife and if that afterlife is contingent upon knowledge, then we are all in a great deal of difficulty, because to live is to plot out time and again all levels of sensation; to live is to deny knowledge, to become a Merrick or Henry (who can make it very well in this stage but may have some problems with the reincarnation). I do not know. I do not know at all.

I used to piss great, heavy streams. I could do it anywhere, anytime, jab it out in a public urinal, do it next to a press photographer, take a piss while standing in the back hall of the convention, waiting to go out and give the acceptance speech; pissing was as natural to me as breathing and a damned sight more pleasant, even sensual in the welling feeling of the bladder and then that quick sighing release. And now, after a lifetime of pissing, after a veritable lifetime of doing it anywhere and anytime I chose and gaining pleasure from it, I am utterly unable to do it at all, unable to exert any control whatsoever. I suppose that there is in a way some justice in this, but in another and more absolute fashion there is not.

Necessary to get it down. *It was not lust* which drove me to Hope— what was that? It meant nothing anywhere in Washington, and for fifty square miles there were women, delightful, available, attractive women, who were as accessible as one's own imagination, and I could have had any of them (in fact, I had a few). It was not that which drove me to Hope, but something rarer, finer, sweeter. I would never have left Eunice if it had not been for this elevation of feeling. Eunice understood and knew exactly what was going on, but she would not have stopped me. She never attempted to. She let me do exactly what I wanted all of the time as long as I kept up appearances. That was the way of Washington marriages in those times (still may be, as far as I know); and in fact that was the way it was with Hope for a while. All of the pressure came from me, not from her; she had no plans other than her column and an interesting life; it could have gone on that way indefinitely … it was my own decision to leave Eunice, to marry Hope, to take the indefinable risks to career, even with the Stevenson example before me—that poor, tormented fool … but not lust. Never lust. That was not any consideration at all. I have always been a considerate and thoughtful man; interested in sex, yes, but never lustful. Just fucking, just fucking Hope, getting in and out of her, moving the tool, digging into her waists, her breasts all around me like flowers, fucking the shit out of her. Who am I kidding? Sanctimonious to the end. How much of this has been the truth and how much the same old lies I will never know, impossible to separate, but I have tried—godammit, I have *tried*.

"No," Goodenough says, "no, it will not be necessary to use force or constriction of any type. He will go without any difficulty at all. Isn't that true, Mr. President?"

I am dictating all of this. I am dictating all of this as it happens, my feet falling below me now with the microphone clenched in my hand and the microphone like a flower, my lips like a child's kissing it. Right up to the end, I will keep on dictating this; they will not get away with it.

"No," I say, "no, I will not come with you." There are two of them, they look like Merrick and Henry in a way, but they are not; they are big, tall, strong men with blank, weak faces, and they make me feel like a child. They make me feel like a child who could cry, because I do not know them. I can only deal with the familiar; I cannot take these shocks anymore, these constant dull shocks. Too much has happened in too little time.

"No," I say again, "I will not go. It is my right not to go. This is my life."

"Mr. President," Goodenough says, kneeling. Sweat is coming out of a hundred crevices on his face, and I can see the dense little hairs growing out of his nose. "Mr. President, please. Bill, please. It will only be for a little while. Don't you see?"

"See what?"

"See the necessity. It will only be for a little while," he says again. "It is highly necessary."

"No," I say, "I do not want to go with you. I refuse to go with you."

"You will," one of the men says. He extends a hand. "You will, right now."

And I see this, I see this now. Truly I see this; they mean business and furthermore they always did. They are going to take me out of here; Goodenough is going to assign me to some institution; and there I will spend the last days of my miserable life. Unable to kill me here, he will drag me into one of his sanitariums; and there he and his trained nurses will do the job. "All right," he says, motioning, "go ahead. Take him."

"Wait," I say. "I want to make a final statement."

Goodenough shakes his head. "There's no time for that—"

"Yes there is," I say. "I'll go quietly when you let me finish, but I'm almost done, I just want to wrap the tapes up. You're going to let me finish them, aren't you?" His blazing little eyes look at the canisters greedily, watch the reels as they loop through the machine. "They're all yours," I say, "my true and final statement. You always knew you were going to get them anyway. Isn't that what you were after from the start? They can make you famous. Well, you can let me finish them."

"Bill," Goodenough says, "you're very sick. The tapes are almost incoherent. It was something that we let you do to keep your spirits in focus but—"

"But nothing," I say. It is shocking to hear this is what Goodenough thinks of the tapes. "They are not incoherent," I say. "They embrace everything. They make every statement. Go out of the room and let me finish."

His eyes become measured and cunning. "You can do it while we're in the room," he says. "There's no need for any of us to leave."

"Yes, there is," I say. "If you let me finish, I'll come quietly, I won't fight at all. But otherwise you'll have to take me out of here screaming." His eyes seem to close in even further, seemingly unconsciously he pats something in his pocket. "You can't give me an injection big enough to knock me out," I say. "You can never shut away the truth, don't you understand that? The truth will come out someday in some form, and then it will be known to the world. How are you going to conceal it?"

"Leave him alone," Goodenough says. If nothing else, he is decisive; he is not an engaging man, but he can, at least occasionally, face the reality of situations and capitulate to them. "Get out of here."

The two men turn and go. In the slump of their shoulders, in their carriage as they leave the room, I can sense relief. They wanted no more part of this than I did; all along they were hoping for a dismissal. They have lived their lives, I think, wildly, their whole lives waiting for some order that would relieve them of all responsibility, cancel out the fact of their lives themselves; and this underlies their submission and their power. They will do anything. They will literally do anything to be left alone. So would I. From the first.

"Five minutes," says Goodenough, standing at the door. "You have five minutes. No more."

"Five minutes will be enough," I say to him. "Five minutes is more than I would need." He closes the door. I am alone now, dust in the room, splinters of light cutting their fragments like knives through the turning dust, the microphone in my hand and—

What can I say?

Say this: that as the returns drifted in that night, as the first pattern began to make itself felt, Connecticut breaking for the opposition and then that slide down the eastern seaboard, all of the New England states on the line, no comfortable majorities but close in every state, as the Midwest started to come in with its dismal projections, as New York went under and we came into midnight realizing that this election was lost, the first incumbent president in more than half a century to be turned out of office, I looked at Hope, who had been sitting through all of this, her face somehow brighter and brighter as the evening went on, rubbed to sheen, the wedges of her face implacable and said, "Well, it's for the best. It really is for the best. Who needed this anyway?"

I expected her to laugh; she looked back at me with an expression I had never before seen on her face. There must have been twenty jammed in that filthy little room, but in that glance it was as if it was only the two of us, the two of us only who existed in the world.

"Don't tell me it's for the best," she said, "I don't want to listen to your easy explanations as to why this doesn't mean anything at all."

My God she was angry! She was taking the election personally, but not in the way that a good wife might be expected to—feeling things on behalf of her husband, that is—but rather as an affront to *her*, her own reputation.

"What do you care?" she said. "You always wanted to lose anyway; losing gave you definition; it was your purpose and your salvation and your strength. You're happy now."

"What are you talking about?" I said. I was really puzzled and confused, sitting there with pad on my knee, making scratch marks in pencil, only to give the hands a business; that was the only purpose. And now the pad slid off me to the rug. "I don't understand what you're talking about."

"You fool," she said, "you love to lose. That's why you ran in 1980, because of the curse. You thought you'd be killed. That would make you one of the biggest losers. But then, when that wasn't enough for you, when it looked as if you weren't going to be killed, you tried to set up things so that the world would be blown up—"

I was astounded. I had never heard of anything like this before; I felt my bones turning watery with astonishment. Pouring through, fusing together like sealing wax. "What?" I said again. "What are you talking about?"

"Nothing," she said. "I won't discuss it anymore. I'm sorry I started, forget it, I said nothing, nothing at all," and turned her attention back toward the television, where the Far West was starting to pour in— Nevada down the pipe, Wyoming not holding, Utah (which was a safe state) swinging the other way, fifty-eight forty-two, the early returns out of selected California precincts wholly disastrous.

But my mind was far away from that, my attention swinging on a long, elevated loop—was she right? *Did* I want to lose? Did that explain Arthur, Eunice, the election, everything that had happened? Was I indeed merely seeking, all of the time, a disaster so enormous that it would relieve me of responsibility? I found myself thinking of the others in that moment—Nixon and Johnson and Kennedy, the need for self-destruction which had united that famous trinity—and an insight burst upon me like an apple exploding into filaments from gunshot under a hot, white light: maybe the presidency was a search for disaster, the point where self-revulsion and the abstract, idealistic purposes which could conceal the self from self fused together … maybe it was that all the time.

"I didn't want to hurt anyone," I said to her then. "That was the important thing, not to hurt anyone."

"It's too late," she said, "it's too late. You're a fool."

"No one," I said again. I meant this; I did not want to hurt anyone. But it was impossible to keep my posture fixated; my attention on the situation had wandered far away. She had opened new territory—the territory was disaster.

I was on a beach with Arthur. He was running from me; I was running toward him, the waves swinging into the shore. I could not catch him, could not even try to catch him; and so after a while I stopped running and began to move slowly back along the shore toward the cabin, the sun collapsing in the sky, realizing that all of my life had been a search for connection *which would not come*, feeling through pain—and that would come only in intervals.

At the beachhouse, Eunice was there; she looked at me. "What are you doing?" she said. "Don't you know it's too late?"

And I said, "Yes, yes, I know it's too late. Everything from now on must be downhill."

This was in 1949 during the Berlin airlift, and it must have been six months after that—no make it seven—that we got our first wind of Korea, the thirty-eighth, the passage into our dreams, the crossing of fire … but to understand then, as the century wound down, that there was nothing, absolutely nothing, that could be said to be ours other than the darkness.

EPILOGUE

The New York Times 4/14/90

... Spokesmen added that no effects were retrieved; the fire which took the life of the President having ravaged his apartment beyond repair. At the behest of the President in a will filed many years ago, the remains were cremated and there will be no services... day of national mourning will commence at sundown 4/19 but federal offices shall remain open since, the President stated, "Mr. Springer would have wanted our business to continue."

THE END

SCOP
BARRY N. MALZBERG

Dedication
"There must be more to life than just living."
—Gully Foyle
The Stars My Destination: Alfred Bester

To my mother and father

PROLOGUE

Scop. (1995–?) A bitter man with bitter eyes and a bitter mouth set bitterly underneath a bitter forehead that leaked bitterness, glowed with pain. "No more," Scop said bitterly, little flights of saliva dazzling their way free from his tongue, dribbling their absent way down his pointed chin to hang suspended in the stop-time an inch above his highly polished, almost fluorescent shoes. "No more of this at all," and wrenched himself, springing the lever, forced himself back then to 1963 where most bitterly—

He stood on a Grassy Knoll with an enormous box camera dressed as a tourist of the time snapping photographs of the Presidential motorcade. (They would never quite figure him out in the investigations but no matter.) It passed by him slowly, lumpish in the Dallas midday, motorcycles front and back, the President waving. Across the way another photographer crouched: Abraham Zapruder. Scop smiled and caught the President clearly in frame open to one tenth aperture just as the first bullet hit twitching back the head. The President screamed (only Scop could hear it but there it was). The President's mouth opened as if he were attempting to ingest the bullet but before the manufacturer's toy camera could get that impossible expression the necessary second bullet hit the occipital zones causing fragmentation. Bitterly Scop launched himself out of there clutching his camera, moved to 1965 in Arlington where he caught a splendid snap of Rockwell's brains blown out in a parking lot, then shunted hurriedly to 1968. Time was running out. He checked into a strategically located motel muttering *oh do excuse* as he pushed his way past businessmen to the swimming pool, ducked under a deck chair, got himself situated not a moment too soon to see the Reverend come strolling into the kind evening light of the balcony and got one, two, three, four angles of the death mask, then whisked to the mosque too late for Malcolm's death but time enough for a lovely portrait of his widow screaming. Bitterly. 1995, the very year in which Scop was born was the last on this swing; he waited out two hours in the public square playing a rented lute and making believe that his camera was alive; onlookers thought him gently crazy but when the Premier was shot in the temple in the motorcade they thought differently. Scop supposed. He had no way of being sure of this of course and with eight exquisite freeze-frames he was already gone.

Back to bitter 1963 and the Grassy Knoll. Terrible times then, slaughter of the infra-structure but there was nothing to be said, event was immutable: you moved on. Sentiment called however; pilgrimage had its role even at the cost of pain. Motorcade on the way again. Two tourists stood behind Scop, women in their early fifties, long-lived for those times, dressed in sunsuits. "Boy get away from me," one of them said and Scop said something unprintable in a foreign language, did not move, looked for the motorcade. Where was Zapruder anyway? "Didn't you listen?" the second woman said, "don't you listen to anything, are you crazy?" and moved deliberately to step on his toe but Scop said *fara fara* in the old tongue and hit her a soft but stunning blow behind the ear, kicked the other unconscious with cunning toes on the spinal regions and then, feeling his failure, knowing his bitterness, winked back to the Time of Origin where he made the necessary adjustments that would compensate for their nonentity, altered lines of flux so that their descendants would be transferred without penalty to others of the nineteenth generation and then returning to the exact spot but three seconds earlier dragged the women away from Grassy Knoll with surprising strength, thirty whole seconds before the motorcade passed.

No one noticed him of course. They were interested only in the events of the day which were clearly Zapruder's; no one had noticed Scop because Scop, originally, had never been there. Behind a hedge he committed rough, quick, unspeakable sexual acts upon the women from vague compulsion and then leapt to the time span suddenly opening, felt it devouring him fleshily. He returned to embarkation. "Enough," he said to the machines against their quick strokes and bird beat, "There must be no more of this. These assassinations … these assassinations were horrible." He had every right to be truly bitter. "It could have been different," he said.

Melodramatically Scop fell to his knees, engineering now for remorse. "Forgive me," he said, "forgive me for this," and then the bitterness overwhelmed to say nothing of the cries of rage of the Temporals as they, having deduced his mission, caught and seized him, shunted him away, four channels diverted to find himself sealed and decked. But not unconscious, oh no. Not unconscious. Bitterly, he considered his failure.

PART ONE

I

SCOP'S FAILURE: If he had not lost it would have been another way, perhaps like this: Scop would have appeared before the old man robed and cloaked at the proper hour, standing deferential yet radiating assurance in the hall of interviews and would have shown his photographs, unfurled them, tripped them one by one like playing cards from his fist, showing them to the astonished Master who would have clutched his own garments withdrawing. "What is the meaning of this? where have we obtained this blasphemy?" the old man would have shrieked.

"Through mastery of the temporal," Scop would have said, "capturing one by one the frozen moments in which our history itself pivoted. Kennedy dead, the kings assassinated. Here at the moment of impact we can see the gong of civilization struck."

"What you have done is illegal. Witness may be allowed under certain circumstance but photographs never," the Master would have said, leaning forward, scuttling the photographs, hiding them in his robes. "You have broken all of the codes; you are asked to submit at once, no delay, to questioning," he says. "You will explain why this was done and how you have circumvented the codes."

"It is of no matter. I have duplicates." Suddenly Scop leans forward, seizes the Temporal Master by the ribbons of his own clothing and pulls the old man closer to him, a faint, fine quiver like that of the machine goes through his hands, a faint, dense sweetish odor penetrates Scop's nostrils, he becomes aware as if for the first time of the acute mortality and vulnerability of the Master and this dismays him because he has not up until now really concerned himself with that problem, being more involved—let us face it—with the reordering of all existence. "We live in a time stream based upon astonishment and disaster, created by a series of accidents, based upon pain and brutality which sends us lurching inch by inch in pain toward a future we cannot divine," he says rather floridly, makes florid gestures with his hands upon the Master's robe, with equal floridity although perhaps some self-awareness wipes his forehead. "Look at these pictures and you will see the proof inviolable. Don't turn away!" he shrieks to the Master whose old eyes indeed do turn inward and who begins to breathe steamily through his mouth exhaling fumes of cabbage, onion, incense and the other mysterious materials which Scop imagines the Masters to eat, "You've got to face it, you've got to face the truth, our world is based on murder," and indeed as he shakes and shakes the old man (becoming more aware of his vulnerability on the instant and by that knowledge also understanding his own power in a world he never made) he can feel the insight driven into him, some spike into the consciousness of the diseased but necessarily gallant old man whose eyes flutter open with that knowledge and the Master says, "Why I do see this, I see it indeed! You're perfectly right: how can an evolution predicated upon the murder of saints lead to anything but barbarism?" and he begins to laugh. Scop laughs also, the two of them laugh hopelessly in the dim clamp of the enclosure while joy fills Scop's heart for he knows that he has made his case to the Master and that all will be changed. The lines will be changed, the dead will walk again, the enormously complicated task of switching over will begin and within his lifetime if not within the next decade Scop will see a world of truth and justice in which the lives of the saints, perpetuated to their natural end, gave impetus to the era of benevolence which follows. "Thank you," the old man says, "thank you for helping me to see this. How unreasonable we were to have thought that this could go on, Scop." *Scop*, he says again, murmuring it, the ritual of naming and places his hand on Scop's head now, the translucent fingers shaking and Scop feels vague warmth, light, distension … he feels joined through the ritual of the naming in some indefinable fashion which will weld him and the Master together for all time, may lead for all he knows, to his own initiation as Master some day … but as this moment flows over him, as he revels in the understanding that he has, almost single-handedly brought the era of barbarism to a close the photographs wink and dazzle before him, they seem to blend and flow together in the murky light and then there are cries, cries all around him, the sounds of the trespassers coming into the hall to seize him with enormous hands and as they drag him away Scop realizes—or then again he tries to avert the realization—that none of this has truly happened and that what he has taken to be resolution is nothing more than a construction, he never got through to the Master, the Master never listened to him, the Master refused to agree … and they tear him from there, he protesting, screaming for his evidentiary photographs but they take him far to a safe place and there he is wrapped layer between layer of stasis while they decide, oh how he hopes that they will decide soon! what they will do with or to him.

II

GETTING THE DALLAS BLUES: Bitterly he ponders his choices. He can present his arguments and be humiliated or he can fail to present his arguments and be humiliated. He decides upon the former course and selects the guise of a rotund appointments secretary on whose appearance he has been able to do a fine mock-up through access to the secret files. As is his custom he is permitted to make direct entrance to the President's quarters before nine where he finds the President in his nightshirt, ruffling his hair and looking unhappily out the window. "I don't like this city," the President says mildly enough. "Every time I come here I get the blues. Getting the Dallas blues," the President adds pointlessly and turns, walks past the disguised Scop and toward a closet. "Now what shall I wear today?" he says, and begins to riffle clothing. "The blue? Or the black? Of course it doesn't matter."

"I would suggest that you leave at once," Scop says.

"I think the black would be better. But then again I look most dashing in blue. It is very difficult to make these decisions because they make me feel like a frivolous person. But occasions of state are frivolous," the President adds mildly, "we really must remember that. At the heart this is a ceremonial position." Humming he takes out the blue and ponders it at extension length. "I might as well," he says. "And they'll probably give me that *hat* at the breakfast but then again—blues for the blue, don't you think that's right?"

Abruptly Scop's control breaks. More and more this has been happening to him; he has tried to slide his way into situations crosswise, moving laterally toward cautious alignment, reminding himself that results are best obtained through indirection but under the circumstances it is impossible to continue this way. Bitterness seizes him. "Leave Dallas!" he shouts, "you must leave this town at once; it is absolutely disastrous for you to extend your stay. You must go, flee, the streets are choked with assassins, at this very moment—" and then he breaks off, tormented, stricken, he has broken the code of information. Whatever he had in mind he had never planned to do this. The President looks at him bleakly and then strokes the fabric of the blue suit, tosses it casually on the bed, parts his robe to reveal himself naked but for his underclothing; a strongly-built man, his body reassembled leaving only residual effects from previous injuries. "That's all well and good," he says, "but we've got only half an hour to be downtown so we'd better hurry."

Scop cries out but no one comes.

III

ALIENATION THEORY: As he has done before but never so desperately he placed himself between the woman's thighs, balanced, inserted, then began in an absent but energetic manner to mime the strokes of generation. He has never been able to comport himself successfully under pressure but this does not excuse him from the obligation to try. He closes his eyes, manufactures images, thinks bitterly that it is not fair that over and again he must go through this without climax before he can proceed but then again he is merely situated within the framework: he has not created it. None of it is his responsibility. After a time when he judges that he has moved sufficiently and that his sincerity cannot be questioned and that it could not be said that he has not tried to do his part he rolls off her, draws up his knees in the darkness and looks at the ceiling waiting for her to speak. She must speak first; there is no way around this. The rules for this part are even more explicit than for the rest: written out. He has checked the list before entering the bleak little simulation of an apartment which she has taken. Finally she says, "What are you trying to do?"

"Save the universe of course," Scop says.

"But why must you save the universe? Would it not be enough to save yourself?"

"We are intertwined!" Scop says. He rolls to his stomach, poises on palms, slowly lifts himself until he thinks he can see knowing that he does not the eyes of the Masters watching him coolly through the prism. "I am the universe and the universe is myself; when I cease to be the universe will wink out of existence." His detumescent little organ, puppylike, flaps agreement underneath him. "Everybody understands that," Scop says.

"But I do not. You must explain it to me."

Yes. He must explain it to her. There is no way around this Scop knows; he must make sense of this to her. This much, at least, is owed for past favors and if he cannot make her understand how can he possibly approach the more diffuse and less sophisticated Masters, many of whom have no conception of the seriousness of the issues involved? "Be reasonable," he says, "remember that you are the framing consciousness and that the universe may exist only as refined through your perceptions. But then consider," he adds, "consider how those perceptions are granted by history, the vast and creaking engines of history at all times lending to these little flickers and glimmers of light the only frame they will ever know … and then ask yourself—"

"I am getting very bored," she says. He feels her fingers moving absently on his organ: the woman will not give up. Either she is insatiable (which he doubts) or she will not accept the humble realities of his condition. "Why don't you try to fuck me again?"

"Because I can't fuck you," Scop says bitterly, "I can't fuck, all that I can do is devolve—"

"Then why do you try so hard?" she says pinching him, "if you do so poorly? Isn't it painful for you?"

"Of course it's painful. Everything is painful. Life is painful, death is painful, likewise the darkness and all motions of passage. Still, I participate."

Her fingernails dig in deeply. "I don't know," she says, "I don't think you so much participate as complain. Why must you complain all the time? Don't you know how tiresome it is," she says, "don't you know how tiresome you are?" and her pressure sends little cylinders of anguish through Scop, "*this* is pain," she says to him knowledgeably, "the other part is merely inconvenience," and he sees what she is saying, he sees her point, Scop is not (despite his monomania) at all a stupid man and he is willing to accept the doubtful realities of his condition to say nothing of the temporal nature of all that he does. He knows that he will not live for a long time and that when he dies his death is permanent; he does not need explication on the permanence of death. "Please stop that," he says mildly enough, "you're hurting me," and then yanks himself from her quickly, she tries to hang on, he feels her little nails digging into his sex and it is all that Scop can do not to scream but he does not scream of course having long been sealed off from even physical sensation: he will not react, he is a machine, he will not show feeling, he is a mechanism and so he merely lies on the bed extended thinking of all the forces of the universe impinging upon him as unnecessarily she tweaks him again and again, a circumstance which he knows will be repeated.

IV

GRASSY KNOLL: "Excuse me," he said to Abraham Zapruder. "Might I ask you for the time?"

Zapruder shrugs, adjusts his camera, looks at his watch. "It's noon," he says. He is an old man, slightly disheveled but kindly. He is here to take pictures of the motorcade which he hopes his grandchildren will enjoy. "Another few minutes," Zapruder says, "I hope that the exposures are correct. The day is beautiful but the weather here is so treacherous and there might be cloud cover."

"I wouldn't worry about it," Scop said. "I am sure that the weather will be fine." He shifted his stance slightly, letting his eyes roll down the thoroughfare where in the distance he thought he could hear the sound of engines but then again it might merely have been heightened apprehension. He and Zapruder after all are old friends, although they have never spoken he has studied the charts and films so closely, dug through the biographical materials with such assiduousness that he sometimes feels that he knows Zapruder more intimately than anyone with whom he has actually dealt to say nothing of the Masters. Of course he must maintain perspective on this, Scop has realized; Zapruder does not have a reciprocal sense of intimacy. For that matter Abraham Zapruder has been dead for seventy years. Carefully, sneakily, Scop inserts a finger underneath the strap holding the camera to Zapruder's shoulder.

"What are you doing?" the old man says. He is a grandfather, a retired toy manufacturer who warms himself on pleasant fall days by planning expeditions for his grandchildren, zoos he can take them to, pictures he can bring home but nevertheless he is no fool. Alertness cascades through his attentive old eyes. "Why are you touching my strap?"

Scop withdrew his finger, cursing the devilish cleverness of the old man, uncertain now but angry within his own uncertainty. In the distance he could see the first flourishes of the motorcade which was now no more than five minutes from this point. It was time for determined measures yet Scop somehow could not summon the will.

"If you will excuse me," Zapruder says, "you are in a position which is somewhat blocking my light. If you would be good enough to move—" He beams upon Scop, defenseless, benevolent, a grandfather whose films will be transferred down the alleys of all the decades and will someday form the Master's justification for their hideous and illegal acts. "I wish to get set up," Zapruder says, "if you will merely—"

Scop inhaled deeply, taking in the dazzle of Dallas sunshine, taking in as well the crucial and complicated implications of the choices he was making and then he said, "Don't take any pictures."

"Don't take any pictures—"

"You don't understand," Scop said hastily, the words pouring out of him then the way that the disastrous film would rattle through the disastrous camera, the touch of Zapruder's finger bringing the mindless reel through and over aperture, casting for all time the dread and unbearable images and the very air around them seemed to contract, so that he was speaking to the man in density rather than open space, all of the others at some far remove so that only he and Abraham

Zapruder were truly at this site which might have been the case in the first place, "You don't understand what you are doing. The results will be absolutely disastrous. These pictures will be printed in the magazines of your time, they will form the basis, the inaccurate basis, for terrible misjudgments, they will eventually be enshrined as perfect realization of disaster. Fifty years from now people will curse your name for them, a hundred years from now your very name will be unspeakable because of what you have brought to them. Must you take these pictures then?"

Zapruder looks at him blankly and Scop realizes that the old man takes him to be mad, that Scop *must* be mad at the Grassy Knoll to have made such statements or there is no objective truth in the Zapruder universe. "Please get away from me," the old man says. "Please leave me alone. I have done nothing to you, I am a simple man, a retired manufacturer, a grandfather, a lover of children—"

"No!" Scop said and made a sweeping, clumsy gesture toward the camera, "no, you cannot take these pictures, you cannot embalm him on these reels forever!" but even as he leapt forward he lurched, missed footing, pirouetted in the grass and then fell heavily, virtually at Zapruder's feet or then again it may only have been an illusion of falling so quietly did the old man regard him, so quickly did Scop recover his balance, stand weaving in front of him. "This must not be permitted to go on," Scop said, "it cannot be, you are dealing with stakes as high as the future of human civilization," and reached out, struck Zapruder, sent the old man staggering back with a walloping blow and then grabbed at the camera, trying to bring it against him with that one lunge but as he did so he felt himself for the second time beginning to fall in the grass, his shoes flailing clownishly on the frictionless grass, Zapruder's face congealing with puzzlement as it looked benignly on and then Scop dove, felt himself falling as if from a great height although it could not have been more than his six and a half feet, falling nose first then in the grass, the scene speeding away from him and from the distance then, as he had always known (and would know again, you bet) the sound of thunder, the sound of drums.

V

SODA ON THE SIDE: It has not always been just this way. He seems to recall an earlier, less difficult time when he lived within rather than without the sanctions of his culture and found them acceptable. "It could be that way again," he says, a little more loudly than he had intended and the bartender in the working class place looks at him curiously over the ridges of the counter, his left hand splayed out at an awkward angle, his right a fist tightly on the cloth which he uses to mop widening circles into the dull finish. "Another one," he says, "and soda on the side," and the bartender shrugs, slams the cloth down, walks to the scotch bottle and taking Scop's glass inverts the bottle, pours clumsily but without haste half-full, puts it down, reaches underneath for a tap glass of soda. The bar is empty at this hour of the day ten-thirty in the morning but later on the workers from the district will come in and stand three deep drinking beer and cursing circumstance. By that time Scop hopes that he will be long gone although he is not sure just where. The bartender gives him the soda, takes some more money over the counter and slams it into the cash register, then walks with a brisk limp down to the rag which has now furled open and continues his slow wiping, looking at Scop now and then with curious, tilted, shy glances as if his manner were mockery and what he really desired was a closer relationship, some perilous intimacy. Scop looks down at his drink, tilts it up, drinks heavily. Alcohol does not agree with him but it is necessary at this time that he keep on drinking for maximum assimilation, the Masters are very strict on this point, and the soda manages to wash away the feeling that he is drowning in the fumes although not the nausea. "Are you all right?" the bartender says for no reason, looking up from his ragging and Scop says that he is all right. "That's good," the bartender says, "I thought for a moment that you were going to be sick. You don't come from around here, do you?"

"Not really."

"I figured that out right away," the bartender says, "I know every face that comes in here and furthermore I can tell the outsiders right off too, those who come nowhere from the section. What brings you here?"

"Nothing much."

"You don't have to talk," the bartender says. "I'm not forcing conversation on you." He considers the counter sullenly, reduces the rag to a knot on his index finger and begins to work in brisk strokes at one limited area. "I just heard you talking to yourself a minute ago I figured you might be better off if you had someone listening to you."

"That's perfectly all right," Scop says, "I don't mind at all."

He does mind, of course and if it were not absolutely necessary for him to be at this place at this time he would leave immediately. His one vocal slip was unfortunate; he is under no circumstances to attract attention to himself nor interact with these people. That he intends to break this most stringent rule of the Temporals within the next hour in the case of a man who is about to come into this bar does not give him excuse to flout it: to the contrary it imposes upon him the absolute necessity to follow the rule in all other circumstances … at heart and for all of his bravado Scop is a congruent personality, a conformist: he accepts and enacts the codes of his society to a degree which even he would not wish to consider closely and all of the time that he is committing most serious violations of temporality he is in craven fear. For these reasons he dreads involvement of any sort with the bartender. He would leave the place immediately, sacrifice everything, return at once … but he cannot, in fifty-two minutes, give or take twelve seconds Leonard Peters will enter this bar and it is vital that this contact be made. Furthermore Scop is almost compulsive about the need to arrive early, the temporal charts have been known to be in error; the coefficient of correlation for fifty-two minutes plus or minus five is no more than point ninety-three and this is not sufficient at least for the high-risk situation in which Scop has placed himself. After all the fate of the universe, nothing more nor less is at stake. So he must stay in the bar, pace out the time, wait for Leonard Peters … "What could be that way again I asked you," the bartender is saying. "Don't you ever answer questions?"

"I was thinking," Scop says, "thinking about something."

"All I wanted to know is what you were saying over there. You don't want to talk about it you could at least say that. I don't like your goddamned manners," the bartender says. He seems to be slightly drunk himself which in this working-class district is not unusual even at this hour of the morning. "Maybe I'll ask you to get the hell out of here."

"That isn't necessary. Let me buy you a drink."

"I don't get bought off that easy."

Scop shrugs. "Suit yourself," he says, hoping that he has a correct grasp on the vernacular of the district. "Anything you want to do."

"The hell with it," the bartender says. He seems to have reached an obscure but exciting sense of resolution, he begins to make circles with the rag on the surfaces again. "Whatever you do is all right with me. I don't give a damn."

The doors slam, someone else walks in. Scop scans him eagerly but the man is not Leonard Peters, that is clear. The life-studies and holographs of the man are exquisite; there is no possibility of mistake. The man gives a long, uncertain stare and then seats himself at the bar, asks the bartender for a beer. The bartender does not seem to know him either. He brings the beer and the newcomer gives him a bill from a sidepocket, then seems confused when the bartender comes back with change. For a moment total dislocation seems to penetrate the crevices of his face, then clumsily he has taken the change from the bartender's hand and puts it in his pocket. He leans forward in great absorption, holding the glass with both hands, drinking in tentative little sips. The bartender mumbles something and returns to his position. The grating sound of the rag against the boards is very loud now.

Scop begins to shake with apprehension. After his first glance at the new man he has returned to his own self-absorption, but that self-absorption more and more, as he feels awareness beginning to sink into him is a cover for a deep and perverse intimation: the newcomer may well have come from the temporals. It is possible that the man is an agent; that he comes from the Masters, that indeed he has been pursuing Scop for a long time and that now in this remote and empty bar he has found him. Surely if the temporals have tracked matters carefully they know what Scop does: That Leonard Peters is critical to any sense of mission. Everything devolves upon the finding of that man and the temporals would know that too. Although Scop has always been a cautious and internalized man, a creature who does not allow any of his moods (he believes) to surface past the bland and affectless panels of his face he now feels the edges of his control visibly shrinking, tearing back to expose the raw and sodden wound of self. Little scars burst open; little lacunae of woe of which he has been unaware for years are exposed. The bartender looks at him strangely. The stranger does not. Scop's hands describe little butterfly patterns on the bar not unreminiscent of the wiping motions which the bartender has made. "Get away from me," he says to the bartender as he imagines the man coming down the railing, enormous, threatening him. "Get away from me now."

The bartender who has not moved at all continues to stare at him. Now with that cool objective sense which has gotten him as far as he has come to date—although not one step further—Scop realizes that he has had an acute anxiety attack; that the aspect of this stranger has thrust him from that perilous and equivocal perch of balance from which he has made search and that he is now falling free in the crazed breezes of paranoia, descending. Only his absolute control and discipline can be invoked to prevent the scene from disassembling before him because *he dare not miss Leonard Peters*, whatever happens it is imperative that the meeting not lapse. There will not be another such opportunity on this cycle, not for twenty years by which time it will be entirely late and it will have been frozen in Peter's preconscious that a man he was supposed to see in a bar when he was thirty-one years old was not there. Scop puts both hands on the bar, tries to still their fluttering. The man on his left continues to gulp from the beer glass in short, desperate strokes, his neck moving peculiarly.

Abruptly Scop, staring at that neck, reaches a judgment: the man is indeed from the temporals. He has appeared in disguise and it is cleverly rigged, shows all of that attention to detail and superficial veracity for which the temporals are famous but as is characteristic of their work it lacks conviction, one inch below the surface it is merely that, a costume and if one focuses the tube of one's attention more deeply it is easy to see, easy to see the lie. "Liar!" Scop shouts and the man turns, looks at him from huge, empty eyes drained of reaction. "Fool! Imposter! Did you think that you could get away with this?"

The man says nothing. He holds his beer glass now like a child might hold a rattle, shaking it slightly, little bubbles of froth steaming and spewing from the rim. Wide, his eyes become wider yet. "You liar!" Scop says. He reaches into his pocket, his hand clings. He feels the weapon hard and smooth within his grasp and tries to remove it but the little lumps and sodden threads of the pocket retain his hand and he finds the weapon half in, half out, its dull gleam visible to the bartender who is suddenly striding toward him rapidly, just as in Scop's vision. It must have been temporal lag; this is what he had seen. "Give me—" the bartender says and then says no more because Scop has yanked the weapon free in one last surge of effort. He points it at the bartender's throat, closes his eyes and pulls the trigger.

He does not know whether or not he has made contact with the man until he hears the shatter of bone, the sound of something pulpous hitting board, then he opens his eyes again and watches as the bartender, semi-decapitated, sits slowly behind the bar, first crouching as if seeking a deep knee bend which then comically did not reverse at the end of its arc but instead continued with gravity until at last the bartender sunk out of the line of sight, only vagrant dazzles from his skull giving indication that he had ever been there. Moist sounds from far below. Scop turns then toward the temporal, resolved that he has no alternative, that he will have to kill this man too because the situation has moved past the chance of easy resolution … but the temporal has already gone; where he was sitting there is emptiness and the bang of the door gives implication that while Scop was engaged in misdirected fire the real enemy has fled.

It infuriates him. He goes to the door, pulls it open and stares at a dismal street which reminds him of the mockups and model of streets of this era which he has studied in magnification for so many lonely hours in the hall. He cannot take the terrain for real; if anything it reminds him of something on which he will have to take an examination … which, of course, at some time in the past he has also done. But beyond the deadening unreality, the sense that he has stumbled into a reconstruction of research materials rather than the consequence he has sought … beyond that is the fact that the street is empty. The wide, flat terrain with neither alleys nor parked vehicles is clear. The temporal has escaped.

Scop gives a bellow of rage and looks back into the bar but the bartender is still dead, then he casts desperate glances through the length of the street hoping at least that Leonard Peters has missed the coefficient and has come plus or minus twenty-five minutes early but Peters too is not there … and screaming futility, bellowing once again his failure Scop runs toward the machine that will take him out of there knowing that when Peters staggers in, looks behind the counter sees the dead man he will be hurt in a very personal and meaningful fashion which will only have outcome ten years later when he is called in to assist on the Final Plans … *Scop trying to alter has merely reinforced the future.* In pain he runs and knows again the wisdom of the Masters: to seek alteration is merely to tighten the threads of causality.

VI

ENCOUNTER AND AT THE END OF IT ILLUMINATION: Thinking of 1995, the convulsion of circumstance, the great hiccup of his father's being that brought him, that miraculous accident, to life, Scop returned to the Grassy Knoll to the side opposite Abraham Zapruder, accosting the two women once again. The sounds of the motorcade were building in the distance; he had lagged through clumsiness to within a two-minute margin: nevertheless he had to go on. There was no time for cancellation. The shorter of the two women was named Elaine Kozciouskos and had been born in 1915. She would die in 1985 hit by an out of control double-decker bus while touring New York City but that was none of Scop's concern now. Generational lines had already been shifted over, albeit clumsily; the Kozciouskos descendants would ascribe other parentage but would go on. One of them, in a minor way, would even play an important role in the reversals of twenty-twenty two he knows. It was her that Scop seized upon and then dragged into the little clump of trees back from the road, impelling her past the three tramps who having other things to witness said nothing. She looked at him terrified. Throughout all of history, a thousand times she would look at him in this way: there was nothing to be done.

"My name," he said, "my name is Lyndon Baines Johnson," picking the name virtually at random, merely trying to reassure her but her face became even more distorted and started to roll away like an enormous vegetable pulled free from the vine, "Now listen here," Scop said, "you've got to get control of yourself," but she had fainted. Perhaps it was his garb which was somewhat unusual for the day; perhaps it had only been his haste and intensity. She lay at his feet. He could hear the sound of the other woman approaching. Her name was Anne Oble and she played no role in his life or that of history, having died childless within the decade. Scop struck her behind the ear for the second time on that cycle and she toppled three yards from the prone figure of Elaine Kozciouskos. He had no time. The motorcade was only a few hundred yards away. He leaned over, wrenched at Elaine Kozciouskos, pulled her toward the machine.

Halfway there he did not think that he would get there, she was unconscious, heavy, unrespondent weight but it was either that or be frozen into Zapruder's reels and that could not happen; it had never happened so he continued to struggle, feeling a little better for the assurance that he would prevail and finally, groaning, was able to insert her head-first into the transmission, stuffed her in, made his own perilous connection and hit the switch. Instantly he fell forward fifty years, using 2013 as the bouncepoint, landing on the towers of the commemorative museum which had been erected on the site in 1994 he believed although the date was not clear and if there was one thing that Scop was not it was a historian, he had no interest in history, only with causation; he came off the bounce and into twenty-forty screaming, at full throttle, Elaine Kozciouskos full weight rolling on the belts, her feeble cries as the transmission took hold sounding like those of the assassinated President himself and then they were back in Scop's bedroom in Dallas, none the worse for it except eternally the worse for it as such things always are. He leaned over groaning, took bags of her flesh in his palms, manipulated her from the transmission and pulled her over to the bed. By the time he was done he was crying with fatigue and yet he knew it would soon pass: emotional excesses always passed, all that there was ever left was the grimness of his duty. She opened dull eyes and looked at him. Scop took off his traveling robes and then he took off his underclothing, standing before her naked except for his medallion and his sandals, rubbing his hands together to simulate confidence. "All right my pretty," he said, "now we fornicate."

She screamed dimly, without conviction. Scop continued to rub his palms and when he judged the moment to be right, sprang forward and tore away her upper garments. He found the task revolting of course and approached the possibility of sex dryly, without pleasure, but it had to be done. Necessity being foremost, he might as well make it as sensuous as possible. He took off the little strands and ribbons to which her blouse had been converted and looked at her sad breasts trapped in their sad covering. Her handbag which he had not noticed before dangled from one wrist to the side of her. She screamed again without resonance. Scop leaned forward, put his fingers underneath her brassiere and lifted it slowly. There was a hiss as of escaping suction and then slowly, without hope but possessed of craft he removed it, looked upon her.

"All right," he said, "now we are going to have sex." Throughout all this she had not said a word, her screams wordless too but now her lips seemed to fuse toward meaning and looking up at him she said, "No."

"Yes," Scop said. *Gently insistent*, this was the quality he was seeking, a sense of communion, slow dance, grasp and enter. Old clichés from the tumultuous decade from which he had plucked her mingled and mixed in his mind but he was not quite able to segregate them so that they would emerge into a coherent, seductive whole. "It is quite necessary," he said. "Observe me. Be patient." Slowly he settled upon her.

His aim was for quick fusion, burning entrance, random twitches and as rapid a withdrawal as possible but at the first instant of contact he could see that this was not going to be possible. For one thing he had forgotten to remove her undergarments; for another he had neglected to remove his own. Sex without the true meeting of genitals was impossible, at least within the context which Scop wished to occupy (the matter of masturbation was an entirely different matter but he had hoped to operate within the tight situational fix of convention now) and his stupidity made him grunt which Elaine Kozciouskos must have taken for uncontrolled lust because she came back at him with a *peep!* of anguish and then attempted to wrench herself from under him, a hopeless response of course—among other things where would she have gone?—but just enough to convince Scop of the need for emergency actions before the moment for connection was lost.

Heavily, mastering her with his weight, he stripped her undergarments in a single, clumsy burst; heavily he tore his own garments free to attempt entrance, all of the time mumbling shy but determined insistences into her ear which, he hoped, would convince her of the uselessness of protest and guide her into an acceptance which would permit Scop to complete this difficult part of his journey in jig time. "It's all right," he said therefore, "it doesn't matter, everything is going to be fine, you're just dreaming this, none of it is happening at all and even if it is happening, well then, it's of no consequence. You'll be able to put it out of your mind," huffing and puffing upon her and she shook her head, her eyes beating like wings, her tongue making frantic gestures against her teeth; in a moment, Scop knew, she would say something absolutely disastrous, something which would yank him from his concentration and cause him to lose the insistence of his rhythm. "Don't talk," he said, "it isn't necessary to talk," and he wedged himself against and then into her, listening to the racketing sound of her breath, feeling her teeth close to the side of his neck as weakly but with determination she sought to bite him.

Well, she could hardly be blamed for that, with that empathy for which he was already well-known and with which he had conditioned himself for his voyage Scop knew exactly how she must be feeling at this time: abducted from a sunny field in Dallas by a maniac, shoved through a transmission belt in pain to emerge into stinking, reeking quarters in which the lunatic sought to clamber above and through her, it was something which would unsettle sterner stuff than Elaine Kozciouskos herself and under the circumstances she had done well in not suffering a fatal sympathetic storm. Still, the gnawing and intermittent penetration of her teeth in his tender and vulnerable neck began to irritate Scop to say nothing of retard his orgasm; forcing himself to orgasm was difficult enough under these hasty and mysterious circumstances let alone with the woman biting him ... absently he reared above her, slapped her open-palmed across the face until her eyes bloomed with tears and then put himself down above her again, closed his eyes, kneaded her sought interior with his organ, placed himself in a smaller and smaller space the way he always did when he was fucking, a feeling of closure and power at last descending upon him as he became closeted in the room of self and effortfully, grunting, feeling pain, little solace in it he began to grind through his orgasm almost incidental to pain and pressure and so in that way he climaxed above her, grunting little painsongs into her ear while her teeth, undiscouraged met once again in his neck with a pressure which outweighed the slender pleasure radiating from his thin organ. Almost immediately he fell off her groaning; rolled to the side. It had not been in any sense a satisfactory sexual experience but then Scop had to remember, cultivating a sense of resignation and larger purpose that pleasure had not been his intention; rather he was seeking an alteration of circumstance, a profundity which pleasure would only have cheapened. He peered cautiously at Elaine Kozciouskos. She seemed to be sleeping but he knew that she had merely fainted from the horror. He began to talk to her slowly in a monolithic, affectless tone, knowing that his words were settling into the pan of her subconscious and that in due course they would have their effect.

"He doesn't have to die, Elaine," Scop said, "the next time that he comes through which of course will seem to you like the first time but we won't weary you with the complexities of that situation, the very next time he comes through if you scream warning, if you cry out you can upset the balance of the conspiracy; you can throw everyone off target. They won't be looking for a woman to be screaming you see and all of them are in a highly nervous state."

Elaine Kozciouskos said nothing. Nevertheless the blankness of her expression, the quiet way in which she inhaled were of themselves encouragements; it was really the first time since he had met the woman that she seemed to be placid. "You are very important," Scop said to her soothingly, "all unwitting you control the balance of history."

Confidential, inflamed by the significance of the knowledge he was bringing to her even if she was not, Scop moved closer, wedged himself hip to hip against her somnolent form. "You can change the course of all history itself Elaine," he said, "your cry, your commotion can misdirect the assassin's fire and possibly save the life of the President of the United States to say nothing of future and unborn generations which but for his death would have lived. Nothing less than the fate of all mankind depends upon you; indeed it is the very universe at issue."

Her eyes flutter, open, her face convulsed with horror. Perhaps he has said this last a little loudly, charged his voice with affect again; at any rate she does not seem to be taking this information well. There is almost no way in which he can tell her that he is driven by large forces outside of himself and really has no choice. "Oh my God," she said, "oh my God, this is really happening."

"Of course it's happening—"

"Get me out of here! Get me out of here before I die. I can't—"

"You are dead," Scop says somewhat metaphysically. "You have already died."

"I can't," she said. "I can't believe this." Little animals seemed to be moving underneath the planes of her cheeks; Scop with his profound grasp of organic and neurological insight sensed that she was on the verge of a cataclysmic cerebral accident "Be calm," he said. "Do not move." He reached a hand to her forehead, patted it absently. "You will understand," he said. "In due course there will come a time when you understand—"

She brought her hands to his wrist, pushed it away, continued the motion in spasm so that Scop lost balance, rolled all the way onto his back, having misjudged her strength he looked at her sullenly. "I can't believe this," she said, "this cannot be happening," and then she began to cry. Scop looked at her trying to measure the depth of her feeling, the temper of his own response thinking that it was strange, it was always strange how it had ended this way time and again: always he had led up to this moment and then in his imagination away from it, little tracks down the other side where she accepted all with quiet and credulous eyes, nodding slowly, tracing little circles on his wrist as she listened, knowing then the justice of what he had done and its necessity: encounter and at the end of it illumination. Instead only this. She cries in pain but all he knows is sorrow.

VII

CLANGOROUS CIRCUMSTANCE: Summoned by the Temporal Administrator Scop tries to maintain a bland and controlled exterior but by the time he has come into the offices he is in a clamorous state, a clangorous circumstance: it is all that he can do to keep himself from falling down in paroxysms of excitement. The colder, darker part of him advises that this would be pointless and would in fact only work against him and it is that to which he listens, settling only for a stray giggle now and then when he feels that his control cannot be absolute. The receptionist looks at him with distaste but takes him into the administrator's office without undue delay and for a while Scop sits there alone, looking at the photographs and drawings of vulgarities on the walls, observing the bizarre sculptures of human copulation on the administrator's desk while he waits for the man to appear. The administrator is often known to do this, to leave his interviewees alone for some minutes before appearing but Scop takes it in stride. He knows that he is being observed through special mirrors but aside from a snort of laughter there, a little cackle of pleasure over here he is perfectly controlled and his snorts and cackles could be taken only for the mild instability of the traveler which he certainly is.

After a time the administrator opens a side door and comes in. He looks like all of the other administrators which is to say completely unremarkable and leaves no physical impression upon Scop, now or hereafter. In certain recurrent but nearly-forgotten dreams he will occasionally see him and many, many months from now when he is on the verge of his last crisis Scop will have a sudden image of the man coming up hard against the preconscious like a dummy on a stick but not until that very moment and maybe not even then will he realize how deeply the administrator has affected him at a subterranean level. On the surface there is nothing. Twenty-five minutes from now he will be unable to recall a single feature of the man or hear his voice.

"You may think you are dreaming this," the administrator begins, "but I want to assure you that you are not. All of this is happening, all of it matters."

"I know that." He chokes on a giggle.

"I am not sure that you are prepared to accept this yet. Certain of your activities indicate that you feel yourself to be in a dreaming condition and therefore in lessened risk but this is not so at all."

Scop knows, of course, that he is being closely monitored but the administrator's offhand confirmation of this gives him a thrill of realization which undercuts the easy hilarity with which he had approached the interview. Everything that he does is being observed; he can perpetrate nothing that does not clear through the mechanisms. "I know that it is objectively true," he says carefully.

"Your conduct in Dealey Plaza raises the suggestion that you may not. You were very offhand there, very reckless and our interview with the old man was suggestive."

"Suggestive of what?"

"And the force you used with the two women was excessive. It went beyond the situation."

Scop shrugs. "I was on a narrow time-line. I felt that I only had a few moments—"

"Whether or not you had a few moments, your actions were excessive. They came close to being unacceptable. Now and in the future you are going to have to be far more aware of the risks here."

"I have always been aware of the risks," Scop says. He is on the verge of asking the administrator how his sexual performance with Elaine Kozciouskos compared with normative standards—he really would like to know—but at the last instant holds back. This is none of his business and to display curiosity would be to suggest weakness which is better not implied in these circumstances. He feels the laughter beginning to churn within him and folds his hands together tightly, his eye caught by a vivid black-and-white of pederasty on the wall to the administrator's right just above a window. It causes him to become solemn again as he turns toward the administrator. They are serious. They have always been serious; he must accept this. Their seriousness is of a different order than his but no less consequential.

"Is something wrong?" the administrator asks.

"Nothing."

"You seem to be a little mystified, a little withdrawn."

"Nothing. I was busy recently and am still, perhaps, a little tired."

"We know you were busy. We are quite certain of your business. But

I am afraid that I suspect some hilarity in you. Do you think that this is hilarious?"

"No."

"Then why were you smirking and smiling in the outer offices?"

"An accident of feature, sir."

"There are no accidents of feature. The face is merely the projection of the unconscious will." But the administrator seems to lose interest in the argument even as he states it; the line runs down, his own face becomes sad and slack as he reaches forward to fondle one of the sculptures on his desk. "Essentially you are doing the work very well," he says. "We have no quarrel with your approach nor with the really admirable energy that you've displayed, at least intermittently. You are doing well in many regards and your *modus operandi* is one of the most original we have yet seen. We are merely afraid that much of this energy comes from your assumption that this is not serious. It is serious."

"I know that," Scop says again. "I can only repeat it. I know that it is serious."

The administrator shrugs. "Very well," he says. "We could deep-probe you to find whether your statement is credible but at this stage of matters it would not be helpful, it would only hold up your progress and it might damage you permanently." He squeezes the sculpture, the metal yields in his hand, slowly it puffs in its grasp and Scop sees a little extra breast beginning to extrude from the material. "We are therefore going to allow you to continue."

"That is appreciated."

"Our decision is liable to constant review of course." The administrator brings over his other hand, rubs a fingernail carefully over the breast, blinks his eyes, his mouth slowly falling open. "But for the time being we are willing to make a continuation."

"That is very kind of you."

"That is very kind of me," the administrator repeats in a different tone, rubbing the breast. There is a long pause into which Scop dares not insert speech. Finally the administrator says, "I think you may be excused now."

Scop stands. "Thank you."

"You must have an attitude of pity and condescension toward me. Admit that."

"What?"

"Or at least some genuine hilarity. Perhaps that is why you were so comedic in the outer offices, thinking about me."

"I'm sorry," Scop says, feeling like a less frightened but equally confused Elaine Kozciouskos. "I don't know what you're talking about."

Squeezing the sculpture with both hands now the administrator says, "You must feel that I'm expressing some kind of abnormal transferred sexuality with this device, that I'm some kind of a pitiable character not in control of himself. Come on, admit it."

"No such thing," Scop says. Indeed he does not know what the administrator is saying; he has long judged this group, of course, to be somewhat emotionally unstable (how else could they perform their stolid, repetitive yet irreplaceable duties?) but the specifics of their perversities have long evaded him. There are certain things about which he dares not think; they would misdirect him from his simpler, greater tasks. "May I be excused?"

The administrator nods. Little pellets of sweat appear at the corners of his eyes; he seems to be sinking deep into himself. His hands flutter over the sculpture, then begin to massage it skillfully and Scop thinks that he hears a bizarre groan. "Go on," the administrator gasps. "Stop looking at me, man. Just get out of here."

Scop turns, moves hurriedly to the door. He fears that he will hear the administrator groan once again and although he has handled the interview up to this point in a commendable fashion he cannot speak for his prospective response if he hears that sound again. He reaches toward the knob, misses it, lunges, catches it and is gone but not before he has heard the high, leaping squeal behind and it is this which splits him open into little mumbles and chuckles and gobbles of laughter which spill from him like dazzling sprays, sprays which multi-colored light his way from the offices although in no private and dignified fashion.

VIII

MEMPHIS: Materializing before Ray too rapidly he waited out the instants of accommodation only hoping that all was not disastrous; that the man, in his shock and rage would not shoot him. Even before the process of entry has fully shut down he is speaking to him. "Don't do this," he says, "you must not do it. You cannot understand the consequences, will not live to see them but they will be intolerable. If not for yourself, for your world, then for those who will follow I beg you to go away from here."

The man holds his rifle in shock, staring. He is a big man who has probably taken one drug compound or another only a little while ago in preparation for the shooting, it has done his reflexes no good but then again it has made him more likely to hear Scop out than would have been so otherwise. His eyes are curiously calm, drifting open. "Who are you?" he says.

"That does not matter. You simply must trust me."

"Where did you come from? Nobody can get in here; they guaranteed me that and I checked the locks myself—"

"It does not matter," Scop says hastily, "it does not matter, all that matters is that you understand what I am saying, that you listen to me. If you shoot this man, if you kill him then you will bring about awful things which you cannot now even comprehend."

The man stares at him sullenly. Assassins are stupid of course; this is something which in his experience has been proven over and again and yet there are certain insights which Scop cannot seem to apprehend emotionally, as fine as his intellectual equipment. Maybe he feels a need to sentimentalize their attention, wants to believe that those capable of such great and vicious consequence do so in complete awareness of what they risk and can summon reason to their defense. This is not the case, he knows that well and yet he feels the old wrenching disgust: perhaps none of this would ever have happened if these men had been intelligent or failing that at least had had some sense of motive. Now there is neither. Possibly the rumors are true: all of them were hypnotized into doing it and have no independence at all, no volition. That is horrible but it is less horrible than what he suspects which is simply that they have no position at all on what they were doing: it makes no impression. "Get out of here," the man says, "or I'll shoot you."

"That would be pointless. You cannot shoot me, I would dematerialize in an instant. No," Scop says, reaching forward, touching the muzzle of the carefully-prepared rifle and turning it downward, "I ask you to listen to me for a moment, that is all."

The motion makes the man tremble, he fights to bring the muzzle up but Scop momentarily is stronger and keeps it in place. The man's hands flutter on the rifle; he is close to panic. "Please," Scop says, "please."

The balance is perilous; for a moment he thinks that Ray will move right through the engagement and attempt to solve it by strength, that he will indeed in his eagerness to commit assassination assassinate Scop himself and the paradoxes of that of course are overwhelming to say nothing of the pain. Fortunately the man does not do this, something blunts his level of response even as the rifle is swinging downward again and then, feet spread, eyes staring at the floor he makes no motion, says nothing as Scop speaks to him with the slow, wheedling insistence of the truly monomaniac, the only kind of voice which would ever get through to the assassin anyway. "Anyway it will come to nothing," Scop says having reached a natural strophe in the conversation, "as sure as you feel now that you are alerting the course of history I would like to make clear to you that you are not; history will mostly be the same. Only your part of it will be different because you will be confined."

"Ah shit," the man says. He circumscribes a little figure on the floor. The air conditioner snarls as if devouring one of its belts, then stops with a grumble and only the fine ticking of someone's watch can be heard in the motel room. "Do you really think that I'm going to believe this stuff? Do you really think that I'm going to take it seriously? Why do I have to believe it anyway? Who are you to me? A man from the future? I don't believe it."

"Accept it on faith then," Scop says. He reaches into his pocket. "Furthermore I can offer you money."

"Ah," the assassin says. He moves back. "Now I see it. You're trying to buy me off."

"Well of course I'm trying—"

"You're from the other side. You must be a communist agent. But I'm not going to be your dupe." The man's little eyes roll, he seems to be transfigured. "I should have known, damn it," he says, "I should have known from the moment you came in this room, the *way* you came in, sneaking that way that you were a communist. I won't be bought off. I'm an American, I'm a real American. I'm doing this for my country and there's no way that you can—"

"Oh come on," Scop says, "don't be ridiculous, there's enough money here to—"

"No *money*. No damned money. Now get out of here now or I'll blow your fucking head off."

Scop sees the seriousness of the assassin's intent. He must have been a fool to have believed that he could reason or bribe the man from intent, now there is nothing left but appeal to conscience and where will that get him. Assassins are utterly without superego. "Your name will be cursed in all the decades to follow," he says hopelessly, "your name will be synonymous with a curse, none of your descendants will live without blemish, in the years to come all that will be known of you is shame—" He cuts himself off. There is really nothing else to say and Ray's intent is quite clear. He must have been a fool to think that this would work. "All right," he says, "all right then. I can't force you not to do this. It lies outside of me."

This of course is a lie. Just as he plucked Elaine Kozciouskos from the Grassy Knoll so he could seize Ray from the motel room and take him elsewhere. The abrupt removal of the assassin would, however, merely leave a void in time which would be filled by even more disastrous events; Scop knows enough of the law of the temporals to accept this. If the assassin is to be dissuaded it must be through volition and conscious choice, this would cast the consequences upon him and not the stress-lines of the culture. All of this he calculates almost instantaneously, thinking of the same time in awe and pity of the man who will be killed. Time and again he must remind himself that these are not abstractions with whom he is dealing; these are people and the pain is real. So he must calculate that too into the intricacies of his situation but the effort is too much, it is too much for him: simple Scop, simple workmen, at the root his affect is bland, his intellect limited, his cerebral hemispheres not choked with the rich blood of abstraction; he is merely trying to get through as best as he can and often it is not sufficient. He moves wearily away from the assassin, bitter and yet not as bitter as he might be in these circumstances because there is something comforting about defeat glimpsed whole. Scop begins to understand that defeat explored and taken fully unto himself might not really be as devastating as he had always feared, there is something enormously satisfying in encountering at least a disaster so great that one has no need for excuses any more. If King is to die so be it; if the century is to turn to waste and disorder because of this sequence of slayings then Thy Will be done. Ultimately there are others who will have to bear these burdens, not him. Not him alone. He goes to the door. "All right," he says. "All right then, do as you will. Goodbye."

"Now wait."

"No," Scop says his hand on the knob, fingers caressing, "I will not wait. There is nothing more to say."

The gun is levelled on him now. "Not like that. I want some explanations."

"There are no explanations."

"Who are you?"

"I said there are no explanations," Scop says. The truth of it delights him; pity that he is so afraid of the rifle. Indeed there are no answers at all. Why did nothing make sense? Because there was no sense. He could have glimpsed this a long time ago if he was not so stubborn; he now understands. All was causeless, unmotivated, disconnected. "Goodbye," he says again and opens the door and steps into the corridor. If Ray shoots him he shoots him, that is all. Death is mere obliteration and besides, he will be reconstituted some day; he knows that this is merely a passing instant of temporality which will be succeeded by a more lasting if somewhat less colorful eternity. At least he must believe this at the present moment in order to function; in truth Scop is not really a religious fanatic and religion plays a little role within his calculations. "Goodbye," he says again and holds his eyes closed and glides into the corridor, glides the door closed, stands there for a moment and then content that there are no sounds of pursuit from within he moves quickly through the bare and sterile halls, his attention elsewhere so that the sound of the shot when it comes as it does merely grazes against the levers of his calculation, making small impact, unhurried rush of the blood as he whisks through the outer doors of the enclosure and is gone.

IX

DECLARATION: "No," he said to the Masters, "no, you are wrong. One man may change the course of history, may change the nature of the rooms which we inhabit. I refuse to believe it is hopeless, I know that it does not have to be that way if we do not accept this as our condition." Even though he was dreaming this there was a great deal of satisfaction in making his case clear even if the Master was a defeated little creature near the bottom of the hierarchy (at least as far as Scop could judge from the insignia of his robes) who could hardly understand what he was saying. "I know that I am doing the right thing here," Scop said, "do you think it's easy? There are enormous sacrifices you know and besides that I'm being exposed to social scorn."

The Master made a defeated motion, ran his hands over the table interposed between he and Scop, the material of the table due to the extreme poverty and transparency of the dream of a weak rubber which yielded easily to his fingertips, damp spots as residue to the pressure when the fingers were removed. "Whatever you say. It is not important to us."

"If it isn't important to you why are you trying to stop me? Why is it such a struggle? Why am I being harassed instead of assisted? After all I'm doing this for all of us."

The Master sighed and leaned away from the table. He seemed acutely uncomfortable but then most of the figures in Scop's dreams had the same aspect; he did not dream images of grace, his life itself being so cluttered and filled with damp, swift motions impossible to dignify under all of the pressures. Then again he had to keep the fact that it was a dream in his mind at all times lest he began to take it seriously and if he took it seriously … well if that occurred the Master might take a different form more reflective of Scop's actual unconscious and he did not want to deal with this either. It was better, it was always better by far to conjure with images which were masks for the buried reality and if you did not have to ever see that buried reality so much the better. "Why don't you just leave?" the Master said in a little voice. "Why must we have these continual arguments? Why must you constantly seek to justify yourself? Isn't it enough for you simply to do what you have to do without looking for approval from us?"

Scop said, "I don't think that you understand the situation. This involves everyone."

"You must leave," the Master said. His figure began to waver, Scop could see little streaks of light coming from behind. "I don't believe that I am going to stay in this form much longer. This is a dream you know and I am apt to become something far more terrible—"

"Why can't you accept?" Scop said rather desperately, not wishing to yield pride but then again the dream was as had been pointed out ending. "You could make it so much easier if you would only cooperate, if you would see that this is being done for all of us."

"Listen you fool," the Master said, his features descending slightly toward him, "this is not being done for your convenience. The world is not manipulated in order to give you pleasure and none of us are here to make matters any easier for you than they must be. If you wish confirmation you will have to find it within your own activities."

Strong language for a dream-image, Scop thought. But then again the unconscious was no more malleable than any other part; he should not have expected otherwise. "All right," he said. "Have it your way." The consciousness of his dreaming, the awareness that he was having vigorous debate with himself caused him to flush although of course discreetly. "Whatever you say."

"You should stop this foolishness."

"Never. I cannot."

"Then you must bear absolute responsibility for what you have become."

"All right," Scop said. "If you say so. I can't argue this any more. It's really ridiculous, you know," he added conversationally and made effort to disperse the image, willing himself toward awakeness in the fashion that a diver might crouch over himself, begin the manipulations for surfacing. "I'm only doing this to help everyone," he continued and waited patiently for the vault from the dream to begin, for the image of the Master to become translucent but it did not, much to his dismay the Master remained as concrete and implacable as he had before. The walls of the room in which they were conferring did not diminish in their solidity. "It isn't so easy you see," the Master said, "you can't simply get away with ending these discussions whenever you'd like;

you have to stay and deal with them and there are certain things which have to be said to you."

Scop cannot bring himself to pay attention to the Master. Nor, it seems, can he cause the scene to disperse; he seems to be caught instead in a perilous middleground where midway between the dream and the actual form which he would take, the Master seems bound now to the necessity to lecture. "You can change nothing," the Master said, "absolutely nothing within and without. Your quest is hopeless. It is not change you are creating but merely slaughter."

"Two by two is four," Scop said, remembering an old assurance from somewhere that the fabric of a dream could be broken down by the fixation upon, the reiteration of irrelevant material. "And eight times three is twenty-four. In 1963 at the age of forty-six John Fitzgerald Kennedy—"

"These mnemonic devices will get you nowhere, Scop. You cannot evade the truth any longer. The constantly reiterated rape which seems to be at the very center time and again of your obsessions—"

"The first President of the United States was George Washington. The thirty-ninth was—"

"Should give you the deepest insight into yourself. What do you really think you want?"

"Ontogeny recapitulates phylogeny. A prime number is a number divisible only by one or itself. The number of sexes is two, the number of chromosomes forty-eight except in the case of—"

"Oh enough, enough!" the Master shouts with disgust and makes a dismissive gesture. "Have it your way. I'm not going to stay here any more and try to argue with you; if you won't see the sense of it it's not going to be from me, you'll just have to undertake all the suffering yourself. But don't blame me," he says and brings fire down with his hand blowing Scop quite free of the fabric of the dream and into a tight enclosure where he lies rocking above—

X

HISTORY AS REDEMPTION:—Not Elaine Kozciouskos with whom he would be quite prepared to copulate even in his rather disturbed state, sleep-drenched, sleep shattered but instead some woman he has never seen before who bears a thin resemblance and then again it may only be misapprehension to a major figure of the time through which he is endlessly looping. "Slow," she says to him with an obscene flourish of gesture, "slow and easy and all will be fine," winding and tightening her little thighs against his entrapped organ, blinking and winking as she brings up her hands then to gather him in. "If you take it slow it will be fine but if you rush it you'll lose it. Big boy," she says as he topples over her then, "fuck me you big, obsessed son of a bitch, you time-traveler you, you crazy little reorganizer of historical cycles," and he begins to moan and gasp within her reflexively, he has never known a woman to talk to him in this fashion although of course he has hoped for it many times. Scop lives in a rather repressed age. "Come on, do it, get it all the way in," she mutters and he wonders whether this too is a dream; circumstance would fit this possibility neatly, it would be in fact exactly the kind of cruelty which the Masters would invoke ... but no, it cannot be a dream, the richness of her flesh, the solidity of the contact, the little grunts which pour from her as he digs in and out are not the components of mystery but have the snaffling awkwardness of the sexual act itself at least as he has always understood it. He doubts very much then that this is a dream although you can never be entirely sure.

"I said don't stop, you big bugger you," the woman mutters, yanking him back to a poised if rather surreal attention and Scop does not know why the matter of his copulation is so important to her, surely she cannot be aroused, it falls almost entirely away from his experience that a woman might urgently need sex but he is nothing if not willing, in a dreamlike state or not he has always shown himself able to meet circumstances on their own terms and so he begins to pummel and paw at her flesh in this state, little obligatory moans pouring from him, small confidences of need as he digs and whines, pokes and kneads, eventually he begins to sense orgasm building within him although it is mostly known as pain rather than desire; sex has never been for him, perhaps as profoundly satisfying as it is rumored to be for some others.

But then again this is not a sexual era. Sex, Scop thinks behind blinded eyes, heaving and bucking automatically, sex went out of the culture sometime around 1970, in the last seventy years the sources of satisfaction have been more inclined toward death. Death and manipulation. There was a time and as a scholar of the period he knows of it when much of the culture was pinned upon sex: all of the anxieties and obsessions of individuals were bound up with it, even the profound political and social interlock of the culture could be unraveled and traced back to that simple and pitiful connection ... but it is gone, gone: he lives in a bleak murderous age, an age of Masters and temporal shocks, an age of halls and machineries and conferences, an age in which only the possibility of travel through time itself to rearrange the artifacts of the society gives hope for some difference ...

and thinking in this rather muddy fashion Scop continues to work upon the woman yielding at last a thin trickle of discharge so bitter, so poisonously wrenched from him that it might not have been love but death which she had yanked. An old obsession of course. He has known it before. The equation of sex with death is too modest and banal to demand much consideration. In his characteristic way Scop rolls from her then, inverts on the bed, looks at the ceiling. Always after intercourse he finds it necessary to look above him as if sex were a return to the bestial, as if the inversion were to express his yearning once again to be free. Mysterious but satisfying. He hears the sound of her breathing beside him.

"Don't talk," he says, anticipating conversation, "there's no need to talk."

"I wasn't going to."

"If you talk I'm going to have to leave instantly," Scop says, "on the other hand if you'll be quiet I'll lie here for a while. It's your decision."

"On the contrary, it's your decision. You control matters, you know."

"Do I?"

"Of course," she says, "you are the subject, I am merely the object. How can you be so stupid? How can you believe otherwise?"

He turns, looks at her. This cannot be a dream, he thinks, or at least it is not necessarily a dream because no dream-image would express itself so forcefully, with such individuality and in a disturbing way she has come closer to him than even the Masters. The Masters have never suggested that Scop might control his world. Looking at her, the soft mask of her face falling across the harder, more penetrating lines so that he can see her too as an artifact he thinks that he is on the verge of recognition, that he knows who she is and that that revelation will in some way change his life but this slides from him as so much else has and he turns away. He is not on an identity-quest and she is by no means the central facet of his existence. Knowing who she is would really prove nothing. "Well," he says after a time, "it's been great but I guess I'd better leave now." He does not know what this really means. Among other things, where is he supposed to go? Where is he now for that matter? But he will find out, all will come clear to him as he moves toward the passageways. One must remain essentially hopeful; one must counsel a reasonable optimism in his life. "It's been very nice," he says, "and I don't want you to think that I wouldn't *like* to stay but—"

"But you're busy. Well of course. That's perfectly all right, it's always understandable. Get on your way you busy man you. Go ahead and change the course of history."

This for some reason makes him bridle; he looks at her in a way he has not before, noting the cunning and artifice with which her body, her manner, her very mood has been put together; there is more art to this woman than, perhaps, in anything he has yet accomplished. Regarding her out of sexual context he is able to appreciate her in a way which was not possible before: dispassionate, beyond challenge. "Are you making fun of me?" he says seriously.

"Of course not. Of course you're going to change the course of history. Isn't that what you're here for?"

"I don't know. What does it matter to you?"

She puts her clasped hands above her head, her breasts slightly expanded although it may be only Scop's eyes that have opened in response to the display. Hard to tell. Everything is hard to tell but on the other hand if circumstantial judgments are not to be made, what then? Life is a series of choices. "It matters a great deal to me," she says. "After all you seek to change all of our lives which would include mine as well since I am a contemporary of yours, inhabiting the same world which you inhabit, lurking in similar corridors, incurring similar doubts."

Is she mocking him? This is possible. Scop begins to seek his clothing. After he gets dressed he will then have to find a way out to be sure but he will handle one thing at a time. "I'm trying to change the world," he says seriously, "there's no reason to laugh at me."

"I'm not laughing at you. Where did you get the idea that I was doing that?"

"From your facial expression. From your tone of voice. From what you are saying."

"Well," she says, drawing her elbow across her chest, concealing her little breasts, a solemn and distressed expression cleaving its way down the little ridges of her face, "I don't think that I like that. I don't think there's any reason for you to say *that*. Of *course* I take you seriously and depend upon you. Doesn't everyone? We can't go on living this way indefinitely in a society framed by murder. Your courageous efforts to alter the social fix are very highly admired I must say, by all of those except the very few whose vested interest in the power and position given them by this society is menaced. But they hardly matter at all. Actually you're a hero for more than you would think. Why else do you imagine that I'd come to your quarters, considering the penalties?"

That solves one mystery at least, Scop thinks. Now he knows where he is. He is in his quarters and she has come to him clandestinely bearing the gifts and danger of herself to render comfort. He is glad to have heard that. It thrusts more context upon their relationship than he ever thought they would truly find. Of course it leaves him with other unsolved problems. He draws his robes tightly around him, grateful for this imagined cloak they give him. "I'm just doing the best I can," he says modestly, "it's a very difficult effort."

"Well of course it is. We all know that. We know how slight the chances are of success. That's why we're so particularly admiring."

"You don't have to be snide."

"I'm not being snide. I'm still lying here naked for one thing. It would have been very easy for me to have gotten dressed and left here just as soon as you did. The trouble with you is that you're too suspicious. You're suspicious of everyone's motives; you can't imagine that someone would really have your interests at heart, just as I do. Look at the risks I'm taking. Why you little revolutionary of the modern consciousness," she says and stretches out her arms, her nipples seem to flare and bounce upon her chest although this too he thinks must be an illusion compounded of fright, "you can come right back here and we'll have sex again. The fact is that you're absolutely lousy in bed and I'm *still* willing to have sex, if only for your sake. What do you think of *that* now?"

Scop shrugs. He feels little dimples appearing, the suspicion of a blush in the corners of his blunt and square features, vaulting upwards. "Well," he says, "well now, *that's* ridiculous." He is not in the least insulted by the suggestion that his sexual performance has been inept. If anything he feels empowered by it. "No," he says, "after all, there are more important things to do. I must be on my way now; I must not abandon—"

"That's why you're so adorable, you little megalomaniac you. You're absolutely dedicated to a completely individual vision of the world." She moves her fingers, trembles on the bed. "That's why you can come back here anytime."

"Oh well," he says, "oh well, it's neither here nor there. I mean it doesn't matter."

She sits in a single graceful motion that seems to carry her breasts below waist-length. This must be an illusion too; he had not imagined her to be so large-breasted at all. Live and learn. "Of course it matters," she says, "you big time-traveler you, you reconstructor of the universe. It matters a great deal, why single-handedly you're trying to restore us to a world of decency and hope, that's what you're trying to do. Now that's a remarkable thing. You're certainly entitled to all the help that you can get. You can come back," she says meaningfully and thrusts a single breast at him, a large, pointed contraption with a marvelous, conical nipple which he had never noticed until this moment, "you can come back anytime you want. Why, anything you want to do is just fine with me here you over-motivated genius you. You can even come back right now if you want to."

"Well no," Scop says hurriedly, "well no but thank you very much, I want you to know that I appreciate it, you're certainly being very kind," and he starts to back toward the door, the door enormous in his consciousness if not in reality; he has to get to the door, his desire to leave the room is overwhelming and yet he tries to do this with a certain minimal grace, a grace which will cover the acute and deadly awkwardness he feels having been seen at last for what he is … a simple and martyred man. He would not have imagined that there would be so much acceptance in the world, not for such as he. At the door he hesitates for a moment; he must confront, after all, the implacable and deadly corridor and he does not know where he is. The situation outside of the highly-defined arena of the room remains ambiguous; it is difficult for him to know exactly how he will come to terms with what is outside.

But he is hopeful. Hopeful and encouraged by what has happened: not the sexuality, not the release but the acceptance. The acceptance has been crucial, it has keyed in upon certain buried needs and made him feel more truly himself than he has for a long time. "Thank you very much," he says. He whisks open the door. "I really appreciate this very much," he says and steps out into the blind but overwhelming corridor and his last vision of her is as she throws him a kiss, the arc of her hand describing a pattern in the air which might be grace itself. "History is redemption," she says and then he is gone.

XI

PAIN LIKE TEARS: "Give me that Aeschylus quote again," Scop said conversationally to Robert Kennedy. It was three nights before the California campaign's end and Kennedy was lying on the bed in his hotel room, shoeless, tieless and in that easy stage between sleep and consciousness where all things, even apparitions from the future seemed possible. Scop knew that the candidate was neither astonished nor disconcerted. No word appeared in the histories of this dialogue so that he knew he was safe. "I'd like to hear it."

"Don't be ridiculous," Robert Kennedy said and closed his eyes again. "None of this is happening. You're not really here."

"Nevertheless," he said and found a more comfortable position against a wall, crossing his legs, leaning into the bare, burnt surfaces of the wall, "whether I'm here or not there is an obligation upon you to accept the found reality. Isn't that one of the subjects of your many fine campaign speeches: the need to deal with reality, to live in the real world? Anyway," Scop added, "no one will ever know whether I'm here or not, the room isn't tapped, you're in complete privacy. Indulge yourself. Act as if I was here. What's the difference?"

"The difference is within me," Robert Kennedy said, "within my sanity I mean to say," but his face seemed quizzical and interested, the famous political candidate and historical personage seemed barely able to restrain his curiosity and ironic involvement in all around him, try as he might. This encouraged Scop. "What are you doing here anyway?" Robert Kennedy said.

"I'm waiting for you to quote Aeschylus. It's a very profound and inspiring quotation."

"See Sorenson."

"I don't want to see Sorenson, I want to see you. You're the one who speaks these things, it's a matter of complete indifference to me who may look it up. Come on," Scop said, "think of me as a time traveler from the future. Imagine a future in which time travel has been developed by private technology at enormous expense so that certain privileged scholars and members of the aristocracy can bear direct witness to fabulous people and events. Think of what it might have cost me to come here and indulge me."

"Is that true? You do come from the future? Are you a time traveler?"

"That's neither here nor there. I said, imagine that this is the case."

"Did I win this election?"

"Come now," Scop said, moved by the cleverness of Robert Kennedy; none of that cunning indicated by the historical texts appeared to have been manufactured. "If I were what I represented to be, you can imagine that divulging information of the kind you ask for would be the most serious crime we would commit. The future is the product of the past; we change the past at our peril for no matter how unsatisfactory it may have been without it we would not have been here at all. I can give you absolutely no information at all which would risk changing the past."

Kennedy stretched on the bed, looked away from Scop, looked at the ceiling again. "I'll keep it to myself," he said. "It's just a matter of curiosity. What harm could it do to tell me?"

"If I told you you did not succeed you might abandon the campaign now which would lead to changes of a different sort. If I told you that you *did* your attitude might change which in turn would change that of others."

"But either way the future would not change."

"I will not," Scop said, "I will not under any circumstances get into the laws of temporal paradox. We simply will not discuss that." He looked at Robert Kennedy, admiring him. Unquestionably much of what had survived about him to Scop's time was true; the man simply had an unusual shrewdness, an acuity and sense of self-definition which was lacking in Scop's rather miserable and self-indulgent era. It would have all been different, he thought, all would have been different indeed if people of this quality were existing in twenty-forty; different conditions would have fully applied … why a Scop himself might not have been necessary. Of course that is not the case now: he realized that such thoughts must be put out of his mind. "You want to give me that quote?" he said, "I really would like to hear it."

Kennedy shook his head. "No," he said. "Definitely not. I don't know who you are or what you're doing here or exactly what the sense of all of this is supposed to be but one thing is for sure, I'm not going to be an exhibition for you. I would suggest that you leave."

"I agree with you. Still, I've come here at such enormous risk and inconvenience that I'd hate to just give it up without staying as long as possible."

"Suit yourself," Kennedy said. He flexed on the bed, closed his eyes. "Just don't bother me if you would. I'd like to get a little rest."

This seemed to complete the issue. Kennedy seemed to fall into a deep and even slumber, the sound of his breathing large and rhythmic in the room, paying no further regard to Scop at all. It was obvious that whether or not Kennedy paid credence to his presence there would certainly be no further discussion with him: the man was sealed into his subjectivity, a subjectivity whose rational dimensions (Scop suspected) would not admit any province of the imagination which this interview would signify. Scop wandered around the hotel room for a little while, trying to pick up from it, from the sleeping form on the bed some indications of the temper of the man, some sense of the persona which would grant him connection but there was none. It was always very difficult for him to establish a relationship with one who was sleeping or otherwise unconscious or dead; all three applied in the case of Robert Kennedy. Moving over to the bed, standing poised, then, above the man Scop had a vision and in that vision he descended upon Robert Kennedy with hands grown ferocious and enormous through need and tore his throat, beat him severely around the temples until he was dead and the need to do it was momentarily palpable, Scop could feel it stalking within him. He could kill the man. He could do this. No one would believe that he was he and when it was over it would all have been for the best anyway because Kennedy was going to die. Kennedy was doomed; whether he died by bullet or by slaughter in his bed his death would be just as absolute as would the world which pivoted from that circumstance.

He could have done it. In fact, Scop leaned forward, thrust out his hands in a rigid, militaristic gesture to do just that, to begin the slaughter and evisceration of Robert Kennedy. But as his hands moved down, as he felt the rhythms of attack falling upon him something stronger than desire came up against him and he stopped in mid-gesture paralyzed, at attention, searching the walls of the room as if for indication of some exterior force that had restrained him, nothing to be seen within the walls but he could perceive it within him nevertheless. He could not murder. He could not do this. There were seemingly limits even to his voyage, his condition: he could not perpetrate. All that he could seek was the obliteration of circumstance, not its renewal. Rape was different, to be sure.

Scop moved away from the bed. Pain like tears moves within the skull of memory. He crouches. He does not want to weep. He waits for the machine to take him out of here. The process is not instantaneous. He weeps.

XII

SLAUGHTERHOUSE: To reassure him of the rightness of his mission—he has stinging doubts, he is not entirely obsessed, every so often Scop thinks that he may be mad and his evaluation of society based upon idiosyncratic perception, not some absolute truth—Scop goes to the Slaughter Games, taking a rear bench high in the stadium in the unreserved section, a place where hopefully he may sink amidst the crowd and be unnoticed. It would not be worthwhile for him to be discovered at this juncture. The unreserved section in which he sits is filled with the Mob: the lowest and crudest elements of the society are here, creatures so brutalized and broken by the poverty of their lives that they do little more than growl at one another while they stare at the Games and then occasionally in a fit of transferred lust turn upon one another and regardless of sexual identity begin to mime the gruesome motions of copulation on the hard planks. The state guards look at all of this without interest, only there to make sure that the disorder does not spill over the gates and into the upper-class sections where the responses if no less savage are at least somewhat controlled. No one pays any attention to Scop as he finds a small space on the long, crowded bench, everyone's attention is fixated upon the arena itself where several Reds and Whites are attacking one another with iron implements, the sounds of impact picked up by the on-field microphones, reverberating hugely from the speakers lined around the stadium. Fifteen or twenty Reds are down to only five of the Whites and the Reds are beginning to lose formation; there is little strategic interest in what will happen now but of course the battle, which is merely a preliminary, must go on to the conclusion. The crowd is not discomfited, only slightly bored by the failure of the Reds to make a better showing and now and then someone in the section faints or succumbs to a quiet, subterranean blow which caves him or her across the bench: only then do the guards become active and take out the struggling form. Scop takes a small bag of candy from his pocket and begins to chew on it absently while he stares at the field.

It is a terrible spectacle, of course. The Slaughter Games are only thirty years old and the formal league arrangements trace back barely a decade but the way in which they have seized upon the imagination to say nothing of the social structure of the populace is to Scop the clearest indication of how dreadfully far the society has run down, how feeling has become obliterated: now only mass murder within the superficial framework of the game format can be said to serve mass emotion. But there is no time for speculations of this sort; rather he finds himself riveted to the field where the advantage of the Whites is now being pressed to the point where the formation of the Reds has completely broken; they scatter on the grass, some of them in open flight, a few others making a last dismal effort to hold ground and to at least die bravely ... but there is nothing to be done about it, the ground cannot be held nor is there any possibility of bravery when the Whites overflow and from the speakers comes the full resonating sound of heavy blows. A Red is decapitated, another is beaten to death by a gang of five Whites and as the last, stricken Reds now in full retreat try desperately to reach the safe area circumscribed outside of the grass the Whites set upon them ... and Scop can take no more. He looks down at his feet. There are limits to his capacity to absorb this; he does not think that he is as cruel as most of the spectators at the games and has always felt that it is a certain sensitivity to this kind of brutality which marks him as finer and better than most of them; that it is in fact this loathing of the sadism of the games which has sent him upon his desperate attempt, the Masters to be damned, to change the past so that the present may live again.

That the present may live again. It is a good phrase, it is indeed one which could become the slogan of his quest itself and he meditates upon it as he stares at his feet. In just a little while he will bring himself to a standing position, lurch out of the stadium. He has seen all that he needs to; has verified his relative humanity in relation to the barbarism of his times and now he may leave but he will just stay for a few moments if he might; standing is such an effort, fighting his way through the throngs who are now screaming for the next round to begin is such a difficult thing to do. Indeed, his companions in these stands are gone mad now with the excitement of the games, they seem to have lost all rationality, any measure of responsibility has been drained from them and looking at them with pity and disgust Scop feels again his distance from the madness and the crowds, the obsession and desires of the culture in which he is trapped. He must be an artifact. He must be some remnant from an earlier, gentler age, that is all he can say because he is totally revolted by the spectacle he is glimpsing and cannot bear to examine the true nature of a culture which could give rise to such spectacle.

Still, he cannot move. Sense tells him to move, also desire and yet he cannot urge himself from the seat. The point is that the games are kind of fascinating, the attitudes of the crowd compelling. The way in which the spectators and various lowlife surrounding him refuse to respond to one another, how their only relationships seem to be identificatory ones with the gladiators is distressing and yet to Scop enriching as well: they may have discovered the secret. The secret is to deny relationships other than abstract, externalized focus. The last Reds have now stumbled from the field and a new troupe comes out, Blacks and Greys this time Scop notices, taller, stronger, more richly attired contestants than those they have succeeded. The Blacks and Greys are, of course, the concluding event on the first part of the program and it would be senseless for him to leave at this point. The program is close enough to intermission; he can leave quietly at that time in the throngs without making an issue of himself as he would, of course, if he were to leave now. It is a strange manner of spectator who would leave the Games just before the concluding event and the Blacks and Greys come very highly recommended; Scop knows from third-hand information if not from direct access (he never reads about the Games or attends them ordinarily) that these teams are among the leaders of the First Division and their contest will decide the standings for the mid-season. Why should he leave now?

Of course he finds the Games repulsive; that is not the point. He does not have to leave to establish his distance from the spectacle, he thinks; he is hardly so uncertain, hardly has such a tenuous grip on his revulsion that he must flee the area. He can test his resolve by witnessing them and not being moved, he thinks. He does not have any ambivalence about his revulsion; he can expose it to the utter fury of the contest and have it remain as it was. But as the teams meet on the field for brief conference, their heads bowing then in the mandatory prayer and exercises of reemission, as he feels an uncharacteristic excitement begin to spread through him, working its way from thighs which seem to blend into his loins with a kind of mutual, aqueous excitement, Scop wonders if this is quite the truth. Perhaps the Games are more important to him than he has ever admitted. He is not a creature who can stand apart from his culture; everyone, even the calmest and most dispassionate researcher is the creation of his cultural ambience and essentially falls within that culture. Can he comment upon it? Can he really stand aside? Damned if Scop knows, he thinks; the Blacks and Greys, deep in conference now, settling the preliminary exclusions do not seem to know either. It occurs to Scop that he really can make no more of an objective judgment on his culture than can these participants themselves; all of them are trapped within the eddying cycles and consequence and so for that matter are these spectators, his fellows for all his disgust: all of them are bound by the spectacle of the Games.

Something lurches within Scop. He is not as strong as he thought after all. He is not as capable as he might have suspected of using these games in the way that they should, as an object of proof. Quite to the contrary. He stands, discombobulated by small breezes, feeling nauseous in the dry air of the stadium. Spectators begin to shout at him. Scop turns, stumbles toward the end of the planking, the shouts rising. He is obstructing view. The formation breaks and the Blacks and Greys return to their separate sides of the playing area. Someone is going to get killed out there. They all are going to get killed out there; in a contest between teams as skilled as these at this stage of the season, as evenly matched as they are some ninety percent of the participants in a given game do not survive. Nor is it important that they survive; all of the continuity of the teams is in their programming and administrative personnel. Scop knows that he should not be concerned about this: the participants are willing, well paid, heavily insured, facing short, brutish lives anyway; to be a Black or Grey, even to be a Red or White is to incur more nobility than they would ever otherwise find. Someone kicks him heavily in the calves and Scop falls to his knees across the next row of spectators, his arms flailing. People curse at him but not in a language which he understands. He wants to explain to them that this is not his fault, that the accident was precipitated by others, that he would never on his own have done anything like this but he cannot seem to frame the words. He is falling.

On the field the Blacks and the Greys approach one another, the speakers amplifying and nicely transmit the sound of their threats. He hears them full like birds in the air. He is falling. Falling.

XIII

REALITY AS THE RECONSTRUCTION OF NEED: He dreams that he was able, somehow, on the Grassy Knoll to deflect the bullet, the angle, the windage factor of the riflist, the aim of Zapruder's camera; he dreams that he was able somehow to call off murder and now he is back in the arena where the slaughter games would be conducted … but there are no slaughter games, never were, the field took an entirely different plan and is now filled with flowers. He strolls among them, aisles and sculpturings of plants, admiring the huge constructions which loom at him at the end of corridors: enormous flowers shaped like bells, their stems like handles on precious artifacts. He is overwhelmed by the beauty of these gardens, particularly since there has been nothing like them in the twenty-forty he knows. He reaches out, takes a large purple flower shaped like a bowl, grasps it by its curiously pendant stalk and twists it off roughly to sniff at it. Thick vapors curl back at his senses, their odor curiously penetrating and grasping him with smells that seem to carry him into the vault of memory: other times other connections. Perhaps he is overreacting to the aspect of these gardens but then again there is no question as to the reality of his sentiment: never has he seen anything quite so beautiful as this or then again he is peculiarly conscious—how could he not be conscious—that he is undoubtedly dreaming.

Nevertheless, Scop continues to wander through the gardens, following a single, circuitous path that takes him through sprigs of displays to a deeper, shadowed portion where behind gates he can see large blooming roses, beyond the roses he can see the trunks of dwarf trees, perfectly formed from the ground to the branches, then strangely misshapen. Leaning against the gate, taking the hard iron into his palms as he might caress a woman's breasts he tries to look into the trees, tries to reach through the gates and merge with their stately, unmoving corporeality in the strange windlessness but the gate does not shift under his hands, his aspect does not quicken or change; he can get no closer, then, to the trees then he is now. After a very long time he allows his hands, one by one, to slide from the gate and turns on the path to wander back the way he came.

He tires now of his isolation, of the strange peace of these gardens. As the demonstration of a world unmade they are moving but sheer symbol has never been able to affect Scop deeply; what he needs is activity, some sense of dramatic heightening which will bring the gardens into closer alignment with his own thoughts, murky as they may be … but there is no one. He feels the surfaces of the dream then beginning to clamp upon him, annoyingly tight and confining in what is, after all, merely an impression of reality and he would like to awaken; he does in fact struggle through the motions of waking, turning in place on the path, waiting for the giant hand of consciousness to reach through the dim bowl of sky and take him out of this, the lesson of the gardens already known, on then to other things … but nothing happens. No hand descends to yank him away. Indeed, he feels more deeply within the dream than ever, the gardens shimmer, reassemble in colors even brighter. A little breeze begins to churn against his face and with it comes the first odors of putrefaction as if the flowers were blooming not petals but little excrudescences of dead flesh. The air tickles his lungs. He feels as if he is about to vomit.

Further down the path, trudging back from its winding departure into a little abscess of magnolias comes Elaine Kozciouskos. What she is doing in these gardens; exactly what the symbolism of her appearance in his dream might be Scop does not know but as she raises her head, sees him, begins to react he finds himself seized with a dread that has nothing to do with the putrefying odors, ever stronger in his nostrils. He is not sure exactly what he fears but it has something to do with her turning upon him, with her running away. Here, more than ever before, he wants her good opinion. This is the world which, in part, he has created for her; he cannot deal with the possibility that even in these places she would turn from him in disgust. "Hello," he says, weakly raising a hand. "Hello, Elaine." He has never used her name before. It must signal a new relationship between the two of them. Maybe not. "Hello Elaine," he says again. "How are you? Where have you been?"

"You fool," she says to him. She lifts her face. Her eyes are luminescent; absolutely excited in a way which he has only associated before this with sexual passion. "You stupid damned fool."

"Me?"

"Of course," she says. "You thought that you could change the future and you can't even change the past."

"I don't want to discuss that Elaine," he says. Somehow he had not imagined himself in dialogue with her; at the corner of his consciousness, in some pocket of the mind when he first saw her, he admits that there might have been a thought of sex, some hint of coupling beneath a sprig of tulips he can just see at the left peripheral vision, a bow of them strung between two bushes … but thoughts of fornication have certainly dwindled; it is hard for him to think of such things when she is being accused of stupidity. He does not think that this is an abnormal reaction. Still, her features are so dusted with light that it might be need which informs them. "Oh you fool," she says again, "do you think that life is a garden?"

"It could have been. It could be yet."

"Nothing," she says, "it could have been nothing," and stretches out her arms toward him, in the very heavy symbolic overcast of the dream it is as if clouds gather around her fingertips although this would be climatologically impossible even in the very advanced technology of twenty-forty. "The past is immutable, you see," she says, "all that you can do by going back and meddling with it is to make it occur over and again in different guises. But of course," she says, her face changing expression, a strange wink spreading a cast over one eye as her hands sink to the level of her waist now cupped gracefully, "if you want to do it you may. No one can stop you. It's your life. All that you'll do is discover and rediscover this on your own and no one ever can make you see that until you see it yourself. You didn't have to take me from Grassy Knoll," she says, "that wasn't necessary at all. I wouldn't have done it. I wouldn't have done it to you."

But Scop has now lost interest in her. He has lost interest in the dream as well, it has been superseded only by an urge to get out of it but the dream is as thick and heavy and clinging as the memory of the shots levelled one and two into the dead form of the President, the body already taking evasive action in the limousine, swinging off-angle at cross-purposes to itself as it hit the purposeless cushion, the head rolling, limbs lolling, the face already kneaded into that high parody of itself which is always known by the dead, the sound of the sirens as they went through Dealey Plaza with the thrill that the ruined blood must have crept into the assassin's loins. "Get away from me," he says to her, "I don't believe in you, I don't believe in anything. I just want you to leave me alone."

"Why should I leave you alone? You summoned me."

"I did not. I couldn't—"

"But you did," she says, "I wouldn't have been here otherwise. Come on. Let's have sex."

"What?"

"That's what you wanted, isn't it? That's what you called me here for. I don't care. It's all the same to me whether you do it or not so you might as well take advantage. You lecherous fool," she adds with a little wink. "You can't change the way in which we live so at least you should be able to change the level of sperm in your vesicles. Don't you agree?" she says. He has never seen her so devilish. Indeed, she is a woman in her late forties, early fifties, hardly sensual, at least as he recalls her from the circumstances of meeting on the Grassy Knoll yet she seems to be absolutely inflamed now with passion. "What the hell," she says, "come on and do it. Don't you think that the symbolism of the gardens is just a little bit transparent? That's what has been on your mind from the first you know."

"Get away from me," he says as she seems to advance upon him, her palms extended, "get away from me right now. I mean it."

"Ah," she says and hooks her arms around him, draws him in, places her lips against his forehead to give him a long if not sensual kiss in that spot, "don't run away from it. It's hopeless and besides you know it's always what you wanted."

"It isn't what I wanted."

"It isn't?" she says. She draws back. "Then why are you here?"

It is too complicated and wearying for him to explain why he is here. He is not even sure that the explanation would hold together. "No," he says. He considers possibilities of flight staring in the distance which dazzles over her left shoulder. Swift calculations almost musical in their regularity, their order, the way in which they blend together assault him. "No," he says again. He crouches in a sprinter's stance. He thrusts himself forward on perilous feet. He flees.

Brushed away by the force of his spring Elaine Kozciouskos stands on the path wiping at her skirt, shouting now with humiliation. He cannot see her but since this is a dream he can see her very well. She waves at him and screams through the flowers. She curses him. He has never heard a woman curse like this before even at the Games. He is immersed in spangles of daffodils.

XIV

TOWARD A HIGHER AND MORE LASTING JUSTICE: Bitter, he is taken before the Temporal Court. Eight solemn old men in the special robes of their office sit above him and confer with one another by passing notes as Scop stands far below in the dock, looking down after that first swift glance at their faces. He cannot deal with them. He knows his failure. It is burnt within him. Later on he knows he will have to deal with the auditors but for the moment they have left him alone and he needs this isolation; quietly, bitterly, he reviews all the events in the long chain of his failure coming to the present time and his humiliation. "I wanted to change worlds," he mutters but this does not give him satisfaction. "I wanted to make this all different, shift the way in which people regarded their lives," but this as well does not matter. There is no efficacy in his voice, no power in his monologue, it is as if the very authority of self has drained from him at some point: maybe at the Games, maybe during one of the rapes, maybe even when little Abraham Zapruder confronted Scop and told him that he was wrong. Who is to say? It does not matter. You go into the machine, you do the best that you can and if at the end of it it has come to this … well then, at least one has made an effort. He made an effort to change. This does not comfort him either. In just a moment, Scop knows, he will disappear into this self-pity in which he is wallowing and never be heard of again, hear nothing himself. He does not want this. For one thing he has an enormous curiosity about the verdict. What will they say? What do they really think of him as measured through their judgment? He can hardly wait to find out.

The head of the temporals rises. He is not head by virtue of seniority but by election; nevertheless he sits at the extreme left being the junior member of the court and otherwise exposed to small indignities imposed by the hierarchical framework. Twenty-forty is full of little inconsistencies and mysteries like this; they do not concern Scop. They are not worthy of his rage. He always felt that his rage had to be saved for the higher, deeper, finer, more important things such as being on the Grassy Knoll. The head of the court clears his throat, shakes his head, allows his little fingers to play with papers on his desk. At length, in a mild, almost apologetic tone he pronounces Scop guilty. Scop is guilty of all counts of unauthorized realteration of circumstance. He is sentenced to obliteration to be conducted in due course.

Immediately Scop is on his feet. He is not really surprised by the verdict he finds; he must have anticipated it as this a long time ago. It could have been in no other way. "May I address the court," he says. "I would like to make a statement."

"You have tampered with the very fabric of our contemporaneity," the head of the court says. His hands are little blotches against the paper, his voice a mild, reedy mumble against the sound of the huge generators which power the autonomous environment of the court. His eyes however are huge and round, it must be the compelling aspect of those eyes, beckoning and deep which made the other members feel that here indeed would be a proper chairman. "By attempting to juggle with the constants you have menaced the lives of every man, woman and child of the planet, not only that but you have ransomed the unborn to your monstrous, megalomaniacal—" He trails off into vagueness, shaking his head, brings his palms together. "It is a terrible calamity," he says and sits down.

"I would like to address the court," Scop says. "I have some prepared remarks."

"I am quite afraid," the senior member, a huge old man at the center says, "that statements are not permitted at this time and in this fashion. You will have an opportunity later."

"I want it now. Each of us, every one of us are being held hostage not to the future but to a brutal mindless past, a past which if the truth itself but be known is the outcome of a criminal conspiracy—"

"No," the senior member says, "no, I'm afraid that we cannot tolerate this at this time and you must be evicted." Scop feels attendants, unseen, but enormous, seize his elbows. "Everything in its place," the senior member points out, "and you will have ample opportunity to make your final statement after you are disposed of. After you are disposed of," he says again and laughs although whether it is from his own humor or merely a random spasm Scop cannot tell. It probably does not matter. "You cannot change the past," the senior member says. "You cannot change the past," the others agree. Their unison is ragged but effective. Scop is speeded out.

His last thought as they take him to freeze him in stasis for a hundred thousand years while they decide what is to be done with him forever or leave that decision to future generations, his last thought is that although they are unreasonable they are not unkind. Perhaps that was what he should have understood from the beginning. They are not unkind. They may have wanted it to be this way but they too have had no choice. He is vaulted through doors. Wood collides with his features. He is taken to a different place. For a while there is immersion and sorrow but after a time there is the immersion only.

PART TWO

I

ELAINE KOZCIOUSKOS: Disguise is not easy. The old features will show up no matter how cunning the plasticine; I know this and know too that to live in mask is to live as a child, convinced that the motions of flight are in themselves concealment. They are not. One learns this and many other things as one grows older.

One must always be the same and those who would know you in one way will know you another. Nevertheless when I am called in and ordered to the Grassy Knoll where I will impersonate a tourist I do not have the will to resist. They promise me that the disguise will be strong, that Scop himself will be mesmerized by the cunning alteration. How am I to tell them that a long time ago Scop and I were lovers and that even if the face conceals the body will, bit by bit, yield its familiar messages? I cannot of course. Our relationship was illicit; confession would be utterly destructive. Beyond that, I have no choice. My gradient does not allow me refusal; a fact of which they are all too aware.

So I tell them I will go and they say that they are satisfied. They are always satisfied in agreement; that is all they have ever sought from the beginning. Not submission, not unending power, not total control … merely the agreement of those they consider their subjects to a direct proposal. This is little enough; I would hardly oppose them even if Scop and I had been lovers. I did not care for him a great deal. Our relationship was one which came out of pain and which ended in perceived hopelessness. Listening to them talk to me it is possible to feel that he may have forgotten my body. Only the administrators in themselves matter, I think. Only they are imperishable.

We are not. Certainly the flesh is mortal; a discovery which must be made when one has reached my stage of life. I do not deny it. Nevertheless, willing to go on for all of my mortality, I take myself to the Grassy Knoll in the most intricate plasticine and given the superficial characteristics of a tourist of this time I blend among the rest of them so easily that it is hard for me to be aware, so deep do I find myself in the role, that the man talking to me in an impassioned way is Scop until suddenly I am hurtled behind the bushes and he begins to shout at me in his strange cracked voice. "Now," he is saying, "you must return with me now."

I shrug, trying to preserve my composure. This is what was urged from the first, that I do not betray emotional distress of a primary nature. Most of my panic can be masked as the understandable terror which a tourist of this time would feel being dragged off by an individual such as Scop. Have I said that he is extremely unstable and presents a bizarre appearance? I do not think that I have made this clear but it is so and the temporal garb of course makes him appear even less rational. Scop is not an unattractive person in some of his moods and given real understanding and patience can respond in a convincing imitation of sanity but there is little question but that to most of us, let alone tourists of the nineteen-sixties he is a preposterous and menacing figure. "Please leave me alone," I say. I think that I have also neglected to mention that another woman standing next to me who Scop has misidentified as being my companion has been knocked unconscious and left in place by one stirring and lunatically energetic blow. Haste, Scop had once confided to me in bed-conversation, makes waste but one would hardly know that he believes this from his conduct at the Knoll. "Away with me," he says, wrapping an arm around me in a close, trembling embrace and I feel the little ridges of his body trembling. People are not looking at us but instead are fixated upon the approaching motorcade which by all calculations is no more than five minutes distant. They must be forgiven for they know not what they do, etc., I think, and let out a low, piercing shriek, not because I am in terror because things are going exactly as I was advised, but simply to encourage Scop into believing that he has control of the situation. I am acting as Elaine Kozciouskos would in this situation. He does not, in embrace, recognize my body. "Now," he says, and hurtles me into the machine.

"No," I say, "no," but of course he has joined me and we are already plunging out of time, toward what I take to be the objective present. Jammed against one another in the enclosure, barely able to fend buttocks from one another there is a horrid intimacy underlying the mutual antagonism; I am seized with the urge to reach out, touch him by the elbow and confide my true identity to say nothing of the plans of the Temporals. It would make us collaborators. But their choice was sound: I could no more establish communion with Scop than I could sincerely beg for release on the Knoll; what happened between us happened a long time ago and now we must be enemies. We are spat out of the enclosure and I find myself in his detestable cubicle. He stumbles out behind me, pulls the door closed, urges me toward the bed. "Now," he says, "we are going to do it now." His eyes are glazed with familiar urgency. His hands began to slash at me, little hammers undoing my clothing. "Now," he says. He is overcome by the urge to copulate. I am told that this would be so, that this is exactly the effect that his plans would have upon him, still it is surprising. I have never seen him this way. Scop was not a passionate man. Our relationship was not characterized by physical passion. It interlocked on other levels. "Come here, you bitch," he says when I am naked. "Get under me now." His face is alight with necessity; truly he is transfigured. It is curiosity as much as duty that causes me to slide rapidly beneath him. I cannot wait to see if there is any change in his performance.

There is not any change in his performance but I do not wish to engage in graphic description. There is no need to dwell upon aspects of the sexual act; they are boring and monolithic the Temporals assure me and the functions of generation have nothing to do with the personality. They offer no insight. They are merely impressed in a kind of universality upon all of us. If purposes were to be served by description of what it is like to copulate under adverse circumstances I would put them down because I am unswerving in my verbal honesty (this is another reason I was chosen) but it is not. In addition, the temporals are embarrassed as well they should be by explicit description of sexual congress. They yearn for it themselves yet it is all behind them. I would not wish to give them pain and will in fact strike these passages when the report is handed on.

After we are done he rolls from me, stares at the ceiling mumbling. *Tristesse*. He sighs heavily as if about to speak, then grumbles quietly and says nothing, waits, starts to sigh again, actually turns toward me with his mouth open and then turns away, shaking his head as if in disgust.

Has he deduced my identity? In the penetration of my body has he learned who I am? Impossible and yet it might be. There is little to be done about this of course. If he knows, he knows; it cannot be changed. I simulate a terrified patience and wait him out. Eventually he will speak. The ways of the Temporals are devious I think: how is my smuggled relationship with him going to misdirect Scop from what seems to be a very careful and well thought out scheme to put the Temporals out of business? What do they have in mind? Or then again do they have nothing in mind and are the reports about the Temporals true at the core, that is that they do not know anything that is going on, that circumstances are utterly out of their control? "I bet you're frightened," Scop says.

I do not think that this requires an answer. Haste to verify would implicate on a different level. So I say nothing.

"Are you frightened?"

I shrug, not an easy gesture while lying on one's back. My breasts bobble. They are the plasticine breasts of a fifty-year-old woman; do I dare to say that he has found them attractive? I inspect them without interest in the work of technicians. "Of course I'm frightened."

"Do you know where you are?"

He will not catch me that way. "Of course not," I say.

"Or what has happened?"

"No again."

He groans, moves on the bed, then abandons that slight collision of thighs which had lent warmth to our conversation. "Your President was killed not ten minutes after you were abducted."

"Really?" I say keeping my voice level. Absence of affect, I have been advised, will work every time. Denial is a stress-reaction; it need never be questioned. "That's hard to believe."

"But it's true," he says, "that's the reason that I was there you know."

"There? For what?"

"To try to prevent the assassination. I'm a visitor from the future. As a matter of fact this is the future that you're in right now."

"How interesting," I say. "I never would have suspected that if you hadn't told me."

"Well, how would you know?" he says, "you've hardly had an opportunity to be about outside and I'm afraid that this is going to be denied you in any case. But the reason that I've gone back there is to try and change the present. We live in a very brutal period here in twenty-forty."

"Twenty-forty? Is that where we are now, where you're from?"

"Exactly," he says and considers me with his strange, insightful eyes. Never, never have I been able to forget that stare of his, even before all of this happened. "You're very intelligent."

"Not really," I say, afraid that I will misdirect him, that he will begin to question me intensely rather than to offer insight into his own motivations, that material which it is my duty to impart, "not intelligent at all. Why do you want to change the present?"

He shrugs, blinks his eyes, shifts on his hips. "Did I say that? I shouldn't have said that; it doesn't matter. It's really not important."

"You said that this was a brutal period."

"Well," he says, "well, every period in human history is brutal. I don't want to convey more of a revulsion toward the situation than is strictly speaking necessary." He seems to be abstracted, discombobulated although then again firm characteristical judgments with this person are not easy. I should know. I above all others should know this. "Get dressed," he says, "I'll take you back."

"Back where?"

"Where you came from."

"Why did you bring me here to begin with if you were only going to take me back?"

"That doesn't matter. I don't want to hear any more questions from you. Do you want to go back or don't you?"

"Well of course I want to go back."

"Then put on your clothing," he says and bounds from the bed, strides toward the mirror pounding his thighs vigorously, "don't ask questions. You should be overjoyed to get back; after all you were abducted to say nothing of being in a state of terror, weren't you?"

"Of course."

"Tell me the truth now."

"I was terrified," I say sincerely. "I still am. I don't know whether I'll get out of this alive or not. Are you really going to turn me back to where I was?"

"Where else?"

"What about the President?"

He pauses in his ritual; in the mirror I can see his face twist, become sullen. "What does that matter to you? Why must you ask so many questions?"

"I won't ask any more."

"Do you think this is easy for me? Do you think that I like to do this? I have no choice; I'm merely following the codes to the best of my ability."

"Of course you are," I say. "I understand that."

"I don't have to put up with your insults and slights. This is my society, not yours. You have nothing to say about this; it's only my generosity that is allowing you to get out of this."

It was his homicidal mania which forced our relationship to an end in the first place. Now it all comes back to me. I reach casually for my dress at the side of the bed, imagine what it would be like to be killed by Scop in role. Would he rip chunks off my body later to see the true identity of the corpse; would he feel remorse? Or would his pleasure merely be deepened by knowing that it is me who he has destroyed? "Yes," I say, "yes, I am sorry, you're right," and spring off the bed and begin to dress and before he can ponder further the significance of what he has said I am dressed and standing before him. "Get dressed," I say to him, "take me back," and his little pubis seems to dimple as if with accusation, "I want to return," I say, "take me, you promised, you promised that I could go back, I didn't make you, it was your decision," and sullenly he begins to put on his clothes, simple garments for traveling, nothing in them to indicate at all the depth and sincerity of his passion and then he is dressed and before me, moving quickly from the room. "Take me back," I shriek, "I refuse to stay here alone," and run after him and he brushes me away and says, "Deal with yourself; do what you will. I don't have to do anything for you," and blunders his way out of the room and I try to follow him but he turns to slap me down with quick force, one absent blow across the head and I fall to my knees sinking, sinking, and he is gone from there; oh no, this is not what I wanted, this is not the way that they said it would be, they did not say that it would be anything like this at all nor that there would be endangerment, I was merely being enlisted to try and avert a serious crime but—

II

THE TEMPORALS:—I should have known better, should have known otherwise. I should have known that they lie to us, will always lie if it suits their purposes. They are interested in nothing but the maintenance of their tyranny, their tyranny locked closely to the nature of the times, and they will do anything to keep the status quo unlike the brave if hopeless little revolutionaries like Scop who do what they can, but always against the grain of the system. After he has left me I return to his cubicle. There is nothing else to do. My dress is ragged and my hair is askew; truly I am disgusted by my appearance. They have made me ugly and they say that this was necessary in order to deceive him but they did not have to make me ugly. I know that now. They did it out of spite.

Knowing my ugliness makes me weep and I raise my hands to tear off the huge chunks of plasticine. I do not care what happens to me as long as I can be restored to myself. But with my hands on my cheeks I pause before the first damage has been done to my appearance and find myself staring as if transfixed at the walls considering what I have become, what they have done to me. There is a kind of justice in this; I may even have deserved it but justice or not if I tear off the plasticine I am done for. If he returns to this cubicle and finds me here and understands what has been done not only I but many will die. I am convinced as to the utter sincerity of his passion. So I let my hands fall from my face and sit there for a time, consciously blanking my mind so that I will think of nothing, so that no estimation of the proceedings will come to me; in that way it is as if, momentarily at any rate, I am free and beyond all of them. Then I hear noises in the corridor and when I look up one of the Masters is staring at me. They must have checked me through to here by a monitoring device implanted; either that or they are watching his cubicle at all times. "What happened?" the Temporal says. I have never seen him before, I think, but then again, they all look very much the same to me and I have never been sensitive to individual differences. They all speak to the same interest anyway. "I demand to know what happened," he says.

"Come in and close the door. Don't shout in the corridors like a fool; do you want to be heard?"

He looks at me with close interest, then steps inside, robes casting little furls and shadows to the floor, reaches behind him to take the knob and eases the door shut. "Why are you showing defiance?"

"I am not showing defiance. I advised you to come in."

"You are wholly within our power. You do this assignment on our behalf; you have no rights or conditions in this whatsoever."

"I don't believe that."

"What happened? You are ordered to tell me at once."

I shrug and say, "I will tell you nothing. You cannot make me."

"Are you mad?"

"Get out of here. I do not wish to be monitored."

His face falls open exposing little blotches and pearls of sweat. "You do not know what you are doing. You have no idea what you are saying."

"Get out now."

"You are being as subversive as he. The consequences will be terrible."

"I don't care about the consequences," I say. The interview is stimulating; for the first time since I was beamed to Grassy Knoll I feel alive, utterly engaged with myself. The risks are great but Scop has taught me something about the levels to which one can be pitched. "If you want me to help you will leave at once," I say. His face rounds. "At once," I say and he backs in a confused way toward the door. "At once," I say yet again and he lurches from the room, I am filled with triumph, he is gone from the room and all unbidden a laugh of sheer relief boils from me and I think how easy it is, I should have known it a long time ago, all that it takes is simple defiance and they are defeated, they are not at all conditioned for the mechanisms of defiance, nothing in their training or position has accustomed them to the fact of refusal and I feel better and leap to my feet, whirl around the confined space in a free and laughing way trying little pirouettes and gestures of release but then as I should have known it would—in fact I am not at all surprised—the depression hits me in overwhelming measure and I collapse to the floor where for a long time I sit pondering, my chin in my hand pondering, sit pondering to consider what has happened to me and whether it is possible that there is any way out. I do not think that there is. I am as confined within the measure of my circumstance as Scop. The Temporals to the contrary. Everything to the contrary.

III

CONSPIRING: The texts are not clear as to the true sequence of events at Dealey Plaza. As preparation for my enlistment it seemed sensible to engage in research, to become familiar with what had happened so that I could play my role on assassination day without bringing undue attention to myself, but although I spent hours rolling and unrolling the Zapruders, although I studied the still photographs and did not neglect the efforts of our very best historians to trace through the motives and culpability I emerged with very little. It is difficult to judge exactly what happened there. There are some who say that there was a conspiracy operative while others feel that the sole assassin was Livy Osborn who was of course killed by Jack Diamonds before he could go to trial. There are some who say that the conspiracy went up to the highest levels of the government at that time and others who say that Osborn was a lonely madman with a good streak of luck. Some say this and some say that but most say nothing at all; it is hardly a topic of consuming interest to most. Scop is an exception; he became obsessed by the assassination long before I knew him but how many are there like this? I think that he fastened upon it, became familiar with the details precisely because it was arcane, an area of dull and private scholarship. He would have gotten no satisfaction from dealing with something where he would have been competing with many others in an area of wide interest.

He was always fascinated with the assassination, however; I cannot deny the sincerity of his interest which appeared to be quite real and which was not based upon self-aggrandizement. "That's when everything went wrong," he said to me once or then again he might have said it several times, all our conversations seem to muddle together in the bowl of happenstance, the cup of memory, "that is when the entire social fabric seemed to come askew, don't you see? If a figure of this importance, the paternalistic leader of the nation, the psychic underlay of the common consciousness could be murdered inexplicably—"

"Others had been murdered."

"Yes," he said, "yes I know what you're saying but not in the era of modern technology. The techniques of diffusion, the communications which had been developed by that time made the tragedy personal and accessible and besides that there was the enormous power which the President yielded before the dispersion—"

"Oh Scop," I said and turned from him, "this is so boring, can't we talk about something else? Is this the only thing that you can talk about?" I was rather dull and frivolous in those days; it must be admitted that our relationship, such as it was, was based upon a mutual sexual attraction and my own boredom, little else. It took the temporals to tell me that there were areas of far greater significance between us than I might have grasped. "I just can't bear to hear any more of this," I said, my back toward him, my little haunches drawn up, pointing toward him my resilient but capacious rectum in which occasionally he would bury himself with small moans and confessions beyond words, "so let's talk about something else," and felt his hands come around to encircle my breasts, "that's better," I said, "that's better now," I was a wanton little slut in those days, interested in immediate satisfactions, unaware as I was for a long time of how deep was his obsession, how serious his intent, "Oh, I like that so much better than all this dull talk about society," and allowed myself to be swaddled in his embrace, taken to his center (or so I thought at the time, lecherous little bitch that I was) but eventually he released me and without turning away, his chin still clamped into my shoulder said, "There's got to be something done about this." I am impacting many discussions of course. He talked about it all the time during the course of our relationship but I am taking highlights, so to speak, from each of the discussions and stringing them together to give the impression of a coherent, rising point of action and view. This is under the advice of the temporals who were good enough to suggest that if I wanted to keep a diary as a tension-outlet I approach my memories in precisely this way. They have had more experience with this than I have. They have had more experience than I have but they do not know what is going on either. "I'm going to have to straighten it out," he said.

"Straighten what out?"

"Everything went crazy then. We're the stillborn product of assassination out of despair. We're a monster, a grotesque; the child that is our age is blind and horribly misshapen."

"Can't you stop talking about this Scop and just have fun?"

"No one can have fun. The Temporals will not permit it. They control everything; they have locked off alternatives not as they say for our protection but merely for our perpetuation. It's got to be changed."

"And how are you going to change it?"

"Well," he said and paused, a long, thick pause which might have lasted some moments or days; there may have been yet another fuck dropped into it (on a level of superficiality we had a passionate relationship, it took the Masters to show me how false it was and how divorced from true feeling) or merely the desire for one but he finally said, "Obviously I'll have to get back to the point of origin."

"How?"

"How?" he said, "by using the convertor of course."

"Unauthorized time travel is illegal. You will be subject to severe penalty."

"You really are a stupid little bitch you know," he said, "if it weren't for the fact that there was a raw, crude sexual attraction here I wouldn't even have gotten involved with you." He shifted on the bed, moved away from me. "Even so, I believe that I am going to get away from you. Right now."

"Be sensible, Scop. You cannot change the past."

"I don't want to change the past. I want to change the present."

"Even so. Even so—"

"I believe that I am going to get away from you," he said, getting from the bed, turning away from me, striding toward his clothing which he began to put on in a rough, absentminded fashion, the glowing insignia of his rank intimidating me as I lay naked on the bed, filled with the desire to get into my own clothing yet not willing to concede weakness. "I don't have to put up with this nonsense. I really don't have to put up with it any more."

"All right," I said. I must have realized then that our relationship was over. He was truly obsessed and when Scop fastens upon an idea he will not let it go, not for anything. "Do what you will."

"I intend exactly that. Get dressed," he said. "Get out of here, get out of my room. You disgust me."

"You did not say that before."

"I did not say a lot of things before. Get out now," he said and lunged to pull me roughly from the sheets but I was too clever for him and had already gained my footing, stood beside the bed then and with real anger went for my own clothing, contorting my emotions into a loathing which I felt would help me survive the humiliation he had imposed upon me. There was no reason for this. There was no reason for him to have done this I thought and while he stood over me raging I drew on my clothes one by one and stood before him for an instant before leaving, I did not know what that look in his eyes meant, was unable to place it for some time but later on it came to me: it was the look that Osborn must have had before he set off the safety and looked down the long distance to the white car in the motorcade.

IV

DESOLATION ROW: His hands are enormous on me as he yanks me away toward the little hidden spot behind. "Come with me now," he says, "don't fight, I'll kill you if you fight," and even though I have been prepared for this it is terrifying to see what he is doing. Even though I have been warned that he will act in exactly this fashion and that I am in no danger whatsoever as long as I cooperate and stay within the role the thought brushes my mind that he is capable of anything, even killing me. We stumble through the grass, his hands seeming to touch me in a hundred hidden places, obscene and yet certain in their persuasiveness and I wonder if he will kill me. If he will kill me right here I will have in one sense succeeded because he will have directed all of his passion onto me but in another way I have lost because I do not want to die. Nothing in or out of this world is worthy my death, my life pivots around the certainty of my continued life; perhaps this sudden insight is worth something. Most likely it is not. I can hear the shouting now, dim applause in the distance as the motorcade approaches and I want to turn, to see, I have never been within distance of this President before and the least I should be able to take out of this experience is to see him but Scop is pushing me toward the machine and I cannot adjust myself within the parameters of this body which they have given me; I cannot adjust and stagger in front of him, the touch of him like insects on my being and we are jammed together in the convertor, heel to heel, the fumes of his breath pattering on my cheeks. "Now," he says, "now," and hits the controls. It seems that we have been through this before but I cannot tell. The sense of chronology has been shattered, all molds as well as the sequential value and it could have been the first or the tenth time that we have been together in the spaces of this machine. I was warned about this too; the faltering and then the breakage of causation so that I might go through one act fifty times and another directly antecedent not at all but the important thing was to maintain courage and perspective. Not to panic. "You damned bitch," he says, "you damned bitch, Elaine," and I say nothing, biting my little lips, clenching my little hands, nothing that I say can possibly affect him. The machine stops and we lurch out together onto the bright pavement of a city, scattered with refuse, facing the large doors of a shuttered building. He grabs me by the elbow. "In there," he says, wrenching me around, "in there," and pushes me toward the doors.

I stagger on the filthy and putrescent stones, fighting for balance, then losing it, going to my knees but being yanked upright by him immediately and he impels me toward the door now in front, dragging me. "Hurry," he says, "oh hurry, hurry, it's going to be too late, you bitch, oh you bitch Elaine," and the pain is terrible. I would not have known that there was so much force in him, would never have measured his brutality even as our worst moments together, even in the clanging and interruption of orgasm as he groaned over me, screaming with astonishment at his discharge he never hurt me so much and I want to tell him then, I can no longer maintain the focus of the lie, I want to tell him who I am and what I am to do to him. "Scop," I say, "Scop," and his face, birdlike, wheels around, he seems at the verge of recognition and as I look at him, as we stand poised, locked on the top step of the building I find that I cannot go through with this; I cannot say to him what I want to and the instant passes. My conditioning has been true; I have been bound in. "No," I say, "no, forget it. Nothing, nothing, nothing."

"How did you know my name?"

"You told that to me."

"No," he says, "no I did not, I *never* told you my name, who are you, who are you?" and there is an instant or maybe several at which time I could reveal everything to him, could indeed break through just as I had fantasized but then it is me to back away from this possibility and I say, "Yes you did, you're so upset, you don't remember anything, don't remember anything at all," and his face blinks like a bulb, astonished at my control and then it is me, me not him who seizes the doors and tugs them open, stumbles into the dense and intolerable spaces of what seems to be a small temple, now in the process of a service: heat, light, dust, crowds, noise, blazing fluorescence from the podium, a tall man shouting and gesturing, cries from the onlookers, perhaps forty or fifty of them in here and a moment with Scop a long time ago comes to me, a promise he made me on the bed, "No," I say, "you're not taking me here, you can't be doing this to me," and he says *stop!* with terrible energy, hurtling himself at me, I tumble over him, hit the floor, feel his own weight cave against me and then overhead I hear the crack of rifle fire from behind, from the door through which I had entered. There is the sound of collision ahead, a gasp, a thin scream, the sound of a body toppling and then the voices, discordant and desperate have broken over us, "No," they are saying, "no, Malcolm, no, no," and another spate of fire, shorter and less purposeful than the last, then the banging of the doors and there is a sudden lush moment in which there is no sound at all, the silence inevitably more provocative than the screams … but the screams begin again, jangled and intermixed this time, as fervent as chant but more ragged and lying on the floor I incline myself toward Scop lying on his stomach, his arms crossed, eyes closed, a strange look of satisfaction carved on his face as if put in there by a clumsy but demonic miniaturist, little pleasure-wrinkles at the side of his eyes which I had seen sometimes while he was coming and underneath the screams, the cries mounting, tumult of movement in the chapel I say to him, "You bastard, why did you take me here, why am I in Harlem now?" and then I remember that the assassination of Malcolm according to what Scop had told me did not occur until a year, almost two years after the assassination of Kennedy and that therefore in my guise as a tourist of this period I am not supposed to know of this. I cannot concede the knowledge of event; instead it is as if I had come to it afresh. I *have* come to it afresh, of course; I can allow my reactions unhindered. My thoughts are confused, disordered, as if little pellets embedded in glassine. "Now," Scop says moving on the boards, "now," and comes to his feet, it is very confused in the terrain surrounding; it is hard to perceive exactly what he is doing, perhaps he is doing nothing, this thought occurs to me, that the events are meaningless, his witness is meaningless … I try to get to my feet in the astonishment but my limbs seem to revolve upon the floor rather than grasping, bodies come in more tightly, it is then that I feel myself lifted, vaulted to a standing position, blocked in by heads, bodies, some of them whimpering, others laying their hands upon me in a way as abrupt and ferocious as had Scop and I see him then through a sudden break in the foliage of witness, at the podium, leaning over the dead body of Malcolm, an aspect of panorama imparted by this, the frieze of his attention as kneeling he stretches out a hand, touches the forehead of the dead man and then the crowd closes in again. I can see nothing.

He has equated the death of Malcolm with Osborn's slaughter of Kennedy; I know that now, knew it before, but I cannot understand why he has taken me to this temple, what he can hope to gain by making witness to further slaughter. Does he feel somehow that I am energized by death just as he is, that all of us can be brought alive only by dead, moody speculations, they are broken, he comes through the crowd toward me, his face blotched and broken into damp and although he is examined no one touches him. He reaches out toward me. "We must leave," he says. Our hands touch. "He is dead."

"No," I say, "I can't go with you, not like that, this has got to stop, sometime it has got to stop."

"What are you talking about?"

"I don't know," I say which is almost the truth, "I don't know what I am talking about," and forms collide: we seem to be at the center of a mass of struggling, weeping people some of whom resemble us but others of whom do not. "Why did you do this?" I say pointlessly, "there had to be another way," and there is the sound of hands beating at the doors, the wood buckling, they must have locked it behind us when we came in although then again it might have been the assassin: who knows? Who knows about anything? "You fool," I say to him, reaching forward, grasping his wrists, impelling him toward me, "You dumb fool, this surely is not the way. This is not the answer, you can't change things by retracing the past over and over again, we are living in a future which will be the product of the past no matter what we do; the future is immutable you see, you have it the wrong way," and he looks at me, looks at me intensely, seems to be trembling on the verge of real understanding, certainly an insight which I cannot bear and then as he is about to break into the speech that will destroy everything, ruin all of the frail plans of the temporals it is too much to bear: "No," I say, "no, don't do it, don't say it, don't do anything at all," and lunge away from him toward the doors which are open, they part, I plunge through them, I run heedless through the wild and the darkening streets.

V

THREE FORTY-FIVE ET SEQ.: "Excuse me," I say to the small man who has been pointed out to me over and over again in the scans as Abraham Zapruder, "May I have a word with you?" It is ten minutes before Scop's materialization, twelve and a half before the motorcade comes into sight. All of this has been carefully, carefully calculated but efficiency or not all confidence seems drained as I face the man. Calculate as you may, work the machines onto the finest point of calibration, the acts will still have to be carried out by humans, the acts will still have to be lived from the inside. The machines can never, never grant us the ethos through which we must regard our condition. "It is very important," I say. He is a shabby old man, frayed but pleasant. He is not bitter like Scop. Scop's bitterness destroyed our relationship; even without the other factors I would have surely left him. One cannot live this way. "I must talk to you." Rolls of film are revealed in the open pouch which dangles from his shoulder. His hands are gathered around his camera like a breast. "Please," I say.

"What is it?"

"You must take no films," I say. "You must take no portraits, no moving portraits." My grasp of idiom is insecure or at least it does not have the fluidity which Scop himself has developed but it will do, it will do, my purposes at least are made clear to him in the sudden shifting of his features. "You must put the camera, put the gear away," I say, "and you must leave here at once."

"Leave here?"

"It's the only way," I say, "if you are here you are going to be implicated. Believe me," I say passionately, finding a level of feeling that I have never entertained in these exercises before, "Nothing, nothing will come out of your portraits but shame, disaster, the confirmation of breakdown. All that will be seen in them is the worst, the very worst that we all have become and your name will be a curse, it will even to this day be cursed among all those whom—"

The old man is backing away from me. Onlookers are staring which is exactly counter to the instructions; I was supposed to attract no attention whatsoever, I was supposed to be as inconspicuous as possible in order that I might float underneath the waters of circumstance. "Please," I say to Zapruder, "I am completely sincere, I mean this, you must not take motions, you cannot do it, if this were not serious I would not ask you," and his mouth begins to move although rather in distress or comprehension it is impossible to say, perhaps both, there are bodies between the two of us filtering contact and I press through them heedless, warned not to use force or the special devices with which I am implanted except in the case of the most dire emergency I still find myself attempting to be reasonable. "Don't you have any consideration for your heirs?" I say, "your name will be reviled; they will be persecuted through all the generations," and of course ambiguity has quite passed from his face by this time, it is quite apparent what the nature of his response is and it is only futility which drives me forward, hurtling forms now adding a real ugliness; I think that in a little while I might be apprehended. "Fool!" I say to him, "fool, coward, liar, cheat!" and his little pouch banging against his forearm, his little eyes clouded with tears or regret Zapruder, completely humiliated, turns to run, this will not work either, nothing will work and something must have happened to my timing, to my control of the instance because here is Scop, he is already at Dealey, bounding from the little hollow where he has hidden the converter, his face dull and murky with the effects of passage but the heaviness already beginning to lift as he sprints toward us. Disorientation is quite brief but disquieting to see; perhaps we really were not meant to travel through time. Scop comes toward me, his uneven, pounding stride easily clearing the grass and now the crowd's attention has shifted toward him, it was never that much upon me anyway; no one really was paying any attention. It is hard and harder yet to realize this, to realize that despite the illusion of consequentially, vast forces, manipulations, the fate of the universe hanging at stake and so on and so forth very few people pay any credence to these events and indeed for all the effect we are having upon the common lives of those surrounding us … well, for all the effect that we are having we might as well be shouting and pounding within dim narrow cubicles at some far remove.

Scop closes upon me. His hands clamp upon my wrist. The odors of his breath, the upheaval of his body pressed against mine reminds me of other times, other places in which we mingled differently but I cannot remind him of these even though the sentiment is overwhelming. Nor can I remind him that this has all happened before; that we have been at Grassy Knoll a hundred times and will be here a hundred times again, that what we are undoing is in itself merely another stop-action frame in the endlessly unreeling Zapruder of our future. "Come with me," he says and begins to push me toward the converter. He hits me on the jaw. "Come with me now."

The abduction has begun. A hundred times he has hurtled me over these slopes, at least as many I have heard the tumult of the motorcade in the distance, seen the fast faces of the crowd pouring past me as heedless of them we hurtled toward our destination. A hundred times this blow has failed to stun me, sending me only as it were to a more solemn level of consciousness, a heightened attention as the singlemindedness of his intent, the desperation of his determinism came through to me as it never had in bed. "Please," I say, "it makes no difference," but he is excited, pulls me harshly. "Please don't do this," I say but he refuses to listen, nothing new here, he has never listened but I go through this over and again not accepting perhaps the simple message of repetition: that it will always be the same. Nothing will change and we will cycle through this over and again to the same conclusion. Nevertheless, if just once, if one time we could break through the pattern—

"Into the converter," he shrieks, "get in quickly you bitch or I'll murder you, I'll really do it you know, you'd better not defy me," and I cannot even breathe cooperation with him; he wants to hear assent as little as resistance. Nothing to do but to keep up with him which I do in my stumbling and misdirected way. "Inside," he says as we duck behind trees, as I see the squat grey oval in which we have traveled so many times. He batters me in the small of the back, I stagger, a plate opens, I sprawl inside. He is over me, raving, pulling the hatch shut with a clang and then he throws the switches. I feel the lurch of passage. It is hard to believe that this is all happening again; there is a feeling of novelty to it, each time new and terrible although to the same conclusion but I must do what I can, must accept the fact that we seem to be in cycle and deal with that. Passage begins. He moans and natters over me. I know that he will wait until we reach his cubicle until the attack begins and yet I feel now as before that it is all he can do, all that both of us can do to restrain from having at one another in the enclosure like beasts.

VI

THE BURNING, THE BURNING: So I go before them and they ask what is going wrong. Why is there no progress? Why does the same thing seem to be happening over and again? Is there no way out of this? Their patience is not unlimited they point out and if there is no real progress they will have to take sterner and more desperate measures, measures which will certainly be cataclysmic and will involve much suffering, torture and death. Not only that but I will be taken off the assignment with all that is implied. No longer will I be eligible for privileges, never again will I be able to participate in the place of honors during the Games. Have I no shame? they wish to know. What is happening? Cannot I even give them an explanation of what is going on?

To all of this I say very little. There is really nothing to be said. What can I say? All my life, I feel as I stand before them in these rooms, watching their faces as dull and blank as board far above me, all of my life I have in one sense or another been appearing before committees of the elders and demanded to justify my tasks, my existence. I can no longer go through these rites. It would be easy for me to point out that I was drafted for these ceremonies, did not volunteer and that it was with very little hope that I was sent on my way. Only later on were their expectations, probably based upon the vast amount of activity between Scop and myself. In the viewers it must have looked, from the frenetic tone of our relationship, as if I was making progress. But I was making no progress whatsoever. I try to point this out to them in a desultory fashion but there is little enthusiasm in my arguments nor much attention in their response. I cannot say that I blame them. Over and over again we have gone through this; at a certain point weariness must set in. There is a time to give up, to admit that nothing can be done, no changes effected but they seem to be incapable of this and so, in a way, do I. We must go on and on, posturing against one another through all the confrontations which are ordained and at the end … at the very end of it there will be absolutely nothing, no more than it is now. I try to explain this too, there is nothing which I would hold back, but their attention is intermittent.

When I am done, it does not take long but the subjective feeling of passage is very intense and I am calling of course on all the other times that I have been in this room, there is a long, dim silence during which they grumble at one another and readjust their positions. The pause goes on so long that I think that I am finished and will be permitted to leave but as I edge myself out of the booth, moving toward the exits, I am retained by a shout from one of them and return to the chair with the feeling that all gestures and efforts will return me once again to this moment: sealed within this interview. "We do not think that you are performing satisfactorily," he says to me. "This is not what you were sent for."

"I did the best that I could."

"Your best is not sufficient. This man is extremely dangerous; he must be blocked. You know the consequences."

I do. I do know the consequences. I have heard them outlined again and again and emotional response has been squeezed out; I no longer feel that these remonstrations, much less my tasks, are consequential. Perhaps this has been the real difficulty, the true cause of my failure. But I do not say any of this. There must come a time, there must come a time to all of us, even Scop, when the premises of a situation are accepted and no longer battled, when one is sealed within the limitations of role. I cannot say this to them of course. There is really nothing that I can say to them. I sit in solemn silence in the dull dark dock and the moments ooze by and they can see from the expression of my face if not my failure to talk that I will no longer try to excuse myself. Finally the leader leans all the way over, looks all the way down and says very gently, "What do you propose to do?"

I shrug. I cannot say that I propose to do nothing because that is not exactly the truth. There is another truth but I cannot get close to it. "Tell me child," he says and there is a tone of emotional connection in his voice which comes very close to moving me. "This is not easy for any of us you know. We are aware of your pain; we have our own. We are merely trying to do the best that we can and that means a severity."

"Leave me alone," I say. Lights wink among the shadows above; the ceiling seems to be broken and through little chinks I can see the sky if I desired. Everything is falling apart; the great hall is in poor repair. Deterioration accelerates and there is absolutely nothing to be done about it; we must face the fact that the devices of the civilization no longer work for us. "Leave me alone and let me do what I must."

"But if you cannot affect him—"

"I am trying. No one can affect him; you asked me to do this because you thought that I might be able to make a difference. At least let me work in my own way."

"But," he says, "but you are making no progress—"

"Let me judge that."

"This cannot go on indefinitely. The tension increases, the time-cycle can be abused only so many times before there is an overwhelming expansion-and-dilation—"

They know nothing of technology. They know nothing of technology whatsoever and yet they will invoke its jargon for the purpose of reproof, this being one of the oldest devises of their repression. I cannot tell them this either of course. In a sense I can tell them nothing. "I will do what I can," I say, "I will not abuse the constructs if I feel that progress is not being made."

"I do not understand this," an elderly member from the side says, leaning his ruined, misshapen head toward the amplifiers. "I do not know what you are talking about. All of this nonsense. The past cannot be changed. The past is simply and finally the past. The present which we occupy can only become the future never a different present. I think this is ridiculous. It—"

Two other members, coming from their seats in abrupt but uncoordinated gestures—all of them are quite old, none of them limber—come to his side and drag him away from the speaker. He fights them, limbs flailing helplessly and gives out little squeaks of anguish which do not seem to move the others as they press him against his chair. There is a long, hollow silence while he is held rigid, pressure to his wrists and then the elder says, "We will forget this."

"Of course."

"We will forget this nonsense. The assumptions upon which temporal rearrangements operate are quite clear and have long been established. You know the dangers."

"Yes, of course."

"Your time is very limited. If you do not begin to achieve satisfactory results quite shortly we are going to have to bring these experiments to an end. You know what will happen then."

"Yes, I know what will happen then."

"You have been warned," the elder says rather dramatically. "Due warning has been given. You will have absolutely no one to blame but yourself. The consequences will be drastic and all of it will be your responsibility. You cannot evade the penalties."

"Yes," I say, "yes," and it is quite enough, Scop's patience and his is not the only that has been drained; I stand shakily by my chair feeling within me the strange and gathering light of anger and underneath that as they rise to file away, even the one who has shouted at me, now unconscious, lolling in their grasp, underneath that the burning: ah, the burning.

<h2 style="text-align:center">VII</h2>

THE ART OF PAIN: In happier times (did we ever have happier times?) Scop and I visit the museum together. Hand in hand we stroll by the exhibits in the outer hall, the animate and inanimate image of our past; the energized torso of Kennedy particularly compelling as we stand before it for a while, listening to him recite certain highlights of his career and collected speeches. The hall is deserted of course, it is always deserted, very few people in the sector we occupy have any interest whatsoever in the past and specialists have their separate facilities in the museum, little carrels in which they exhibit the minutiae and miniaturizations of the Golden Era, seeking esoterica which such as we can never understand. Scop is affectionate, memories of death and disaster seem to bring us closer together, open up a warmth in him previously unsuspected and as we stand before the film exhibit of the events at Dealey Plaza he leans against me, rubs his thumb in my palm, mutters little private obscenities into my ear which in less stricken circumstances might cause me to feel a sexual longing ... but of course I cannot, unlike Scop I am made quite solemn by recollections of these terrible events. In fact if it were not for his immoderate obsession I would never come here.

The clips are old and somewhat strained but even through the cracks in the filter, the poor and wavering quality of the projector, the horror of the assassination comes through quite clearly. In black and white, in color, in reverse and in freeze-frame Kennedy dies over and again, the first bullet a fly bite at the side of the neck causing him to absently swat it away, the second the enormous reflexive sneeze that blows half his brain and all of his life away while his fingers absently pinch the spot of first entrance as if by holding that together he could deny the terrific impact. Without sound the films acquire a power which they could not possibly have had in the real, Dealey Plaza—I have been there by now many times—cannot compare at all with the representation of it caught in Zapruder's fix. The miracle of art is that it can transform the hurried and aimless, give it a sense of purpose which it could not possibly have had without the framing of the artist ... and Zapruder, for all of his limitations, is nothing if he is not an artist. Scop stands in the booth, pressing the buttons, running the scene of impact over and over while little lines of concentration appear and disappear around his eyes, his mouth pursed to solemn attention.

I know that if he were to put out my hand to verify I would find him with an erection. I have found him so at other times. But even though he would enjoy this, even though—I am sure—every cell of his body leans toward, claims that shocking touch with which I would grasp and unload him, I stand perfectly still, do nothing whatsoever. There would be an impropriety about this which even in our bleak and painful age I could not possibly tolerate. There are limits to all human conduct. Not only that but seeing the films is exceedingly depressing; it reminds me of the rot of human life, the mortality of kings. "God," Scop says. He is deeply moved. "God, that's something." He turns off the projector. In the dense spaces of the booth I become aware of an overwhelming putrescence which the odors of the projector had only masked. "Something's got to be done about that," he says, "that's all there is to it." In his voice I hear a determination that, perhaps, I have never sensed before.

"What are you talking about?"

"That," he says. He must gesture but of course it is too dark to see. "This slaughter. We cannot exist in a world predicated upon slaughter."

"I do not know what you mean." There is no dissemblance in my tone. At the time to which I am referring I had no conception of his obsessive search for a "different" past; it was only much later that I became aware of the specific dimensions of his lunacy. At this time I was quite young, quite naive and emotionally involved with him in a way which could not continue but at the time seemed all-encompassing. "Please let's go. It smells here."

"It's all clear to me now," he says, "why did I never understand this before?" He reaches out, flicks on the projector once again: here is Zapruder frames 345 *et seq.* stop-action at the moment of the second impact. The film has been thoughtfully spliced to always start there; the custodians are quite aware of what the few onlookers who come here want to see. (The Games are much better on all counts). "That's where it went wrong."

Dimly I sense the outlines of his purpose. "That's ridiculous," I say. "It all happened a long time ago. Maybe it never really happened at all."

"Oh, it happened all right." He is transfixed by the film, stops it, runs it through again. "It is the central fact of our history."

"But how can we be *sure*? Maybe it's all a myth. Maybe it's something that they made up, that they gave films and talks about just as a fantasy. Well," I say aggressively as he turns on me in the darkness his eyes wide, I know, with astonishment or maybe then again it is rage. "This is possible."

"That's ridiculous. Scholars and writers have been back through the converter any number of times; this has all been precisely verified—"

"But how can you be sure? Can you be sure of any of this? Maybe it's a lie, all of it is a lie; I mean it could be a compact to deceive." I am floundering and yet I cannot accept the films without protest. Is this not better for all? Should I have let him go on without argument, would it all have been easier if he had not felt that he had to prove something to me as well as to himself? I will never know. Now, I will never know. "Never mind," I say, "forget it."

His grasp is harsh on my upper arm. I never knew that those fingers which had brushed me so delicately, a witch's kiss in the places where the soul lies embalmed could bring such pain. "Then why do you say it? Why do you say something like that?"

"I was only trying—"

"You bitch," he says against my ear, "you bitch, you won't ever leave me alone, will you? You won't ever accept the truth of this, the truth of what is going on, you've got to protest—"

"Please," I say, "please, you're hurting me," and this is true, he is hurting me terribly, he is hurting me in a way which cannot be described but his hand is tight and tightening upon me and suddenly he yanks me free of the booth, we are out in the dusty and musty, the nearly lightless but still dimly illuminated area of the museum himself and he is dragging me through the exhibits, dragging me past them while he is saying, "You've got to face the truth, you can't go back, can't go back into lies, we are what we are because of what *they* have been," and I can say nothing, the pain is terrific, also the realization that he can do this to me, me who he says that he has loved who, in a sense has been closer (he told me this) to him than anyone he has ever known. We stand before a monstrous diorama, the younger Kennedy in the act of receiving the shot in the pantry that killed him, one hand raised, the other down, the head exploding in the impact, the bodies around him in those strange postures of attention which can be captured only in frieze, trapped movement is grotesque and he puts a hand in my back, pushes, sends me lunging through the serim and I am literally in the pantry, the dead air coursing through my open mouth, the dead forms surrounding me and closer to the plasticine than I am meant to be I can see all of the tiny flaws driven into their faces, the cracked and broken places where the dead spaces of wire and putrefaction begin. These figurines have not been treated for fifteen years, they stink but even though they are more dead in proximity they are more alive as well; the immobilized eyes retain the aspect of recognition, the cardboard appendages seem shaped for caress and as I look at Robert Kennedy, it is as if I am transported to the pantry itself, this is not twenty-forty but the nineteen-seventies which overtake and here I am and *the next shot is for me*. The assassin's gun is levelled, he has killed the Senator and *I am next* and I do not want to die, not in this place, not in this fashion, I must be screaming, sunk to my knees, my forehead against the waist of the dummy, curiously resilient and ponderous under the cheap fabrics. I cannot believe that this is happening; I do not want to die and it must be then that my screams begin although there is very little conscious sensation and the screams might come from outside. I am dragged away from there, the scene diminishing as something takes me from the diorama and onto the floor of the museum and when I come back to myself I am on the floor. Scop leaning over me. His face is implacable.

"Do you see?" he says.

I say nothing. There is nothing to say. I cannot control my voice, little broken sounds emerge which may or may not come from me. They may emerge from the diorama. They may even have come from Scop.

"Listen to me," he says. He puts his hands on my cheeks, cups them, brings my head slightly off the floor so that he is looking at me at close range, the same small spots of ruination around his eyes as I saw in the Kennedy figure. Are they all artificial? "Do you see now what I was trying to tell you?"

"See what?"

"You fool," he says staring at me, "you fool, try to understand, damn it," and now he leans in even more closely, the conjunction of our faces is absolute, as absolute as in the motions of intercourse itself but there is something other than desire in his eyes, something even more necessitous. "You thought you were going to be killed," he said, "the diorama came alive for you, the figures were real, you felt your death in their assemblage, you damned fool," he says, "you damned fool don't you see now that that's exactly the way I feel living in this time? They are killing us? They have already killed us. *We are the victims*."

And it falls away (so many things fall away but then again there is the lurching sense of recovery also) and I see weeping on the floor the message that he has tried to bring to me: that there is an art to pain.

VIII

I WANDERED LONELY AS A CROWD: On the Knoll after the assassination. Curiosity takes me here; just once it would be interesting to see what it is like afterward, in the part that is unrecollected. Here it is not five minutes after the car has gone away, the sirens pouring through the eaves of the city and still the crowd is here in little broken pieces, wandering over the landscape, looking for a bit of information or if not that some shared memory as to what has occurred. No one seems quite sure exactly what has happened and I would not enlighten them. They do not pay any attention to me nor I to them; it must be understood clearly that I am not part of their time nor they of mine and now that I do not in this new cycle have to be disguised in the garments of their contemporaneity that disjunction is clear; it is impossible that I could be regarded as one of them. But my appearance is not bizarre. It has been carefully modified to avoid undue distraction; the colors are soothing, the cut modest, I look very much as a proper citizen of twenty-forty should look adorned for the Games where the object is to take as little attention away from the field as possible.

There is confusion here but it is of the most modest sort; there is pain but it is well controlled. No one, after all, knows exactly what has happened. *I* do not know exactly what has happened although at this moment the President, of course, already dead must be in the emergency room at Parkland, the top of his skull being checked for cosmetic changes. There is very little to be done about it. Someone, taking offense at me for no reason which I can understand, casting me for an outsider, suddenly comes against me heavily, a young man in his twenties and begins to push me back against the trees, screaming. I do not know what he is trying to say but it has something to do with the man in the big white hat. The man in the big white hat is out to get him. His motions appear ferocious but have no force in them; he strikes at me with limbs like pins and his efforts to thrust me to the ground are successful only because I cooperate, because I allow myself to fold slowly from the waist and go into the grass. It is always best to cooperate. It is best to make as little of an example of oneself when traveling out of time as possible; dislocations are to be minimized. These lessons I have absorbed well from the temporals if none other. Nevertheless, the sheer accumulation of blows begins to weary me after a time and no one from the crowd seems inclined to help. In fact, they seem quite pleased and interested at the antics of the young man who seems to be acting on behalf of all of them. Have I, after all, managed to make myself that conspicuous? It is a dismaying thought to say nothing of being filled with pain. "Stop it," I say to him as he begins to kick at me, "now just stop that."

Oddly, he does, as if the suggestion were something entirely outside of his ken; something so astonishing that it needed fuller consideration. He looks at the sky. "Why?" he says. A little spittle falls from the corner of his mouth. The crowd sighs. "Why should I stop?"

"Because your President is dead."

"He can't be dead; he was just here. He just rode by us in a big white car."

"He was shot and killed," I say, "didn't you see that?"

He bends toward me. Like all young psychopaths he is incredibly flexible; his body conforms to laws which only his strange brain can emit. Hands on hips he says, "How did you know that?"

It occurs to me that I am not in an optimum position, sitting on the grass, giving out news of the assassination. "It doesn't matter," I say, kicking my legs straight out, "it might not have been that way."

"What do you mean he was shot and killed?"

"Maybe he wasn't," I say. "Everybody has a different point of view on that. I might have been looking at it from a bad perspective. Now—"

"What the hell are you talking about?" he says and kicks me. There is no power in his kick either but a weak blow with a foot is more dangerous than one with a hand. I feel little waves of anticipatory pain moving through my upper thigh and draw up my legs, reel over, crouch, haul myself into a standing position. There are forty or fifty of them in a loose circle looking at me with expressions which I cannot deduce but which do not look helpful. I realize that the converter is at a good distance from me, more than a hundred yards, tucked securely behind a bench. This was stupid; Scop always kept his converter at much closer range and now I can see exactly why. It was unwise to take this situation as frivolous. I should not have done it but who was to know what it was like in the Plaza after the assassination? For one thing no one had ever been here before. "You bitch," the young man says and moves forward to kick me again, "tell me the truth now. Tell me how you knew that he was killed!"

I seem to be in trouble. I seem to be in some kind of trouble but all is very confused and bedazzling; perspectives alter even as I sit and the rising of sound from the circle might only be the own blood's messages ringing distantly. I never anticipated this kind of difficulty when I came here. Scop would not have anticipated either, that is my only comfort. He would have been in even worse difficulty. "Now just stop it," I say. I back away from him, three steps that carry me toward the edge of the circle. "Now there's no reason for this at all; you know that this is ridiculous," but my voice is carrying toward a shriek the way that it almost always does when I am tired or tinder pressure. "You're not being reasonable," I say, "how would I know that he was killed, it was just something that I was saying."

Someone, an old man I think grabs me by the elbow, wheels me around. I look into the ravaged face which brings back momentary impressions of the Robert Kennedy diorama but there is intensity as well as corruption to his gaze. "I think you ought to answer some questions," he says, "we're not fools here you know," and swings me to pull me in tighter and at this I break. The situation is clearly more serious than I took it to be until a few moments ago and now I can see the risks. It might not be only the President who is slain in Dallas on this day and the implications, of course, burst upon me: the alteration of history will be grievous. Everything will be changed if my death too becomes a historical fact. I push my way out of his grasp, tearing his hands from me as if they were paper claws, something seeming to tear within him as I do this and then I blunder my way past him pushing hard, falling to the grass, coming erect and just as Scop has so many times so I do it as well: run. I run.

I must make it to the converter and the advantage of my surprise start gives me at least a chance of achieving it but as I begin to work my way in clumsy winding course toward the place where the machine is hidden I can hear them behind me beginning to gather for chase. Some part of me gifted with observation and great acuity paces behind is a part of the crowd, sees them massing, gathering, then coming toward me in a great overpowering rush which gathers up the slowest and weakest and sends them along with the rest, an undifferentiated mass is the phrase that I think that I am seeking, not that I am exactly "seeking" anything in this undifferentiated and terrible chase but the converter itself. Where is it? Where did I put it? Exactly why did I think that it was necessary to come back to Dallas at this time; what did I expect to find here? Well, it would be interesting to say that I was able to deal with such complicated and abstruse questions in flight but of course I did not, fear and self hatred carried me along and helped me to shut out their sounds but I became aware then of footsteps alongside me, someone drawing up to match pace and as I threw a frantic glance over the left shoulder I saw the thin and terrifying youth with which all of this had begun and I tried to run faster but no hope, no way, I was extended to my limits and not used to physical action in any case, breath coming unevenly, coursing through my lungs and burning. "Keep running," he said to me, the words distinct, "I'll guard you."

"What?"

"You'll get there," he said, "just trust in me and don't worry about any of this, just keep on running," and astonishment disappeared into the reservoir of pain, everything sunk into the pain, all of it falling away from me as if now in the true historical past of the nineteen sixties, none of this happening now, all of it a long time ago and I could see the bulky shape of the convertor jammed against the bench where I had left it, gaping open like a mouth. This gave me heart and I extended my stride, tried with what little strength left to allow the will to enter me freely and the youth was ahead of me now, the crowd slightly behind, he dove for the convertor, flung it open. "Now," he said and gestured but I did not need the gesture, needed it not at all; instead I plunged within, he followed me; I knew what would happen even before it did, life contained no surprises, all possibilities had contracted, the convertor closed, it lurched, I felt the moments of passage: turned toward him then, the youth in the converter and saw him looking at me in the dim and protected light of course: it had to be that way it could have been no other. No other.

Scop!

IX

GAMES: On the field, in the little shadows cast by motion, they strike at one another. It is difficult to make differentiation between them in the poor light; the teams are nothing but a struggling mass of men, some of them on the ground, others swirling around them. Try as I may I cannot concentrate my attention: my thoughts are elsewhere.

I do not wish to go to the Games. The Games repulse me. Nevertheless it has been insisted that I go there at least once; it has something to do, they assure me, with form. Form requires that I go to all the places that Scop has gone, that I touch the events that touch him. Only in that way can our cycles truly mesh; only in that fashion is it possible that I will be able to make recovery.

I did not want it to be this way. Looking at the men in the distance I understand their predicament in certain ways to be the match of my own; they have been caught by circumstances, plunged into a brutality which is not of their making but which nevertheless are the only gestures that may be theirs in order to survive. So it is for me; I did not want to do this but it was made clear that there was no alternative. If I were not to accept my fate, if I were not somewhere along the way to pursue and dissuade Scop from his terrible mission then civilization as we know it would fall. I could not bear this. I do not want civilization to fall. It is not much that we live in, I believe that Scop is right in saying this, but it is the only reality which we have and to that degree it must be cherished. Must be protected. I think.

I am in an isolated part of the stadium. This at least they have allowed me; to watch the Games by myself and behind glass. No sounds other than those I wish to hear through the controlled speakers assault me, no smells or winds from the field can touch me behind this glass. None of the onlookers will bother me with curses or with his own clumsy response to the Games, no one in an excess of identification will throw up on my lap. Somewhere across the field and if I wished I could throw a beam of light there and find him, somewhere far across the way Scop sits surrounded in the public sections seeing what I see now but I do not have to deal with him. They have given me the most elegant quarters available to one of my rank. That at least they have done for me. They could have done no more.

I know that they are dying on that field. Death is no abstraction to me no matter how reduced it may be for the participants. (There are those who say that they have no sensation whatsoever, that they are bred and trained for the Games and that their nerves have been severed, that the cerebral cortex itself has been reduced. There are others who say that this is a canard and that they are just like us but the Administrators say nothing at all leaving the argument essentially irresolute. I think that this is best for all of us; not to have that final knowledge that is of what it must be like for them. We will never know. It is a mystery.) But the death which they feel is less complex and extended than what is happening to me; what is for us, Scop has warned, is not the simple termination of life but its slow evisceration over the forty or fifty years that we have left to us until, at last, the machines and the temporals have won everything. This is what Scop says; that soon only they will remain; that the rest of us, like the participants in the Games, will be merely their functionaries. I do not know.

I do not know and I take this quiet moment in the sealed booth to at least put all of these thoughts away from me, in some different place. It is not necessary for me to have any awareness of the implications, I have been assured; it is only necessary that I do my job. Far out on the field they are struggling and dying but I have turned off the transistors and none of their cries, none of them at all, penetrate to these spaces.

I am alone; I am sealed in ice. There was a time and it was not so long ago when I was possessed of feeling; when Scop himself could give me feeling over and again but that is not so now. Much has been purged from me and willingly. I do not wish to feel.

I sit in the booth and watch the Games. "You can get out of this," he said to me a long time ago. "You can be anything that you want to; you can change things and make them different. The future lies within you; now with the convertor the past itself can be changed." His touch was insistent, his hands sliding against me in the night added their own pressure and insistence, at that moment it seemed possible. God help me, he reached me at that time: I will never tell them this but he made it seem as if it were so. "Help me," he said, "help me and together the two of us will control the world."

"I do not want to control the world."

"Yes you do. To live is to want control; you must control in order to live. If you did not have this there would be utter chaos and you would not survive at all. Go that one last step, admit what you want it to be."

"It will be the same," I said to him, "no matter what you tell me, you know that it will never be any different."

"That is not so. Trust me. Believe in me."

"Unauthorized use of the convertor is illegal. The penalties are terrible. You cannot—"

"Yes I can," he said. "Let me worry about that too. Let me deal with them. They no longer know what is going on, you see. Control has passed from their hands which means that they are dead and now we may come alive. I will be able to use the convertor. Do you care for me?"

That he would call upon emotion at a time like this! But of course that was always his way; there was nothing he would not call upon if he felt that it would help him. This may for all I know form a definition of greatness. He might have been a great man. But now like me he is at this field watching the Games and there is no more power that he can exert to change them than could I. I must understand this. "Caring has nothing to do with it," I said. I was always sensible in all of the spaces of our connection; perhaps this is what destroyed us. I do not know. "What you ask is impossible."

"Trust me if you care."

"Trust has nothing to do with this."

"Trust has everything to do with it," he said. I felt his sex upon me, lying against my thigh, then making the absent motions toward penetration and I felt myself clench inside. "Now," he said, "now."

I squeezed shut, turned, cast him off me. "No," I said, "no I will not deal with it that way. You cannot use this against me."

His breath was full against my shoulder for a long time but he said nothing. In the darkness I could see the little rectangular outlines of the grid coming up and realized yet again that we live within iron. They have made us metal; we are the Convertor, we are the machines. Then he said, "You are crazy."

"No I am not."

"You do not understand what you are. They have done this to you. Step away and see it; see it clearly and what you have become."

"No," I said. On the field most of them are down now; I can see in the wreckage of that collision only a very few of them still standing and they are severely damaged, bracing themselves against falling. "No," I said to him then, "I cannot help you. I will not work with you. It is hopeless, don't you see that?"

He broke contact; I felt weightless in the bed. "I should have known," he said, "but I held out hope even until now. That makes me a fool."

"Go away," I said. "Go away from me, please." It seemed to me at that moment as I considered our past with complete and total objectivity that everything, all of it, had passed between us in small, huddled spaces, that we had never really done anything, that we had not been outside of this enclosure for a moment, had never been able to partake of those spaces which he said were possible and I was sickened as one must always be at moments of true insight; it is too much to deal with those hollow platitudes which turn out, as in the case of everyone else, to be at the center of existence. "Please go away now."

"I'll go," he said, "I'll go and never come back. I thought you were different," he said after a while; I could hear the rustling of the clothing of his rank settling around him once again, "I thought that somehow you would not be like any of the others—"

"You said there *were* no others."

"In a way there weren't. In a way you don't matter either. You could have helped me," he said. "Everything could have been different, could be different yet. But you won't. You won't do anything. You're like everybody else. Don't worry," he said then, "I'm going to leave. I'll just have to do it myself, that's all. I'll do it myself and it will be only that much harder but that is the way it is going to be," and he was gone. I lay there in the darkness for a while, trying to deduce whether or not it made any difference being alone, whether in his absence I would feel differently about what he had said but I found that it did not and after a while passed into a watchful, uneasy sleep.

The field is cleared. It is time for the survivors to be taken to the wards; it is time for the harriers to come through on their one sweep; soon the final events of the day will begin. And somewhere over there in that slash of color which I can see as blood against the grey of concrete, somewhere over there, at this moment, Scop is thinking of me.

PART THREE

No one wants this job but someone has to do it: that is the way I feel about it. No one is interested in taking the responsibility and putting up with the problems; everyone would rather be off fucking or at the Games but if it were not for us none of their little lives would be possible. This is something that I force myself to remember when things get too difficult and I feel the need to go over the edge myself. Someone has to do it and take pride in it as well because without pride where are you? We are making the whole damned system go. That's all. That's clear.

They brought up this greenshift before us; Scopolamine, Scop for short, forty-five years old, third level East. Scopolamine used to be a kind of drug, truth serum I believe, this Scop took his byline seriously. He was out to tell the truth. He was out to change the course of lives as if they had never been changed before.

Greenshift is crazy. That is why they put them there, over in the Easters. There is not a cycle which passes without serious trouble in the sector and almost always it is a greenshifter who is causing it. Perhaps it has something to do with the hydroponics labs themselves, chlorophyll in the skin or brain or somesuch but I do not regard this theory highly. They are crazy because they are crazy, that is all. You do not have to look any further than that for a total understanding of the situation.

He stood before us, having been brought in on some minor checkup of one sort or the other. Even before we could give him the readout, the standard stuff about the reasons for him being there and what he could choose to do he began to address us. "I demand the use of the Convertor," he said. "I insist upon it; it is my right."

Convertor-use, for researchers and certain kinds of dilettantes, of course, is purely within the province of the Temporal Board. We explained this to him very reasonably but Scop was having no part of it. He said in that case *we* were the Temporal Board and could act upon the request on our own choosing. "Every man is entitled to the Board of his own choosing," the greenshifter said, "and this is mine. May I have the convertor or not? I warn you that if it is not granted legally I will obtain it illegally so whatever you decide here does not matter. I am going to have my way whatever you decide but I would prefer to do it amicably." Then he said something very strange which we passed by at the time but which turned out, at least as far as I understand it, to be the key to everything that happened. "We live in times that have come about because of murder," he said, "and this is unspeakable, we cannot live that way. We must eradicate the murder and then we will live in different and better times." I should have known right then that he was crazy and taken measures but what could I have done? What could I have done? I was only one of many and none of us (despite his insistences) was on the temporal board.

But none of this came up at the time. Greenshifters are not taken seriously; less so in routine cases of slackness and missed cycles such as this and we continued the interview as if this was nothing out of the ordinary, as if his case was completely routine which it seemed to be, which in fact it seems to be at this moment. There was no reason to apply unusual emphasis to what he had to say, we never had any cause to consider it for a moment. I will not take any blame and I resent, I might as well say this, I do resent the necessity for masking this statement. It should not be necessary. None of what you say happened had anything to do with any of us regardless of Scop's insane accusations or whatever other sources you may have heard of.

The matter of advising the greenshifter was passed along to me. This also was right and proper; we work in ritual order and it was my turn. If it had not been my turn I would have said nothing and would even have had trouble in remembering him. There are so many of these routine appearances and they mean nothing. As it happened it was my turn to speak. "What do you mean based on murder?" I said merely as a way of establishing his confidence, of bridging a relationship. There are numerous little devices we have as a means of keeping our attention on what we are doing. It is not as easy as many think to be on the boards. It is quite a difficult and testing position as a matter of fact and we have gained less understanding and sympathy than I think is truly our right. "I don't understand what you are saying." For a man of forty-five his physical appearance was impressive. This is something that I do remember about him; that enabled me to recall him instantly or at least with very little effort when you brought up the subject. Otherwise I might not have remembered him at all. I hardly keep all of this in the forefront of my mind you know. This for me is a routine job which I do without pleasure out of the sad sense that someone must do it in order to keep the cooperative order but that does not mean that I have to have any affection for it, does it? I am not, after all, a Gamesman.

"I have made myself very clear in the papers on file."

"I'm sorry," I said, "we do not review the preliminary papers in routine hearings such as these." What else could I have told him? Should I have tried to give him the impression that he was more important than he was? Then I would have built his megalomania out of all proportion and I would have been judged guilty in another way. My position has got to be considered also. I think that it is fair and legitimate and will eventually be justified. "Perhaps," I went on, "you would like to explain yourself in a little more detail." I did not have to allow him this option. It was an unusual courtesy.

"No," he said, "I will not explain myself; my conclusions are the same that you would come to if you thought about it for a while. I wish to use the convertor so that I may straighten out everything. I ask no help; I can do all of this myself."

"That's ridiculous. We cannot grant you use of the convertor. It does not fall within our purview. In any case you know that the past cannot be tampered with; you know the protectorate and the penalties."

"Leave it to me," he said standing there, holding his ground, quite unintimidated and I do not think that he is entitled to any credit for this, "you leave it to me to make the judgment as to protectorates and penalties." He came up against the boards and grasped them, his fingers changing color under the pressure, the surfaces cutting into his hands in a way that must have been most painful. "Don't you understand what is going on here?" he said, "don't you realize that we are living not in a present but in a dream of waste, an extension of all the terrors of the past; don't you realize that we live awash in blood?" I did not know what he was talking about. "Blood is everywhere; we are awash in it and we cannot bear this," he said, "we must change the situation at the base; we must return and correct. Otherwise I tell you we will see the end of it in our time and that is the truth; I have seen it clearly."

It is evident what kind of lunacy I was dealing with at this time. At least a transcription of the dialogue, as I recall it should furnish all the evidence (if evidence truly be necessary) of how unbalanced was his state and what there was to be done under the circumstances. My own handling of the situation was dignified, sensible and the only proper means of coming to terms at that time. If this is not clear then reference to the reports should make it so without the need for further discussion. I am making this statement under duress and under protest and despite the threats feel that my position is clear and that I am adequately protected under the codes.

"We are not the temporal board," I said, "your objections have nothing to do with us at all, greenshifter. You will have to apply to them for an authorized use of the convertor for all the good that this will do because they will surely deny your request."

"You are the temporal board," he said, "you are appearing under disguise because you do not want the unpleasant and difficult publicity of having it known that the temporal board is meeting on simple matters in greenshift. But I know devices; I have plotted your cunning evasions and I know exactly what you are. I am not here for review as you claim but rather for the most intense observation and I want you to know that this is exactly how I feel so that there will be no doubt in your minds when I begin the adjustments that you were amply warned."

"Let's dispose of him," someone said. I turned to find out who it was but the statement was not repeated and I met seven fierce, bland old faces to my right and left, none of them ready for statement. Sometimes I think that the random selection of these boards is really a poor way of managing the process; you get a lot of weak elders who are eligible only for senescence, death, removal, who pass out the useless final days of their lives in filling out the statutory requirements and now and then you meet a non-Elder who has psychopathic illusions that his functioning in board of review will somehow change his life to say nothing of those around him. I belong to neither class of course; I approach these duties as a responsibility which must be met and do so with unusual firmness and perspicacity, fairness and insight but I have never confused what we do with possessing any significance. Greenshift is full of small failures of conduct and absence of integration but they are at the crudest and least consequential level: who really cares about greenshifters anyway? Most of their lapses can be seen in terms of personal corruption, that is all. Raking my keen and intelligent eyes from right to left through the faces surrounding me it was impossible to see who had said *let's dispose of him*; no one really wishing to admit to the statement but it did not matter, of course, any one of them could have said it … they might have said it as a body as a matter of fact. I was the only one on the panel with intelligence and acuity and what difference, after all, does any of that make? Intelligence and acuity is not necessary here. "We have to read the complaint," the elder next to me said. At least his voice was distinct. "It isn't fair if we don't spell out the particulars."

"I know what the complaint is," Scop said, "it is specious."

"What is it?" I said. "You tell us then if you're so much in control of this."

"No," he said sullenly, "I don't have to if I don't want to. And I don't want to."

"All right," I said. The interview had become wearying to me no less than to the rest of them. All that one can attempt to do is to meet the superficial requirements of the statutes and then go beyond them a little bit; there are limits to what can be done, however, with the unresponsive or the insane. "We are going to terminate this with a warning."

"Warning against what?"

"Against continuation of the pattern of conduct which has brought you here."

He stood. "I'll fix you," he said. "I'll deal with your pattern of conduct. I'll show you a few changes around here. You cannot continue to do this to people. Sooner or later you have to face the truth; that you are the descendants of the murderers of the past. Your time is transitory. I will change everything."

"Is that your final statement?"

"You mean you have nothing to say? You can listen to this and say nothing?"

"I don't know what you would have us say," I said and drew encouragement from the nods I sensed around me. Certainly I received full support from the board for the actions taken: this much is clear. If there is any responsibility it is shared. It does not devolve fully upon me. "You refuse to admit complicity, you show no sense of guilt, you do not even seem to acknowledge the reasons for your being here. All of this will become part of the report."

"You are fools and understand nothing. You do not even realize why you are here or whose work you are doing."

"Unless you have anything further to say I am going to terminate this interview at the present time."

"Fools," he said, "I'll get the convertor and just destroy you all. Children of murder. You'll be wiped out of the time scheme."

He was raving. "Use of the convertor is forbidden to unauthorized personnel. You are unauthorized personnel. You will no longer make these threats."

"Fools."

"Suitable entries will be made on the record," I said, "now leave."

"Leave?"

"Exactly," I said and gestured toward the wing *apparat* behind him. "Through there."

"You really are mad. I knew it a long time ago but you keep on proving it over and over again. All of you are crazy."

"Go," I said to him and he turned, began to make his labored way up the ramps and into the distance, I found my interest beginning to flick away even before he had left, my mind scuttling ahead toward the next case, the next candidate for review. It is impossible to get too involved with any of these situations, otherwise feeling is totally dissipated, absolutely destroyed and one winds up completely ineffective. Certainly a greenshifter who has fallen out of cycle, who is brought before board for a mild admonition, who makes wild threats about stealing a converter and altering the past in order to make a different present … certainly such an individual cannot be handled in any other fashion but expeditiously. That is how he was dealt with. Expeditiously. I see no reason for complaint about our behavior.

We went on to Case S103 and then Y1014; we went through Z12 and even the clamorous and difficult B1411 that day and in all of those situations as this our decisions were fair and quick, correct and biting and I do not know why this one has been selected as a special instance; I cannot understand the course of your inquiry. What was done was done and would happen again, unless of course it would not happen again and this the thrust of your inquiry by which I mean that a mistake has been made but if a mistake has been made I have not made it. I am perfectly innocent in anything to do with this affair and would repeat my actions again and have done absolutely nothing to incur any of your blame and am not guilty at all and did not take his threats to get the convertor seriously how could anyone believe that he would get a convertor? Everyone might have gotten hold of a convertor and the case was of the Temporal Authority and would not be released under any circumstances to a greenshifter with problems like his why it is absolutely impossible to think that he might have gotten hold of a convertor and the case was handled perfectly, why he was not even admonished and I resent having to fill this out and I have nothing more to say I did everything perfectly properly in every detail and am not to blame and any one of you would have done the same thing if you were me and if there is anyone to blame the rest of the board should be questioned since I was obviously the only one among them with intelligence and alertness and am extremely resentful and will refuse to cooperate any further and *did not make one single mistake through all of this* and all of the mistakes were those of the others and …

PART FOUR

I

DREAMT AS IF IN CUNNING AND POWER: Lee Harvey Osborn (1934–1963) has a dream and in that dream he has killed the President of the United States of America. The course of history has been changed enormously: seventy-seven years later the consequences of his action are still being examined, still being enacted in the common lives of six billion citizens of the Greater and Lesser Earths but in the dream Osborn has no time to consider such large matters; he is in desperate flight. He has not wanted to kill the President or then again he has, it is difficult to disentangle his motives; it is even possible that he has *not* killed the President but has merely come to this flight through an excess of desire … but be that as it may as he flees through the alleys and motion picture theaters, the bars and buses of this large American metropolis of the pre-dynastic epoch his thoughts are cluttered with images of the gallows and electricity, slow evisceration and constant pain. He has not wanted it to happen in this way. If he had to do it all over again it would be different.

But in the dream there is no returning; what he has done is irrevocable. Even as he mumbles and twitches On his miserable pallet in an Army barracks dreaming not only of this but of the novel that he will someday write … even as he retreats against the edges of the dream, it coalesces, becomes sharper and now in the abscesses of a motion picture theater he thinks he sees a nest of patrolmen in the outer lobby, prowling in, cutting open the darkness with lights like knives looking for him. There are very few people in this theater; there cannot be more than twenty altogether what with it being a Friday afternoon and the President's visit having brought the whole city to curbside or its television sets, that part of the city which does not work that is to say. Lee Harvey Osborn is also unemployed; sometimes he is quite bitter about this and at other times he is not knowing that his is a much greater destiny than ordinary employment in an obscure office or factory but what controls him now more than anything else is fear, the fear that the patrolmen will find him.

He does not know exactly why he is so frightened. In the dream he has killed the President of the United States of America and that is certainly reason for him to be sought but he is also outside of the dream in a simultaneity of conviction and here he knows that he has no more to do with the police, then, than anyone else within these walls. But the dream is peculiar and gelatinous, it drapes around him like a garment which he both is and is not wearing and he decides, finally, that the fear must take precedence, it is the fear with which he must deal since it is possible, at least possible that he is the man they are seeking … and slowly, slowly he arcs himself out of the seat, stumbles past a fat old man clutching himself so quietly in the darkness and into an aisle. He will try to leave the theater as inconspicuously as possible. He will leave the theater and return to his bedroom and there, silent and alone, he will try to work out these difficulties in his mind.

Lately something has been happening to his mind. He does not seem to be thinking with the same clarity and insight which he used to muster, his thoughts seem jumbled and strange to him (the dream is part of that disturbance) and hypochondriacal to the last moment Osborn believes that he may have a brain tumor, something terrible and inoperable which is eating away at the corners of his cerebrum and will soon tap the gross motor at which time he will be dead. He will not see a doctor because he cannot bear to have these fears confirmed; it would be far better to die, to be eaten away, to perish from the center than to sit in an office across from a man who would lay out for him the fact of his own death. He is almost at the door toward the lobby, his undershirt coming against him in tight, streaked blotches where he has sweated it through when the lights in the theater go on, all of them, hit by some master switch and in the glare he finds himself facing a patrolman; the next thing he knows he is braced up against a wall facing the drawn gun and other police are coming in from the sides. Their faces are angry and yet unyielding; he feels that he has never seen such faces before and as he confronts them, as in that continuing silence they bear down he realizes that he has never been so frightened. He tries to speak but he cannot. "You son of a bitch," the nearest patrolman says, "you son of a bitch, we've got you. We've got you now." He reaches out and slashes Osborn across the face with the back of his hand. His condition is such that he does not even feel the pain, only a greater panic.

"Don't kill him," someone says, "don't hurt him bad, just take him in; we've got all the time in the world to deal with him later," and they close in nodding; feeling their hands on him, the whisk and stutter of their grasp Osborn decides then that he has had enough of the dream, it is a bad dream, one he does not wish to continue and he tries to vault himself out of it *but he cannot do it*; he cannot escape the parameters of the vision embracing him and so, struggling, he submits but submission is not easy either; they seem no more willing to accept his collapse than they were his struggle. Humiliation is in the transversal of their hands as they put them upon him; humiliation also in the way that their eyes seem suddenly and terribly knowledgeable as they come in closer, putting handcuffs on him, their fingers beating at him. Again and again he tries to will himself out of the dream like a man trying to batter his way through an orgasm that will not occur, that the very motions deaden; again and again he tells himself that this cannot be happening, that all of these events come from within his own skull but as he tries again to heave himself out of that lobby, as he tries repeatedly to either leap or go under the dream so that he is back again in his bed the first outlines of understanding begin to appear to him as if in the dazzle of fluorescence through which they take him to the waiting car. He wanted to do it, that is what he sees; whether or not these events are really happening they partake of what must have been his real desire to become the Killer of the King and he finds this insight so shocking and yet so absolutely correct, such an utter confirmation of what he must have long known about himself that he gasps, inhales, shudders in their grasp and that is the way they put him into the car and so he is taken away from there and toward the police station where in due course he will find the true and final explanation of what he has become.

II

THE TURNING POINT: Scop confers with his teammates, the Greens, before they take the field for their climactic battle with the Blues for the challenge rights in the third division. Only a very few of them will return to this room alive he knows but this does not make the warnings he gives them any less imperative. The Games, although they result in death for almost all of them must be dealt with as if the choice for life was in their own hands which in certain senses it may be. And in other senses it may not. "Gather around," Scop says, motioning them into a tight circle. Carrying their gear they troop toward him, their sullen, bleak faces as clean of feeling as the dead stones in Daley Plaza. Segregated and trained for the Games from their tenth birthday almost all of the Gamesmen are completely lacking intelligence, it has been drilled and tortured out of them but in a very few there seems to be a kind of awareness seen only as an unwillingness to join the tightly-packed circle. It is those, Scop knows, who he must reach; the Games, being evenly matched for size and weaponry are almost completely random for all of their brutality. Results will turn upon marginal factors which in turn depend upon complete motivation. How many of these marginals will eventually be willing to die? Can they be motivated no less than any of the others to the reality of their survival? They seem trivial factors as compared to the overpowering brutality and pain, the utter seeming disorganization of all the movement on the field but as Scop knows these are the factors which will determine outcome; the blood and the death must be taken for granted. Bodies will fall, lives will run away without any reference to his (or their) feelings on the matter.

"You realize," Scop says, "that there will be no turning back when we get onto the field, that from that moment forward everything we do can move us in only one direction? We must kill them all, the Blues, we must kill them to the last one because otherwise they will kill us." Is he reaching them? He cannot tell. "Do you want this to be a Blue world?" he says. "Do you really want to feel that in the generations to come the Greens will have perished from this earth? Is that the legacy that you want to leave?"

They look at him without comprehension. He knows that the concepts are too difficult for them, the words too puzzling but he had hoped that a certain mood could be conveyed, a level of feeling to which they would respond. Sometimes it is not so much meaning as rhythm which can energize them. Also they are not as stupid, he believes, as everyone takes them to be and at a certain level they take in everything. They can be reached. He has to believe that anyway; his presence would be utterly futile otherwise. "All right," he says to them, a sudden chilling sensation that he is a fool choking himself, "let's go out then. There is nothing else to say."

They move away from him pounding their gear, moving toward the corridors in a flourish of movement that does not conceal that they are merely responding to verbal cues. There does not seem to be any feeling in them. There does not seem to be any interaction either; what has been said of them is true, they are not social creatures, know nothing of relationships, may not even be conscious of one another as living beings because of the conditioning that has taught them that they are machines and that their one purpose is to destroy those of other colors. Scop alone in the corner now watches them go, realizes that they are utterly outside of his ability to reach them but that this is no insult to him; they are outside of anyone's ability. They merely perform their dreadful actions and die but none of it has anything to do with human persuasion.

Well, he thinks, well, it might have something to do with the culture itself. It is a barbarous, mechanistic construct in which he lives; the purposes of the machines are at all times greater or at least clearer than the purposes of the populace who lives entrapped within them and it is pointless to look at the Gamesman as anything extraordinary; he is simply, stripped bare, the final and most typical product of his culture. As he walks down the corridor, following them through the close concrete and into the arena it must be that the thought comes to Scop for the first time: the thought that the entire culture is ruinous, barbarous and insane. It is not just the Games. The Games are merely that point at which the culture asserts itself most clearly, at which it is easiest to see exactly what is going on here. But the Games do not matter except as diversion. The trouble is that he, the Gamesmen, everyone … they are living in a culture which is completely mad.

Then he must change it, Scop thinks as he walks slowly up the steps, staggering a little at the simplicity or then again it might be the complexity of his insight, then if this is truly the case then it must be changed and it falls upon him to change it. Ultimately responsibility must descend upon the individual who will take it; it cannot be shirked once acknowledged. If the culture is mad and he has seen it clearly then he cannot let it go by; he must do everything within his power to change it.

Wondering how he can possibly change it Scop walks upon the field hearing as if from a great distance the sound of the shifters roaring as the teams take their places to the side and doffing their superficial gear prepare for death.

III

THE TRUE AND THE REAL AND THE FINAL MEANING: Still in the dream which has now become familiar, comforting, almost reality itself, certainly too close to all the secret places of him to fight against, still deep in the dream which is the only reality he will ever again know Lee Harvey Osborn now takes himself to have been in the basement of a police station for almost two days, submitting to interrogation with only short interruptions for food or elimination; once a brief nap. They are not trying to torture him they have made clear, only to try to work with him to obtain the true and the real and the final meaning for what he has done. By this he gathers that they want a confession but of course that is the one thing that he cannot give them since he is not sure as to whether or not he shot the President. Everything seems so terribly unclear; his memory of the events of recent weeks is blurred, chiaroscuro. All that he is clear about recently is the movie theater and what he was doing when they caught him: he was thinking about masturbating, tell the truth and be done. It must be the brain damage. He knows he has a brain tumor. For months it has been eating away into his soft, vulnerable grey tissue, chewing up little parts of his memory and reason until at last, within only a little time he would have had nothing up there at all except the neural sockets that sent instructions to his hands to pull off. This is better. At least he is under custody now. Eventually a doctor will examine him and at that point they will be clear as to what has happened to him and they will not bother him any more. He may even get an operation. He may get the help that he needs.

But for the moment they try to coax out of him a confession. Why did he do it? Where was he when he did it? What did he do with the rifle and for that matter how had he gotten the rifle to begin with? Had he planned this for a long time, mapping out the President's route or rather was it an impulsive thing decided on the day itself? He gathers that they have been in his apartment but there is nothing that they could find there. He does not even remember what is in his apartment. As far as his wife; that means nothing. He is not even sure that he has a wife. It has been so terribly long since he has thought of her. It has been so terribly long since he has thought of anything. Mostly he is interested in going to the Bijou and beating it off.

They want to know what his plans were for escaping. Did he really think that he would get away with it? Where was he going to go? Did he have assistance from a foreign country? Did he have contacts in some foreign port which would enable him to flee? They are quite polite for all the brutality of the process. He has dealt with a lot of police in a lot of cities through his time and certainly these must be given credit for courtesy; the southern accents, the curiously formal tilt of their faces as they ask the most shockingly intimate questions in the most distant and apologetic fashion is remarkable and would be something worth remembering in other circumstances, if he believed that he had any kind of a future. He would put all of this down in his novel except that he is pretty sure at this point that there is not going to be a novel that he, Lee Harvey Osborn, is for all intents and purposes finished. Maybe not. How has his sex life been? Not too bad, he says, like anyone else's sex life. Of course with the baby recently and certainly the problems they had had with his not being able to get a job … Maybe he would like to talk some more about that. Except that he would not. There are certain things it turns out and to his surprise which he really cannot talk about. Like his wife. He begins to cry.

But crying is no more helpful to him in this dream than it was ever outside of it. It seems that they are not impressed and that indeed his crying, as a sign of weakness, gives them encouragement to pick up the pace of their questioning, to dig into him in a way that they had not before. The politeness begins to drop out of their voices. They begin to ask their questions in a more strident fashion, facing him now, hurling the questions to him in grunting passion, one syllable at a time and they start to get through to him, the emotional significance of the questioning that is: they are serious here, they are serious, *they believe that he has killed the President* and it is possible that until this moment he has not taken them seriously, has not believed that they could possibly have this on their minds. How could he have killed the President? He loved him, revered him, didn't everyone? The President was going to occupy a very important role in the novel that he was writing, a whole chapter devoted to his life and works and in praise of the man to say nothing of his beautiful wife; that was what he thought of the President but they do not believe this. They do not seem to take him seriously. No one took him seriously, that was always one of his problems Osborn thinks but this is in a more dangerous fashion because he begins to see that these people want him dead. They really do. They will not be satisfied until he is dead despite the fact that their tempers are still well in check and they maintain the outer edges of their politeness. How could he have believed that essentially these people were on his side and willing to help him, to work with him? What a fool he has been! Of course it is too late now. He keeps on denying however. That is the only thing he has to hold onto, the denials, the fact that he has not done what they have accused him of. He knows that he could not have done it. Everything is a blur right up to the movie theater, the brain tumor, that is it, has wiped out his memory but still he knows himself. He must have faith in what he has been. He could not have done something like that.

If he did what they said he has, if he indeed killed the President then he is mad. That is something which Osborn cannot face. His brain may be turning to pulp because of malignancy but what remains of it would be good, sane, decent up until the end. The other way means that he would be totally out of control. He tries to tell that to them. He tries to make it clear, to gain their confidence, to show them that what they are suggesting is wrong but it does not seem to make much of an impression upon them. They have their own problems he can surmise. It must be very bad for them.

Of course he has no idea of what it may be like outside the police station. He is denied newspapers, reporters, rumors of any sort: everyone who comes into his presence has obviously been instructed to say nothing. This for Osborn is the worst. At least he wants to know what has happened out there; whether or not the President is dead, whether his wife knows that he is in this station. The President must be dead or they would not be doing this to him … but as for the other part, he does not know. They will not let him get a lawyer. They allow him nothing except piss call and coffee and a sandwich now and then and in off-hours a slight nap. Nor do they show any signs of breaking the schedule.

After a long time, it may be a week but he has utterly lost perspective; it is impossible for him to judge how many hours he has been in this basement the questioning stops. They tell him that he may be alone for a while and then they withdraw leaving only the mighty strobe focused upon him in the locked and guarded basement and in that time Lee Harvey Osborn makes his last and greatest attempt to escape from the shackles of his dream, to return to the bed of choice which he has deserted a long time ago. He closes his eyes and squeezes his fist, wills himself out of the basement and into the enclosure of his bed where he wishes to awaken and find that all of this is a construction and that now it may pass from him. The physical effort involved in renouncing his circumstances makes him literally ill; he feels weak and drained, little patches of color passing in and out of his face, uneven respiration, nausea and a feeling of self-revulsion as profound as any that he has ever known … and yet try as he does he cannot take himself out of the basement. It is as if the dream has contaminated his being and left all of him foul and corrupt, not only the part of him that is in this station. After a very long time he opens his eyes and finds that he is still there, still indisputably there and it is then that he finally accepts his position as if for the first time. It may be a dream, it may not, there is no way that he can tell right up to the moment of termination but he will have to act, henceforth, as if it were real. There is no way out for him any more than there is for the poor dead President. *The poor dead President!* and an image of Kennedy flips up in his mind like a placard, the face, the broken little lines at the corners, the strange vulnerability of the eyes and he begins to see some of the pain that might have been involved; a pain that is no longer his own. He would weep but he cannot. He is drained. The time for weeping is past.

After some time they come back into the room and tell him that the questioning is over and that it is now time for him to be taken somewhere else and formally arraigned. For the murder of the President of the United States. He comes to his feet, starts to say something and then realizing the futility of this sits down slowly; there is nothing to say. There is nothing that he can add. They ask him if he is ready and he says that he would like something to wear; how can he go over in an undershirt and work pants? Isn't he at least entitled to some dignity? People will see him. They assure him that there will be no pictures and that an area has been cleared for him which he can come through without ever having to see the press or they him. That relieves him a little and then he asks if he will be able to see his wife, if he will be able to call a lawyer. They tell him that there will be time for all of this soon just as soon as they get the formal arraignment out of the way. They are very calm and reasonable, with a reasonableness which matches his own new feeling of confidence. After all, the worst has happened. It has come to this and he is still dreaming. He cannot come out of it then. The worst that can be done to him has already been done; all that they can do now is to kill him. And then he will wake up.

They help him out of the chair. Walking he feels disconnected, translucent somehow, barely making connection with the floor and he stumbles, they have to support him with large, kindly hands, then take him down the long line of the room and through the door which opens into an even longer corridor, smoke through it, voices at the end of it. He rears in their hands. "No," he says. He is overtaken by fear. "No, I won't do it. Please don't make me."

"Come," they say but he balks, roots in place. They tug at him. He feels his face freezing into hard lines, lines of stone; nothing like this has ever happened before. "What is wrong?"

"I won't go," he says. "I won't go."

"Come on," they say and pull on his wrists. "Move now."

"No," he says. "They'll kill me. They'll kill me out there."

"No they won't!"

"They will!" he says and he knows that this is the truth. When he has a conviction of this sort he has never been wrong, not once, not ever: he has it now. "I don't want to die," he says. "Not this way."

"Let's go, Osborn," one of them says. "Let's go or I'll knock you unconscious."

"No you won't," he says with sudden cunning. "I have to be awake when you walk me through there. I tell you I can't go."

"What's wrong with you?"

"They'll kill me!"

"The area has been cleared. Everyone is standing back."

"I don't want to die," he says. He knows it is the truth. He has wavered from time to time but always he has tried to hold onto life and it is not living which he regrets so much as how much he has maimed, detested his mortality. "Please," he says, "don't do this to me."

They begin to pull at him again. He is really quite helpless. He has balked them for a moment only by the force of will but, of course, he has absolutely no control; there is nothing he can do that they will not permit him and at that moment they want him to walk the corridor. He resists for another moment and then he gives himself over to them, something nearly exquisite in the yielding, in the realization that he has at last gone over the line of option and is now completely in their hands. He is utterly at the mercy of others and this is something entirely new for him; it has never been this way before. "All right," he says as he begins to move with them, quite briskly now considering how impeded his circulatory system has become, "all right, have it your way but they're going to kill me; they are as sure as hell going to kill me."

He feels almost cheerful about this. There is a heartening sense of progress, of self-realization in accepting one's own imminent death. It is a great adventure; that is what a lot of theologians say and although Osborn has never had much to do with religion believing that it is essentially an oppressive device he is interested in knowing after all these years whether the theologians have something on the ball. Maybe they do. Who is he to say that they do not? As terrified as he was before he finds himself almost euphoric now; violent swings of mood: great underlying depression is indicated but what the hell. What the hell, it is out of his hands now. Almost jauntily he swings behind them through the corridor and at the end of it a door is open, he sees the teeming blankness of the room ahead, understands that it is crammed with more police, press, photographers, reporters, observers ... he is going to be famous. He is famous already. His life is not to be measured in beating it off in the bijous; rather he has achieved at last some measure of that to which he was always entitled. He always knew that he would make a big reputation and even if for all the wrong reasons here it is. Maybe it is for the best. He has to believe this. He feels that the police surrounding him look at him almost enviously now as he walks into the light. There is a pressure in his chest. Someone has shoved a gun into his chest. He knows the unmistakable feeling of a pistol; he has dealt with weapons in the army, now he looks down to verify and only then in a quick, vaulting instant does he move up, seek recognition but all that he sees is the hand, the splayed hand against the gun and before he can catch the eyes to find out who is doing this to him, who has done this to him something tears its way into his chest with the ferocity of a snake striking and it all falls away. He does not feel himself going down. That has already happened. It happened a long time ago. It has nothing to do with him whatsoever. He does not; he absolutely does not give a damn.

IV

A SOLEMN DECLARATION OF PURPOSE: He takes himself then to be at the bedside of the dying Robert Kennedy, trying to make it all clear to him in the few moments that he has. Kennedy is hooked up to life-support mechanisms and does not seem to be very attentive; the oxygen pumps away, the intravenous burbles its hearty burble as it sends sugar into the concealed wrist, all of Kennedy is shrouded underneath a sheet and yet Scop keeps on talking; his time is limited, he must do the best that he can under the circumstances. "Listen here," he says, "you know that this was the only way that it could be, I had to turn the times around; I had to take drastic action." Kennedy says nothing of course; Kennedy is legally dead, the brain stem destroyed, only the gross motor functions continuing and those under mechanical assistance. He will remain legally dead for another twelve hours and then upon the decision of the family he will be declared absolutely dead and all supportive mechanisms will be removed. For the moment however Scop can persist in the illusion of connection. He is alone in the hospital room. It is one of those moments when family and doctors and friends having nothing else to say have retreated once more to the corridors and the exhausted nurse dozing off in the corner will never remember this. The convertor has brought him close to the bed and he can communicate with Kennedy without raising his voice, without even moving his lips. "We've got to start again," Scop says, "we've got to act as if this had never happened and try a fresh start in a different direction. We cannot go on this way. You must understand."

The intravenous flask chucks another two cc of pure dextrose into the Kennedy veins, a merry burbling sound coming from its center. It is not a response, not really, but it serves the same purposes as one might provide; it gives Scop the feeling that he is obtaining response from the form no matter how shrouded. "Now there are those," Scop says, "and I have met them and I have had the opportunity to discuss these issues, there are those who think that I'm a little obsessive about all of this business, that I've taken a single-minded attitude and won't really change my mind but they just don't realize the seriousness of this as you do. I'm sure that you agree with me; you were always a serious-minded man and you can see that a future based upon a series of murders wouldn't be a very happy one. I want to tell you that twenty-forty is a terrible place to be alive and I'm not even getting into the matter of personal unhappiness, just looking at this objectively. So you see, I've got to do what I can to straighten the matter out even though it makes things even more difficult for me than it might be otherwise."

In the corner the nurse stirs, mutters something in a thick doze, relapses into sleep. She must be having a dream, Scop thinks, a dream very much like some of his own: blood, death, pain dripping from the walls of the night but she will recover from hers in time whereas he will not and as far as Kennedy, there is no way in which he can apprehend what is going on in that brain at the present time. The higher nerve centers have been destroyed but that may only give the nightmares a rawer tinge. "Right now," Scop says conversationally, "I'm concentrating, on Dealey Plaza and that business with your brother. It's my opinion that if the basic changes can be effected there then this will never happen to you; that that's the place of original sin so to speak and that if we can straighten things out there everything else will fall into place. I hope so," he says, "I certainly hope so." He moves away from the bed then, stands at the doorway. The nurse snorts, comes to a posture of attention with her eyes closed, her hands outstretched, grasping as if to seize some object intensely visible, then subsides to her original position, eyelids fluttering. It will not be long now until she has awakened. "I'll have to go," Scop says. "I just wanted to tell you what I was doing, to let you know that I was trying to do this for you also. It's your future too." This does not sound quite sufficient: he knew what he wanted to say when he came in here but now it seems to be spinning away from him. "It's a shared future," he says, "don't you see that?" and he imagines that the body sits straight up in the bed, that Robert Kennedy looks at him with great compassion and understanding, bonded to him in that searching glance which restores his features, smooths out the ruined skull, turns him once again into the person that he must have been and that Kennedy now says, "Yes, I see that, I see what you're trying to do, it's all right, it's a good thing, I'm glad, everybody's glad, no one can blame you for this, you've done the right thing, just keep on doing it, you've got to keep on struggling, struggling, Aeschylus, pain like tears, the darkness, the darkness," but then again none of this may have happened at all; Scop may have invented this scene out of his great need to give some justification to his excessive activities and in any case he cannot remain to wonder about it any longer; he hears noises in the outer hall which can only indicate that relatives are once again going to come inside. Perhaps they have decided to remove the life-support equipment at this time. In that case they would be most surprised at how active and lively has been Robert Kennedy's recent participation. But enough, enough. He looks for the convertor, finds it jammed under some tubing, quickly compacts himself, dives inside and is taken out of there. The equipment, at least, never fails.

It is strange, he thinks; it is a strangeness. He thought that he felt for these icons; that at the center there was a deep and profound emotion, a complicated grief to speed him on his way, that all of the time what was taking him onward was that quality of feeling … but looking at Kennedy in the bed he had realized that he felt nothing, that was it; he felt absolutely nothing toward any of them but weariness and the sensation that history had made abstractions of them all. Of them all. It was not pain but circumstance which he had chosen to relieve.

V

TAKING LEAVE: So it is time then; it is time to say farewell. Farewell before embarkation and his quest which can have only one result whatever its outcome; his death. He knows that he will die. He sacrifices himself willingly. Farewell to Elaine Kozciouskos and just one last time he appears on the Knoll to touch her, a clanging touch, her skin like brass as he comes against her and then is gone. Farewell to Dealey Plaza itself, to Abraham Zapruder and the motorcade; farewell to JFK and Lee Harvey Osborn who was only trying to stay out of the Bijou: he soars way, way above them, three hundred feet or more through the stasis device of the convertor and here they seem absolutely reduced, insignificant, roiling in their convulsions on the dead brown and green below although their pain too must matter. Farewell to the Games and he appears five hundred feet above the stadium, suspended, oddly at peace in the lift and thinks of giving a speech except that he has no amplifying devices and no one would hear him; they are too interested in what is going on below; farewell to the Masters also who were only trying to do their job, doing what they could to preserve the order that had been given them, not their fault, no one's fault at all really that that which they occupied was unspeakable; farewell to all of them and then finally taking the convertor back for the last time to the hotel room in which he made his various preparations, drawing on his gloves, setting up and sighting the rifle, reading newspapers, eating sandwiches while waiting for the proper time, here in that hotel room past the formal goodbyes it is time for him to take leave of himself because no less than the others he must cut off his own persona. The leavetaking must be final, he realizes. In order for it to work he must divest himself of everything and that means his own identity as well. Fair is fair. Certain things are absolute. "Goodbye," he says to himself in the hotel room, "goodbye now."

His persona barely looks up, being otherwise occupied. "Goodbye then," he says.

"Had to be done," Scop says, "there was no other way; you must see that now."

"I can't be bothered," his persona says, inspecting the rifle, the gleaming surfaces, shaping his hands around it, shaking it for solidity. "As you see I've got other things to do."

"I just wanted to make it clear. I wanted to make it clear to you as well,"

"You've made everything clear. You've done everything that you could. Now leave."

Scop sees that he is right. There can be no search for justification; the only answers must be within himself. "All right then," he says, "all right if that's the way you want it," and before his persona can look up he has whisked himself out of the room, has detached himself utterly, moved elsewhere. Perhaps taking formal leave was a mistake; perhaps he should have left the situation as he found it but he has always been inclined toward sentimental gestures of this type. It may be for the best in the long run; no one can say that he did not make it clear at exactly what point he had given up. For he has given up. He has gone as far as he can within the present context, even further if he may say so (he will allow himself to say so) and now there is nothing else to do. There comes a time when history must be permitted to work out its own terrible equations, when a rational man out of a decent sense of awe will remove himself and allow that to be done. He has thrown himself into the machinery and done what he can; now it is out of his hands.

"Live," Scop says in Dealey Plaza, "live," he says, hovering over the Games, "live," he says to Malcolm and to Robert Kennedy and to Jack Kennedy, "live," he says to Lee Harvey Osborn in the corridors and to King on the ledge in Memphis, "live and live," he says and then he pushes himself to the fullest exertion, the fullest and most terrible exertion he has ever known and falls with the convertor wraps around him, the engines off, the convertor merely a shell, plunging and plunging a thousand yards beneath circumstance and as stone closes over him he knows (or at least he thinks he knows) what must happen next. And before. And over again.

THE END

Thoughts on *Scop*

By Barry N. Malzberg

SCOP was written as a conscious tribute to the work of Alfred Bester. The dawn of the day after I finished it in mid-March, 1975 I was driving in darkness to the Post Office at some unspeakable hour and Bester was live on a radio show called "Hour of the Wolf"— reading *THE MEN WHO MURDERED MOHAMMED*. No story is better heard in the dust of early dawn in this suburb of the lost.

Bester read splendidly; later I called in live and spoke to him for a minute or so not mentioning the novel I had just finished. He had entered full twilight but the reading was up to the story.

A couple of years later someone in Martin Harry Greenberg's "Science Fiction as Literature" course asked me telephonically (I was paid $25 for that one-hour gig), "What do you think is the best single work to ever come out of science fiction?" Reflexively I named *THE MEN WHO MURDERED MOHAMMED*. Many years later, Robert Silverberg's response in an interview to the same question was "Alfred Bester's *FONDLY FAHRENHEIT*." That's as defensible a choice as mine. Bester was our best and I wrote *SCOP* in his honor.

One Amazon commentator stated about *SCOP*, "This is not the worst Malzberg novel but it is close." Individual predilection drives the bus. *SCOP* remains among my favorite novels because the published edition represents almost exactly what I wanted as I began; it came out like that idealized sexual partner we all fantasize. It was the novel I had in mind as I addressed the first line. No gap between aspiration and achievement. I had that experience just twice—once with *SCOP* and once with *THE MEN INSIDE*. Too bad they couldn't all be that way.

—Teaneck, NJ

Barry N. Malzberg Bibliography

FICTION (as either Barry or Barry N. Malzberg)

Oracle of the Thousand Hands (1968)
Screen (1968)
Confessions of Westchester County (1970)
The Spread (1971)
In My Parents' Bedroom (1971)
The Falling Astronauts (1971)
The Masochist (1972, reprinted as Everything Happened to Susan, 1975; as Cinema, 2020)
Horizontal Woman (1972; reprinted as The Social Worker, 1973)
Beyond Apollo (1972)
Overlay (1972)
Revelations (1972)
Herovit's World (1973)
In the Enclosure (1973)
The Men Inside (1973)
Phase IV (1973; novelization based on a story & screenplay by Mayo Simon)
The Day of the Burning (1974)
The Tactics of Conquest (1974)
Underlay (1974)
The Destruction of the Temple (1974)
Guernica Night (1974)
On a Planet Alien (1974)
Out from Ganymede (1974; stories)
The Sodom and Gomorrah Business (1974)
The Best of Barry N. Malzberg (1975; stories)
The Many Worlds of Barry Malzberg (1975; stories)
Galaxies (1975)
The Gamesman (1975)
Down Here in the Dream Quarter (1976; stories)
Scop (1976)
The Last Transaction (1977)
Chorale (1978)
Malzberg at Large (1979; stories)
The Man Who Loved the Midnight Lady (1980; stories)
The Cross of Fire (1982)
The Remaking of Sigmund Freud (1985)
In the Stone House (2000; stories)
Shiva and Other Stories (2001; stories)
The Passage of the Light: The Recursive Science Fiction of Barry N. Malzberg (2004; ed. by Tony Lewis & Mike Resnick; stories)
The Very Best of Barry N. Malzberg (2013; stories)
Ready When You Are and Other Stories (2023; stories)
Collaborative Capers (2023; stories)
Collecting Myself (2024; stories)

With Bill Pronzini

The Running of the Beasts (1976)
Acts of Mercy (1977)
Night Screams (1979)
Prose Bowl (1980)
Problems Solved (2003; stories)
On Account of Darkness and Other SF Stories (2004; stories)

As Mike Barry

Lone Wolf series:
Night Raider (1973)
Bay Prowler (1973)
Boston Avenger (1973)
Desert Stalker (1974)
Havana Hit (1974)
Chicago Slaughter (1974)
Peruvian Nightmare (1974)
Los Angeles Holocaust (1974)

Miami Marauder (1974)
Harlem Showdown (1975)
Detroit Massacre (1975)
Phoenix Inferno (1975)
The Killing Run (1975)
Philadelphia Blowup (1975)

As Francine di Natale

The Circle (1969)

As Claudine Dumas

The Confessions of a Parisian
    Chambermaid (1969)

As Mel Johnson/M. L. Johnson

Love Doll (1967; with The Sex Pros
    by Orrie Hitt)
I, Lesbian (1968; as M. L. Johnson)
Just Ask (1968; with Playgirl by Lou
    Craig)
Instant Sex (1968)
Chained (1968; with Master of
    Women by March Hastings & Love
    Captive by Dallas Mayo)
Kiss and Run (1968; with Sex on the
    Sand by Sheldon Lord & Odd Girl
    by March Hastings)
Nympho Nurse (1969; with Young
    and Eager by Jim Conroy &
    Quickie by Gene Evans)
The Sadist (1969; with Flesh by Max
    Collier)
The Box (1969)
Do It To Me (1969; with Hot Blonde
    by Jim Conroy)
Born to Give (1969; with Swap Club
    by Greg Hamilton & Wild in Bed
    by Dirk Malloy)
Campus Doll (1969; with High
    School Stud by Robert Hadley)
A Way With All Maidens (1969)

As Howard Lee

Kung Fu #1: The Way of the Tiger,
    the Sign of the Dragon (1973)

As Lee W. Mason

Lady of a Thousand Sorrows (1977)

As K. M. O'Donnell

Empty People (1969)
The Final War and Other Fantasies
    (1969; stories)
Dwellers of the Deep (1970)
Gather at the Hall of the Planets
    (1971)
In the Pocket and Other S-F Stories
    (1971; stories)
Universe Day (1971; stories)

As Eliot B. Reston

The Womanizer (1972)

As Gerrold Watkins

Southern Comfort (1969)
A Bed of Money (1970)
A Satyr's Romance (1970)
Giving It Away (1970)
Art of the Fugue (1970)

NON-FICTION/ESSAYS

The Engines of the Night: Science
    Fiction in the Eighties (1982;
    essays)
Breakfast in the Ruins (2007;
    essays: expansion of Engines of the
    Night)
The Business of Science Fiction: Two
    Insiders Discuss Writing and
    Publishing (2010; with Mike
    Resnick)

The Bend at the End of the Road (2018; essays)

EDITED ANTHOLOGIES

Final Stage (1974; with Edward L. Ferman)

Arena (1976; with Edward L. Ferman)

Graven Images (1977; with Edward L. Ferman)

Dark Sins, Dark Dreams (1978; with Bill Pronzini)

The End of Summer: SF in the Fifties (1979; with Bill Pronzini)

Shared Tomorrows: Science Fiction in Collaboration (1979; with Bill Pronzini)

Neglected Visions (1979; with Martin H. Greenberg & Joseph D. Olander)

Bug-Eyed Monsters (1980; with Bill Pronzini)

The Science Fiction of Mark Clifton (1980; with Martin H. Greenberg)

The Arbor House Treasury of Horror & the Supernatural (1981; with Bill Pronzini & Martin H. Greenberg)

The Science Fiction of Kris Neville (1984; with Martin H. Greenberg)

Mystery in the Mainstream (1986; with Bill Pronzini & Martin H. Greenberg)

Uncollected Stars (1986; with Piers Anthony, Martin H. Greenberg & Charles G. Waugh)

The Best Time Travel Stories of All Time (2003)

www.ingramcontent.com/pod-product-compliance
Lightning Source LLC
Chambersburg PA
CBHW050334160726
48002CB00001B/311